THE
LAST
TEMPTATION

ALSO BY AMY O. LEWIS

A Mountain of Evidence
Half-Told Truths

THE
LAST
TEMPTATION

A NOVEL

AMY O. LEWIS

ARROW ROAD
PRESS

Published by Arrow Road Press, Denver, CO
www.amyolewis.com

Edited and designed by Girl Friday Productions
www.girlfridayproductions.com

Cover design: Emily Weigel
Project management: Mari Kesselring and Laura Dailey
Image credits: cover © by Shutterstock/Backgroundy, Wikimedia Commons

ISBN (paperback): 978-1-7372977-4-1
ISBN (ebook): 978-1-7372977-5-8

Library of Congress Control Number: 2022916151

For Jim and Pam Lewis, with deepest thanks

PROLOGUE

It was decided. They were going back to France.

Yesterday's startling announcement rattled around in Laurie Beltran's mind as she ran up the side of the mountain. Two years living in Santa Fe had done nothing to improve her parents' marriage. At least in Nice, or wherever the family settled this time on the French Riviera, Peter and Marilyn Beltran would be free to pursue their separate agendas.

Their separate affairs, their eldest daughter amended bitterly.

Beads of sweat glistened on her forehead as she sprinted up the Atalaya Mountain Trail. When a rare trickle of perspiration tracked toward her eye, she backhanded her wrist across her face to catch it. At seven thousand feet above sea level, the air in Santa Fe was thin and dry. It was completely different from the air along the Mediterranean coast. Laurie reached back in her memory to when her family had last lived in Nice. She recalled the gentle sea breezes blowing in from offshore and, more strongly than that, the stunningly clear blue of the Mediterranean Sea.

It hardly mattered to her what her parents did. Three months from now, she would be in college in Santa Barbara.

She smiled at a different thought.

"Just do it with Brent, Laurie," Melanie, her best friend, had said in something akin to a frenzy last night. "You're out of your mind if you don't! You're leaving for the summer anyway, what's there to lose?"

Laurie's smile spread. Her breathing grew more ragged, possibly from the incline, more likely from the turn of her thoughts.

Brent was the senior class president and state track star. She'd had a crush on him for months. Last week, he broke up with his longtime girlfriend. Two days ago, he asked her out. Tonight they were taking his Jack Russell to the dog park and, later, going to a classmate's graduation party.

"I don't even know if he wants to do it with me," she had exclaimed to Melanie.

"Trust me. He does."

She wouldn't. She knew that. Not the first time they went out together. Not even when she felt herself going crazy, wanting to.

"Yeah, and what if he never asks you out again?" Melanie said, getting in the final word as always.

Laurie tore into a sprint on the steep incline. She survived fifty yards before the terrain got the better of her. Hands on her hips, she swallowed great gulps of air while she gazed at the view of treetops cascading down the mountain. Below, the city built on a broad plain spread into the distance beneath a cloudless crystalline-blue sky.

The kids in her class couldn't wait to get out of Santa Fe. Talk about being stuck in the middle of the desert, they complained, lamenting there was nothing to do here and no decent places to hang out. She supposed that was why Brent had invited her to go to the dog park. "He's taking you to the *dog park?*" her sister, Natalie, had exclaimed when she'd heard. On Natalie's last date, she'd insisted on going to Geronimo for dinner.

Laurie was perfectly happy with Brent's invitation. She couldn't imagine what they'd find to talk about seated across from one another in a fancy restaurant.

She resumed her run. Halfway down the long hill, she left the street for the maze of roads that wound in serpentine fashion into the hills. Her family lived a mile east of the historic Santa Fe Plaza, opposite St. John's College, in one of the most prestigious neighborhoods in a city that prided itself on such things. It wasn't, strictly speaking, their house. Her grandparents owned it, a detail that troubled no one. Laurie loved the house for its sunset views and its proximity to the mountain trails, not to mention it was near enough to Santa Fe Prep for her and her brother and sister to walk to school. Not that Natalie ever did. Laurie didn't think her younger sister had walked once in the past two years.

She rounded the last curve. As she did, the house came into view. Her new BMW was parked outside.

"I assumed you wouldn't mind if I washed it. *Her,*" Ricardo said, smiling, standing alongside the dark-blue car with a soft cloth in his hand.

"Of course not. Thank you, Ricardo."

Laurie lightly fingered the buff-dried trunk as she walked past. Even the feel of the gleaming steel seemed to reverberate with excellence. She glanced inside a side window to reassure herself the interior was exactly as she remembered.

"Will you be taking her out soon?" Ricardo asked. "Or should I return her to the garage?"

"The garage is fine. I need to shower."

She entered the breezeway outside the kitchen. The spicy aroma of tomatoes and chiles wafted from an open window.

"Hello, Anna," she called to the woman inside the house, who was stirring something in a tall pot.

"Hello, Laurie," Anna called back.

The BMW was a surprise graduation gift from her grandparents. It had shown up yesterday morning before she left for school. A waste of a day, really. Classes and tests were over. Graduation itself wasn't until next week. She'd had to wait all day to get behind the wheel. With the music cranked up, she'd tested the car out on the steep, curvy road leading up to the Santa Fe Ski Basin. It hadn't disappointed.

The BMW was her grandparents' second gift to her recently. A few weeks ago, after she'd turned eighteen and it was clear she was going to graduate from high school, her grandmother and grandfather had given her the first disbursement of her trust fund. It was a stock portfolio valued at several hundred thousand dollars. There was more to come. Under the terms of the trust, she would get the second disbursement when she graduated from college, and the remainder when she turned twenty-five. She didn't know exactly how much was in the trust. Plenty, her father had said once when Natalie pestered him about it. Identical trusts existed for Natalie and Danny, but they wouldn't get theirs for years.

For the first time, Laurie felt like the chosen one in their family. She harbored no doubt that Natalie truly was her parents' favorite. Just this once, it felt great to be singled out and rewarded. She grinned. And just this once, Natalie was being punished for screwing up. Natalie had failed two classes this year. Natalie wasn't going to France. She was staying in Santa Fe to attend summer school.

Laurie entered the house through the mudroom. At the end of a long hallway, she jogged up the steps leading to the great room. She turned the corner and bounded up the staircase to the second floor. Passing Danny's room, she heard the blare of a TV and a single woof from Hutch, their black Lab.

Though she'd meant to go straight to the shower, the sweat she'd worked up on her run had already evaporated. She grabbed her phone and flopped into a chair, slipping in her earbuds. She turned up the music in the hope of breaking down her inhibitions.

Melanie had said it didn't matter if Laurie had sex with Brent. There was no possible downside to seriously making out with a guy. Anyway, he would have a condom. Melanie said the first time was kind of a waste anyway. It took a while to get a feel for doing it.

Laurie tried to let her imagination run free. It wasn't as if she never fantasized about making out. She wasn't a prude. She just wasn't sure that Brent was the right guy. Or that tonight was the right night. She held her breath and pretended she could feel him reaching for her. She imagined his fingertips on her skin. She released her breath, and she knew. Melanie was right. It would be okay if she didn't overthink it.

A loud bang sounded from somewhere in the house.

Jarred, Laurie opened her eyes, unable to tell if a door had been slammed shut or something large had been dropped. She listened, and when no other sound followed, she closed her eyes and tried to slip back to where she'd just been.

She and Brent were only going to the dog park. And later, to a party. It was casual. They were two friends wanting to hang out together. No big deal.

A second loud bang sounded. This time, it definitely sounded like a door slamming. Next thing Laurie knew, her bedroom door flew open. Natalie stood at the threshold.

Instantly enraged, Laurie leapt from her chair. "You're not allowed in here!" she yelled.

Natalie ignored her.

"Get out!" Laurie screamed.

Natalie, two years younger, strode into the room. She bore down upon her older sister with a determination Laurie had never witnessed in all her years of living with a very determined sister. Too late, Laurie saw the knife in Natalie's hand.

She retreated, falling back into the chair as a rush of terror flooded her.

Natalie drew close. Without hesitation, she raised the knife and plunged it into her sister's chest.

Laurie's fear fled with the first bolt of pain.

Blood spurted from the wound. Laurie gasped for breath, unable to comprehend the sight of her sister looming above her. Natalie raised the knife a second time, plunging it deeper. Laurie choked on her own blood. She fought for a clear swallow of air. Natalie raised the bloodied knife a third time. Knowing she was about to die, Laurie searched for the reason in her sister's eyes. All she saw was a rock-hard intensity. It was as if Natalie were possessed. Yet Laurie knew she had never seen her sister more alive than she was at this moment.

The words sprang to her lips out of nowhere. "The Lord is my shepherd," she prayed.

CHAPTER 1

The overhead light was too bright. The acoustics were sharp and brittle. Despite the room's shortcomings, the woman's voice carried through the cavernous space with melodious authority, sounding more like a spoken song than a sermon.

Kim Jackson leaned her head against the wall and closed her eyes. She didn't attend Sunday services in the basement of the town hall in Creede, Colorado, seeking spiritual edification. She came for the pleasure of hearing Laurie Beltran speak.

"It is springtime, the season of rebirth," Laurie said. "The first tiny buds are showing on trees and shrubs. Lying just behind the protective fold of pale-green leaves, blossoms await their moment to explode in an array of vibrant colors. Nature brings itself forth, without intervention. So, too, can we bring forth from within ourselves what is natural to each of us and is, in its own way, as vivid and beautiful as the flowers we will soon see bursting into bloom."

Laurie continued in the same vein. Kim tracked her voice as it rose and fell, seeming to burrow deeper toward some promised treasure. Occasionally a word or a phrase caught her ear, and for reasons she couldn't explain, she smiled. For a few blissful moments, she was released from both the past and the future.

When the sermon wound to a close, Laurie announced the final scripture reading. Something from Luke, Kim thought, recalling the verses posted on the chalkboard.

"Forgive me," Laurie said. "Instead of reading from Luke, I'd like to read one of my favorite passages. The twenty-third Psalm."

There followed the sound of pages shuffling and a faint undercurrent of grumbling among those who had marked the reading and now had to backtrack to the book of Psalms. Kim glanced at the rows of people seated in folding chairs in front of her and saw what she always did: one pair of eyes after another riveted to the sight of the woman standing at a lectern draped with a cloth, a simple cross woven into the fabric.

Laurie wore a long-sleeved navy-blue dress. Its shapeless form hung loosely on her slender frame. A hairband held back her straight, dark hair. It took no effort to imagine Laurie Beltran wearing the triangular-shaped dark-blue headpiece of a Catholic novitiate, the attire she was recently rumored to have worn. It required a massive leap to picture her in the black and white of a nun's habit, the garb the same rumor mill reported as her destiny.

"'The Lord is my shepherd; I shall not want. He maketh me to lie down in green pastures: he leadeth me beside the still waters.'"

Kim warmed to the sound of the familiar Psalm. She resumed her former posture, head against the wall. A verse or two later, her reverie was disturbed. Laurie's normally fluid speech grew stilted. Puzzled, Kim straightened. Laurie was standing stock-still. Her gaze was fixed on a point on the rear wall. Kim glanced that way and saw nothing. The Bible lay open in the young woman's hands, but she wasn't reading from it.

"'I will fear no evil,'" Laurie said tersely. She soldiered on. "'And I shall dwell in the house of the Lord forever.'"

The words sounded like a prison sentence.

Strummed guitar strings sent haunting notes through the air. Several people coughed or cleared their throats. With a decisive modulation, the guitarist lit into a chord pattern that became the opening of a favorite hymn. The congregation rose. All traces of Laurie's torturous recitation of the Psalm disappeared with the joyful song.

The service ended with a prayer.

Afterward, Kim observed the predictable swelling of the crowd around Laurie. Voices rippled throughout the room. It took a moment for the resumption of normal life to displace the hour of quiet. For the fourth time in as many weeks, Kim was surprised to find herself at the conclusion of a religious service in Creede's town hall basement. But she was long past the point where she relied on logic to account for the shape of her life.

She picked up her jacket and threaded her way through the rows of chairs toward the stairs.

"Kim—wait, please."

Laurie had succeeded in separating herself from the throng and was headed for Kim, who, at a distance in the rear of the room, was not an easy target to reach. When she drew close, Laurie lowered her voice. "There's something I was hoping to discuss with you. It's a small matter, really."

The dismissive tone of her words was belied by the urgency in her eyes. Kim smiled at the incongruity. Laurie evidently mistook her reaction for something else.

"Oh, you don't ordinarily stay for the group talk. Maybe we could arrange to meet another time."

"It's fine, Laurie. I'll stay today and we can talk afterward."

"Thank you. I promise I won't take up much of your time. You could join us," she said, pointing at the circle of folding chairs presently being drawn together. A plate of cookies sat on a side table along with two pitchers, one of ice water, the other fruit punch.

Kim eyed the emerging formation dubiously. "I don't know. I don't think I have anything to contribute."

"There's no requirement to participate. Besides,"—Laurie paused to smile wryly—"even if you wanted to, there's little chance you could get a word in edgewise."

Kim poured a glass of water and took a vacant chair, nodding casually to the woman next to her.

Laurie had no sooner tucked the fold of her dress beneath her and sat down than a woman named Valerie Crane spoke peremptorily. "I don't have a clue what the point of your message was today. With Easter only a few weeks away, you go off half-cocked on some bizarre notion about the merits of self-sufficiency? Would you please explain to me what that has to do with the death and resurrection of Jesus Christ?"

Valerie was a broad-shouldered woman with dark hair and an imposing presence. Neither tall nor overweight, she possessed a striking force that found expression, at least at the moment, through her shrill voice.

Laurie smiled disarmingly. "I had thought to talk about that," she said, faintly sardonically. "Yesterday, as I was preparing my thoughts for this morning, I found myself humbled by the beauty of the day and of the season it so perfectly represented. To my surprise, I found I was forcing my thoughts around the subject you've named. It seemed a travesty to force anything when, all around me, new life was simply springing into being. I thought of the wonder of that. Then I thought of the wonder of who each of us is as a unique individual and how poorly we sometimes appreciate that in ourselves and in each other."

It wasn't clear that Laurie had finished. Valerie gave her no chance to go on. She launched a second assault, more vitriolic than the first. Others in the group chimed in, some agreeing, others not. Laurie took the part of referee until the allotted time had passed, and with a sigh of relief, Kim realized the session was over.

"Honestly, I should have known better," Laurie said when she and Kim reached the top step outside the building. Kim had expected their meeting would take place in the basement hall. Laurie had a different idea. After turning off the lights, lowering the thermostat, and locking the door, she invited Kim to her home, a five-minute walk from the town center, she promised. The proximity hardly merited distinction. As Kim had learned in her brief sojourn in the former mining camp, nearly everything in Creede, Colorado, was a five-minute walk from the center of town.

They passed tourist shops, most still closed. This early in April, the town snared few vacationers, though Kim was always surprised by at least one car with an out-of-state license plate parked on the street. Creede's natural beauty never went out of season. Today the mountains were dwarfed by low-hanging clouds. Yesterday the sun had shone, lighting the rock towers standing sentinel to the entrance to the canyon in a golden glow beneath a brilliant blue sky.

Laurie turned left at the next street. When they reached the section of road spanning the creek, Kim's eyes were drawn to the rushing water, still weeks away from the height of spring runoff, according to John Carlos, her boss. A thunderous roar accompanied the muddy froth on its downstream surge. This was a different breed of water than she had ever encountered before. The novelty of seeing and hearing it hadn't worn thin.

Midway down the block, Laurie said, "This is it." She opened a picket-fence gate and led the way around the main house to a small wooden house at the rear of the property. With a twist of the doorknob, she entered.

"You don't lock up when you leave?" Kim said.

"No. The lock broke. I latch it from inside when I'm here. Well, at night, anyway."

Having entered, Kim inspected the locking apparatus. The broken lock was of the flimsy push-button-on-the-doorknob variety. The latch was even less substantial. It was a simple slender hook that slipped into an eyelet on the opposite wall. "You have to be kidding," she said.

"About what?"

"Your home security. This is terrible."

"Oh well. It's fine." Laurie pointed to a chair. "Make yourself at home. I'm going to change clothes."

Still frowning, Kim turned from inspecting the shabby lock to acquaint herself with her surroundings. She stood in what passed for the living room. The smallish space had a congested feel, furnished with two chairs, a coffee table, an end table, a lamp, and a bookcase. Laurie had disappeared behind a closed door to the adjacent room, presumably her bedroom. The kitchen was to the left. Kim took two steps and saw a small refrigerator and stove, a porcelain sink, and a plastic dish rack on the countertop with a single bowl and cup set out to dry. A narrow table with two high-backed chairs occupied the space against the wall.

Bright light filtered in from the window above the sink. By contrast, the living room was dark. The one window was adorned with a lowered blind and curtains. There were no photos or framed pictures hanging on the walls. No TV, no music system. However compact and sparsely outfitted, the cottage's interior was cleaned and scrubbed thoroughly.

Prior to today, Kim had done no more than exchange introductions with Laurie. It felt odd to be standing inside her home.

"Was today's discussion group fairly typical?" she called through the closed bedroom door.

"Are you really asking whether Valerie is always so belligerent?" Laurie called back.

"Yes, I guess I am."

The door opened. Dressed in blue jeans and a wool sweater, and with her hair hanging loose, Laurie appeared completely transformed. No longer a prim, religious devotee, she looked like a young college student. The change went deeper. Laurie was a beautiful twentysomething woman. Kim checked her surprise at the transformation.

"To answer your question, no, Valerie isn't always so angry. She and I have had our disagreements, but she's never lashed out in public before."

Kim was about to say she had enjoyed the day's message before realizing she hadn't paid enough attention to be sure what it was. More to the point, she had no desire to share any opinion.

Laurie indicated the chairs in the living room. "Please, have a seat."

Nearly an hour had passed since Laurie had begged a few minutes of her time. Kim was no closer to knowing what the young woman wanted than she had been when she agreed to the meeting. For no clear reason, she began to suspect Laurie Beltran had a hidden agenda, a prospect that both intrigued and irritated her. "What was it you wanted to talk about?" she said.

"You're an accountant, right?"

Kim flinched. The words sent an arrow-like bolt through her scar-toughened flesh. "Not an accountant, exactly," she lied. "I've been working with the local tax guy, helping him process tax returns."

"John Carlos," Laurie said, and she laughed.

"What?"

"From what I've heard, you're a welcome addition to his office."

Kim refrained from commenting. It was nothing to her what kind of business John Carlos ran. She had been hired a few weeks ago to help with the crush of tax returns that needed to be filed before April 15. In that time, she had seen plenty of evidence that her boss had failed to get his customers their full due from the government in years past. She also knew she had earned the gratitude of many townspeople for her efforts on their behalf. But the fact remained that she would leave and he would stay, and life would go on as it always had for John Carlos and his clientele.

"You wanted to talk about a tax problem?" she said.

It was Laurie's turn to flinch. "No. I wanted to ask whether you know anything about nonprofit organizations. We do have a problem. The church, that is. If you can call it a church."

"What kind of problem?"

"Several months ago, shortly after I came here, I joined a weekly prayer group. It was a large group, even before I joined. Several people asked whether I would be willing to lead a Sunday service. I had never done anything like that before, but it seems to have worked out. The problem is, we have no official status as a nonprofit, and I'm afraid we may need to do something about that."

"Why?"

"Because of the collection money. Our expenses are few, but we have them. We have a secretary who has been keeping the money. Or, I should say, had. When it got to be too much, she wasn't comfortable having it in her house. So she brought it here."

"How much money?"

"It's a bit over five hundred dollars. I haven't added in today's collection."

"You're telling me you keep that much cash in an unlocked house?" Kim said incredulously.

"Only two people know it's here, our secretary and me. Besides, no one could find it even if they did know."

Kim doubted that. "What do you want from me?"

"We need a safe place to keep the money. I've been told we can't open a bank account in the church's name without first establishing ourselves as a nonprofit. I don't know that any of us want to go to that trouble. If we have to, I thought maybe you could help."

"I know very little about nonprofit organizations." Kim flashed to the few occasions the subject had been mentioned in lectures taken while she was earning her MBA. "I suspect it's a matter of filing certain papers with the IRS, establishing a board of directors, submitting tax forms annually. That may be all there is to it."

"That's all?" Laurie said sarcastically.

Beyond the curtained window, Kim glimpsed a patch of blue sky breaking through a thick band of clouds. Her heart leapt at the hope for another springlike day. Oppressed by the dankness of the room and by the curious fusion of Laurie's simplicity and willfulness, she stood up, finished with this conversation.

"It's probably less complicated than it sounds. Even John Carlos could walk you through it." She added the mean dig before realizing her esteemed boss would no doubt charge in fees nearly the whole amount the group had in reserve. Another thought occurred to her. "If all you're worried about is keeping your cash safe, you could get a safe deposit box at a bank."

"A safe deposit box? What is that?"

Laurie's ignorance came as a surprise. Kim couldn't remember a time when she hadn't known what a safe deposit box was. "You rent a metal box that's kept locked in the bank's vault. You would have a key to it. Anytime you wanted access, you would have to sign in and present your key. No record is kept anywhere of what's inside the box. Your money would be safe." She took a step and reached for the front doorknob.

"Kim—wait."

Laurie's face was rigid. Kim saw fear in her eyes. She glanced down to Laurie's hand, grasping her forearm.

"I do have a tax problem. I need your help."

CHAPTER 2

Shades of gray and brown dominated the world Kim found after leaving Laurie's house. The paved streets wove ribbons of gray through the neighborhood. Brown was everywhere else, in tree trunks and branches, also on the clapboard houses she passed. Overhead, scattered patches of blue fought against the banner of prevailing clouds. Not confident about the day's chances of turning nice, she set a quick pace toward her home in the canyon. If it started raining, she wanted to be inside, safe and dry.

On the way, she took a mental inventory of her pantry. She had the ingredients for a quiche. Or she could scramble eggs for lunch.

She dismissed both choices. The one would take too long to bake; the other didn't sound nearly hearty enough to sustain her through a cool, rainy day.

At the far end of town, she stopped at a restaurant called Miner's Haven. She waved to Francie, the waitress, and the cook, who were standing along the back wall, talking. Francie waved her to a booth.

"What can I get you, Kim?" Francie said as she slid a glass of water onto the table.

"Just a burger today. No cheese."

"Fries with that?"

"Sure." Despite the warmth inside the place, Kim shivered against the chill that had settled in her bones since leaving Laurie's house. "Any chance you have split pea soup?"

"Fresh made this morning."

"Great. I'd like a cup of that too."

"You got it."

Two minutes later, a steaming cup of soup sat in front of her. Kim spooned it slowly, savoring the warmth and flavor. It worked magic, restoring her to a sense of ease she hadn't felt for a couple of hours. Not since Laurie had approached her at the end of the service. She laughed at the connection. Of all the people she had met since settling in Creede, Laurie Beltran had to be the least threatening.

Creede hadn't been Kim's destination when she had set out from western Colorado a month ago. She'd spent the previous five months living in the Four Corners region, working the night shift at a convenience store in Cortez and tramping through Mesa Verde National Park on cold winter days. It was no mystery she was passing time there. No message ever arrived on her doorstep, summoning her back to Durango, fifty miles away. She was waiting to hear from Lena Fallon. Lena wasn't in Durango, but Kim believed Lena would return to the place she had always called home, and when she did, Kim would be invited back into the ex-cop's life.

Some days, Kim thought it was a hopeless dream. When a string of those days fell one after the other in February, she came to a decision. She would go back to Chicago and face the life she had walked out on a year earlier. She would find someone in the Department of Justice who would listen to her story. Crimes had been committed. Some of the evidence pointed to her. Her former boss had seen to that by framing her for a murder. But much of the evidence *had* to point elsewhere, to offshore accounts and a fraud scheme she had played no part in. Six months ago, Kim had counted on Lena Fallon's help to expose the web of lies that riddled her past. Now she was on her own.

The day she left Cortez, she drove one hundred miles across southern Colorado. At the summit of Wolf Creek Pass, she stopped. The air was crisp and cold at nearly eleven thousand feet above sea level. Ignoring the chill, she gazed at the panoramic view of her beloved San Juan Mountains, wanting to imprint the sight of the jagged peaks forever on her soul, knowing no memory, however vivid, could replicate this moment. Twenty miles farther down the road, the bottom fell out of her plans. She stared hopelessly across a broad valley floor. There were no mountains ahead. Unable to bear a landscape absent of soaring spires, she turned left at the one intersection in town. Tall peaks loomed due north. Determined to go as far and as deep into those mountains as possible, she drove on. At the mouth of a canyon, the pavement gave way to dirt. She made it around a curve before the road disappeared beneath a mound of snow. Mission accomplished, she backed out. Driving at a crawl, she came to an apparently vacant cabin. Before the day was over, she had arranged to rent the place.

"Thanks, Francie," she said when her waitress returned with a plate of food.

"My pleasure, Kim. Hey, do you have any time this week to take a look at my sister's taxes? My fool brother-in-law swears he's gonna do them, but we all know he won't get around to it."

"I think I do. Tell your sister to call me first thing in the morning to set up an appointment."

"I've been telling her to call you for two weeks."

The subject reminded Kim she had promised to meet with Laurie Beltran tomorrow night. To do her taxes, supposedly. She laughed, wondering what Laurie really wanted from her.

She finished her lunch. While paying her bill at the cash register, she noticed a flyer taped to the window. The word "MISSING" was printed at the top, followed by a photo of a man and a single paragraph detailing the little that was known about Trip Garrett's disappearance.

"Yeah, how 'bout that," Francie said, sidling up next to Kim. "That notice just went up an hour ago. A real shame, what with all that family's already been through."

"You know him?" Kim said.

"Oh honey, haven't you figured out I know everybody in this town?"

"What kind of trouble has the family had?" Kim asked.

"Their little boy died last fall. Cutest little son of a gun you'd ever want to see. Trip took it real hard."

Kim moved toward the door, ignoring questions that were none of her business. "I hope he shows up soon."

"We all do," Francie echoed.

Outside, the sky had turned dark and threatening. A sharp gust of wind tore at Kim's jacket. She hurried against the first drops of rain. Within a few steps, she broke into a jog, which became an all-out sprint as she raced the storm for home.

Damp but not drenched, she shivered standing outside the cabin while she dug in her pocket for her key. Once inside, she flipped on the overhead light, then made a beeline for the woodstove at the far wall. Adept at coaxing the warm ashes into a blazing fire, she stirred the embers before adding kindling. The dry wood flamed quickly. She added the next layer of fuel, four skinny logs set in a crosshatch pattern. Cast-iron door closed, she sat back on her knees, satisfied that the fire would grow.

Belatedly, she thought to remove her outer layer. She stood up and threw the jacket over the back of a chair, then went to her bedroom to find something warm and dry. Back in the living room, she checked on the fire and found it ready for larger logs. Still, it would be a while until the stove took the chill from the room. She sat on the sofa and pulled a down sleeping bag to her chin.

A rare feeling of contentment washed over her. She slouched deeper on the cushions and remembered the cabin as she had seen it that first day, austere beneath a winter sky. Without paying any especial mind to the fact that she was trespassing, she had proceeded to investigate the premises. She was standing on the porch when she heard a voice behind her.

"What the hell are you doing at my cabin?" a woman, presumably the property owner, had demanded.

Kim grinned at the memory of the day she'd met Paula Rowe. She had broken off from peering inside the rustic cabin to see a woman on the near side of middle age heading straight for her. She half expected to see a shotgun in the woman's hands.

"You live here?" Kim had asked, thrusting a thumb at the structure.

"I live there." The woman emphatically pointed toward the vastly larger home on the adjacent lot. "Who are you?"

"My name is Kim Jackson. Would you consider renting this place to me?"

"Why should I?"

That quickly, Kim realized she didn't have a decent answer. Rather than reply, she sank onto the top step. Her gaze wandered to the vertical wall of rock towering over the landscape, and she thought, *Because I want to sit here and look at that rock.* "You probably shouldn't," she said.

The woman reacted with surprise. "Why shouldn't I rent it to you?"

Kim had no chance to assemble a list of perfectly good reasons. The woman spoke first. "Are you an artist? Did someone send you to me?"

"No, I'm not an artist."

"Then what are you?"

By then Kim had given up hope of entering into a contract with the woman. They weren't even close to proving they could complete a simple conversation. "That's not a question I feel able to answer."

"Oh for chrissakes. What kind of work do you do?"

"Oh. I'm a bookkeeper. I do some accounting work."

"And you expect to find work in this town?"

"No, I hadn't really thought about it."

"All right then, here's the deal. You pay me a couple hundred dollars a month and agree to do my income taxes. Either leave by May first or commit to staying through August. I rent this cabin seasonally. I'm an artist. Usually I rent to a young artist. By the way, there's no central heat, only a woodstove. The stove does a good job of keeping the place warm, once you get the hang of using it. Still want to see inside?"

Kim did.

It was nearly as cold inside the cabin as out, but Kim's mind was made up. She nodded while the woman, who by then had introduced herself, ran down a description of the place: sink, stove, refrigerator, all in working order. A table and two chairs. Had she mentioned the place came furnished? Kim continued to nod. When they turned at the next entryway, Paula muttered, "Oh."

Perplexed, and suddenly worried, Kim stepped around her soon-to-be landlady to see what had provoked the atonal exclamation. "What the?" she blurted. On the far wall, next to the toilet, was a door. A fully functioning exterior door, complete with dead bolt.

"I forgot to mention this particular feature," Paula said. "You can't build a house without providing two separate points of egress. Did you know that?"

"Not specifically."

"I didn't either. I had this place designed and mostly built before some county inspector showed up and made me install a second door. It wasn't a great choice of location," she said, clearly not bothered in the least.

Kim smiled at the memory of that first meeting. Warm now, she cast off the sleeping bag.

Within a few weeks, she would have to answer the second of Paula's leasing terms and say whether she meant to stay on through the summer or pack up and leave. Seen in one light, the answer was simple. She wanted to stay. Since moving into the cabin, she hadn't felt a single impulse to go anywhere else.

The problem was the need to give any answer. For some time now, Kim had felt unhinged, for lack of a better word. She moved without troubling herself overmuch about the direction she took. In general, she kept up appearances. She maintained a minimum air of responsibility, at least when it came to preparing tax returns. But there were other times when she felt herself teetering, as though she were edging far too close to some abyss. In good conscience, she failed to see how she could commit to anything.

CHAPTER 3

"Before we get started, I need to ask whether you'll keep everything I tell you confidential," Laurie Beltran said the following evening.

Taken aback by the young woman's detached voice, matched by sober brown eyes boring into her, Kim sought to reassure her. "Of course I'll keep your financial matters private, Laurie. As I would anything you asked me not to reveal."

"You have to understand. Nothing like this has ever happened to me before! I don't have a clue what these papers mean or what to do with them."

They were in Laurie's living room, seated on chairs that took up nearly the whole of the meager space. A thin folder lay on the coffee table. There was no white pad riddled with questions, no pen lying atop for note-taking. By all appearances, the meeting was shaping up to be blissfully brief.

Laurie reached for the folder. "This came in the mail." She thrust it forward.

Kim took the folder. Inside there were three sheets of paper. The first was a business letter bearing a Santa Fe return address. It had been sent to Laurie at a post office box in Pagosa

Springs, a town larger than Creede some forty miles south. The letter described a stock transaction and urged Laurie to seek professional help in dealing with the tax implications of the proceeds. Kim flipped to the second page. It was a standard 1099-B form reporting income from sales for the previous tax year. Kim scanned the figures in the columns and did a double take. The tally at the bottom was six figures. The truth slowly registered. Last year, Laurie had realized a gain of $245,000 on the sale of stocks.

"Jesus Christ, Laurie," Kim muttered. She glanced up, alarmed at her thoughtless curse. "Sorry. I didn't mean to say that."

Laurie appeared not to have heard. Kim returned her attention to the tax form. "Did you pay estimated taxes last year?"

"I don't know that I've ever paid taxes. I don't know a thing about any of this."

Kim sighed. It was worse than she had expected. "Then at a minimum you're going to have a whopping big tax bill."

"I don't know how I can possibly pay it! I don't have very much money."

But that wasn't true. Laurie did have money. Kim reread the 1099-B. Somewhere, Laurie had $245,000 sitting in an account. Kim read the third page. According to the document, Laurie had owned eight thousand shares of a company that had been purchased by another in a straight cash deal. From the company's name, Avalon Storage Devices, Kim gathered the business was in the high-tech industry.

"The stock was a gift from my grandparents. I didn't have a thing to do with it," Laurie said.

Kim smiled. "Hey, let's back up, okay? Let's forget about the money for a minute and spend a little time getting to know each other."

"Okay."

Kim tossed the folder on the coffee table. She wished she had more time to weigh what to say.

"Why do you come to church?" Laurie asked. "You don't believe in God, do you?"

Touché, Kim thought, amused by Laurie's cheekiness. "I enjoy attending. There's not much else to do in town on Sunday mornings," she said, answering but not telling the truth. She tried again. "I like listening to you. And no, I don't believe in God. At least not in the God of your Bible."

"Which God do you believe in?"

"I think the answer is no God, but I haven't worked that out yet. Laurie, can I ask you something? I've heard that you lived in a convent before you came here."

"That was a while ago."

"Where was the convent?"

"In Santa Fe."

Kim noticed that Laurie was dressed in the same clothes she had worn after church on Sunday, blue jeans and a worn wool sweater. Despite her pallor, she was an attractive young woman, blessed with fine skin, clear brown eyes, and long dark hair.

"How long were you in the convent?"

"Two years."

"Do you mind my asking how old you are?"

"I'm twenty-four. How old are you?"

"Thirty. I think I see now," Kim said, musing over the information. "You haven't had to pay taxes before because you haven't had income."

"I may have paid taxes in the past. Someone else would have handled that."

Kim drew a long breath. "Laurie, it really is nothing to me what you do with this money. But the government will have rather severe expectations concerning the part that is due to them. I'm afraid there will be nothing negotiable about that."

"What do you mean?"

"You're going to have to pay the amount you owe, whatever it turns out to be. I suspect you may owe as much as $30,000. I won't know until I plug these numbers into a computer worksheet. Somewhere, I don't know where, you have $245,000 sitting in an account. So you do have plenty of money to pay your tax bill."

Kim thought anyone else would have been staggered by the sum. Laurie was unfazed. Glassiness returned to her eyes. Feeling her slipping back into a too-quiet state, Kim abandoned the subject of money. "Hey, how did you know?" she asked.

"Know what?"

"That I don't believe in God."

"I don't feel God in you. That's not to say I think you're a godless person. It's the opposite. I feel something good and true in you, and I don't know whether you're still searching to find your way with God or you know something else that lets you be the way you are, good without walking in the path of the church's teaching. That's why I felt able to trust you with this." Laurie nodded at the folder.

"What would you have done if I hadn't been here?"

"I'm not sure. Probably nothing."

"Do you mind if I ask a personal question?"

"It depends on the question."

"How did you get from a convent in Santa Fe to Creede, Colorado?"

The last bit of color drained from Laurie's face. Kim had no chance to try and understand the reaction her question had provoked. There was a knock at the door. Both women jumped.

"Are you expecting anyone?" Kim said.

Laurie shook her head.

Kim went to the door. "Who is it?" she called.

"Andy Preston, Mineral County sheriff."

Kim gave the knob a twist. A tall man with a handlebar mustache, dressed in a brown uniform and displaying his badge, walked in without invitation. "Laurie Beltran?" he said. Kim pointed at Laurie.

"What's this about?" Kim said.

The sheriff ignored her. "Ms. Beltran, I have a few questions for you about your relationship with Trip Garrett."

Kim recognized the missing man's name from the poster she had seen at breakfast yesterday and others she had seen around town since then. "Have you found him?" she said.

Andy Preston turned and gave Kim a considered look. "Yep, we've found him. Pulled his body out of Willow Creek late this afternoon. 'Scuse my manners, miss. I don't believe we've met."

CHAPTER 4

"Stay still. Why are you so jumpy tonight?" Paula Rowe said.

Kim grimaced. "Lack of oxygen. I'm suffocating."

"From what?"

"Other people. I—"

"Quiet."

The only sound afterward was of charcoal striking paper, a scrabbling sound made large by the backdrop of silence. When Kim twitched again, Paula roared, "You're useless to me tonight! What is your problem?"

They took a break. Kim closed her eyes and drew a welcome breath while she stretched her neck one direction, then the other. She rolled her shoulders forward and back. Feeling marginally better, she twisted around to look at Paula, something she rarely did while sitting for her. "Sorry, Chief. It's been a long couple of days. I guess I don't have it in me tonight."

Paula closed her eyes in a withering display. "Tonight of all nights."

Kim didn't take the bait. She doubted there was anything special about tonight.

"Can you please give me five uninterrupted minutes?" Paula said.

"Maybe. Give me a minute."

Kim raised her arms and swung them back in the hope of coaxing new blood through the limbs. Gradually, she resumed her former position sitting on the barstool: body turned, profile offered, nude upper half of her body revealed to the artist. Her gaze settled on a distant wall. Expression ebbed from her features. It was the pose she was meant to hold.

Most nights she was able to enter a semidetached state while sitting. Typically, she was able to achieve an almost surreal stillness for up to thirty minutes at a time while Paula sketched her. It no longer bothered her when Paula occasionally came close, circling her with tablet and charcoal stub in hand, angling for another perspective.

Becoming an artist's model was nothing Kim had ever imagined doing. The first time Paula asked, Kim's answer was an unequivocal no. She didn't think about it again. She certainly didn't feel coerced, but the next time Paula asked, Kim had said yes.

That day, Paula had found her where Kim often was back then: lying on a cheap and broken chaise longue outside her cabin, bundled in two sleeping bags, looking up at what she had come to think of as her rock wall. A snowstorm was swirling down from the canyon. She was beginning to be buried beneath a glaze of white.

"You're as weird as I am," Paula had said. "I didn't think I'd ever say that to anyone." When Kim failed to reply, Paula said, "Do you want to come to the house for dinner tonight?"

"Yes. I'd like that," Kim had said. Thus began their curious friendship.

A sharp sound of a tablet closing jarred her from the memory. "We're done here," Paula said.

Kim moved. She had no idea how long she had been sitting. She took the light-blue men's dress shirt from where it was hooked over the back of a chair and put it on, slowly fastening the long line of buttons. She could have dressed in her own clothes, but she liked wearing the shirt and she knew Paula liked seeing her in it. She rolled back the sleeves and walked over to the kitchen counter.

"Why are you feeling oppressed by the great sea of humanity tonight?" Paula said.

Kim shrugged. Even if Laurie Beltran hadn't exacted a promise of silence from her, Kim wouldn't have told Paula what she had learned the previous night. But Laurie had been too much on her mind all day.

"You're not going to tell me, are you?"

"It's nothing worth telling, Paula."

"Have it your way."

Paula refilled her wineglass. Kim took a glass of water and joined her at the kitchen table. A casserole was in the oven. A bowl of salad was on the counter.

Kim hadn't yet spent enough time inside the artist's house to have had her fill of admiring it. All gleaming blond wood and windows, the open living space—kitchen, sitting room, art studio—ran the length of the house on the south side. Industrial lighting hung from the vaulted ceiling. Stainless steel appliances shone in the light, as did the polished surface of the hardwood floor.

Kim had never seen the rest of the house, other than the adjacent bathroom, where she would remove her blouse and bra and then don the overlarge shirt prior to each session.

Paula stabbed the base of her wineglass with two fingers. Wisps of wavy blond hair fluttered in the tension around her face. The rest of her long, thick hair was held in place by a clip. An intense but attractive woman, Paula's blue eyes and jutting chin were her most distinguishing features. Her eyes welded her to a world she was committed to transforming through art. Her chin gave her face depth of character. An inch shorter than Kim's height of five-seven, Paula's build was sturdier, softer around her stomach and hips. She was forty-two years old.

"What have you been reading in that nasty little book of yours?" she said.

"'Epigrams and Interludes,'" Kim replied. "My least favorite part."

"What round is this, three? Four?"

"Something like that." Kim had been reading Friedrich Nietzsche's *Beyond Good and Evil* off and on for months. It was one of a handful of books in her collection and was not precisely hers. It had once belonged to Lena Fallon.

"So you don't have any good stories for me?"

"Not tonight."

Kim walked to the counter and poured a glass of wine. On turning, she saw Paula's eyes firmly fixed on her and thought this was at least an improvement over the artist's earlier fit of pique. She returned to the kitchen table and sat down.

Their eyes met. Kim started the game. "Do you believe in God the father almighty, maker of heaven and earth?"

"Of course I don't."

"Do you believe in friendship?"

"I don't find it necessary to believe in friendship."

Kim mulled over the reply. It would be easy enough to get sidetracked. She didn't let herself. "Do you believe in color and line?"

"Yes."

She hesitated. "Do you believe in justice?"

Paula snorted. "Justice is a negative concept. It's a victim's best friend. It only gets hauled onto the stage when there's a perceived need to right a wrong. No wrong can ever be set right. It will stand forever, alongside all of the other wrongs that have ever been committed."

Kim drew a shallow breath. Accustomed as she was to Paula's harsh line, even this took her aback. "So you're saying there is no such thing as justice?"

"I'm suggesting you would do better to inquire about the tools of your rarefied notion of 'justice.' The punishment and control of human beings, that's what the question really comes to, don't you think?"

"I don't know. Maybe."

It was more than Kim could bear to think about now.

The buzzer on the oven went off. Paula laughed as she stood up. "Someday I'm going to solve these puzzles of yours." She started to walk away. "Someday I'm going to know what the hell we've been talking about all this time."

Much later that night, Kim lay in bed gazing through a window unadorned with any covering. Outside, the perimeter of the property was well lit. Normally the lights didn't bother her. She didn't blame them now for her sleeplessness. Without turning her head, she traced the line of wooden fence posts from where they emerged in shadow at the western edge of the property to where they disappeared beyond her view to the east. Tufts of scrub grass were dark in the foreground. In the background, Paula's house loomed large as a castle.

Kim replayed Paula's words from earlier that night. *Justice is a victim's best friend. Justice is about a perceived need to right a wrong. No wrong can ever be set right.*

The words teased her. She didn't quibble with them, only let them rattle around in her mind. Behind their echo she saw a man dressed in brown interrogating a scared-to-death twenty-four-year-old woman about a dead man. "I've been told you argued with Trip Garrett on Friday afternoon," Andy Preston, Mineral County sheriff, had said to Laurie last night. "Mind telling me about what?"

"He wouldn't pay me," Laurie had replied, her voice rising in a tone half exclamation, half wail.

By degrees, the story came out. For two weeks Laurie had failed to be paid for childcare. She babysat the Garrett daughters, ages three years and eighteen months, while the mother, Cathy, worked at the elementary school and Trip Garrett worked for himself, operating a home repair and remodeling company. The Garretts were in arrears to Laurie for $250.

"So you confronted Trip while he was unwinding over at Alvie's bar?" the sheriff had demanded to know.

Kim didn't think she had imagined the insinuation—that Laurie was the aggressor, and that she had a heck of a nerve, talking to a man about money while he was wetting his whistle at the end of a week. She didn't want to credit Preston with more savvy than he deserved, but she suspected he was goading Laurie, trying to spark a flare that might signal something more explosive lurking inside the doe-eyed woman of God. When Kim pressed him for more information, Andy Preston admitted that Trip Garrett was last seen Friday afternoon in the bar with his buddies, and later that night, at home with his wife and daughters. He went out in the evening, never to return.

While the stars moved stealthily across the sky and the shadows imperceptibly changed shape on Paula's land, Kim mulled over a deeper mystery. Why would a woman who had $245,000 bother with a job where she earned twenty-five dollars a day?

Laurie's argument in the bar had netted her thirty dollars when Trip Garrett opened his wallet and handed over a twenty and a ten. It had also netted her a less welcome honor. From Sheriff Andy Preston's questions, Kim gathered Laurie was a person of interest in Garrett's death.

CHAPTER 5

The oak desktop in the spare room at John Carlos's accounting services office was a mess. A stack of client folders, a laptop computer, two notepads covered with black scrawls, and a variety of pens and pencils cluttered the surface, along with an ancient telephone inching precariously close to the edge. An open newspaper lay atop the debris. It was the last thing Kim should have been reading on a morning booked with appointments. She had read the Trip Garrett story twice and learned the local man was thirty-five years old when he died. He was a born and bred Coloradoan. He and a partner owned a remodeling company that had them doing all manner of jobs from simple repairs to large-scale additions and renovations. His work took him away from Creede, most recently to a strip mall in South Fork, twenty-odd miles away. For other jobs he had traveled to Del Norte and Pagosa Springs, larger towns a bit farther afield.

Trip was described as an avid outdoorsman who loved hunting and fly-fishing. He was the father of two girls. He and his wife, Cathy, had tragically lost their son, Cody, last year.

Kim reached for a notepad and jotted down a list of questions, beginning with, What was Garrett's state of mind leading up to his death? Was he depressed over the death of his son, and possibly suicidal? Had he taken pains to obscure the manner of his death in order to guarantee life insurance would be paid to his family? Did he have a life insurance policy?

How had Cody Garrett died?

Sharp rapping at the door interrupted her. "Kim, your next appointment is here," Dee, the receptionist, said.

Kim looked up. "Great."

She made a stab at clearing the desk by piling folders and notepads into a wobbly stack. She pulled a clean pad from a desk drawer, opened the laptop, and was standing, ready to greet her client when he walked in.

Forty-five minutes and three new pages of scribbled notes later, she escorted the mining engineer from the office while reminding him of the supporting documents he needed to provide. He was no sooner out the door than Kim turned to greet her next client, who was waiting in reception. "I'll be right with you, Mrs. Johnson," she said, hastily retreating into her inner sanctum. She spent two minutes jotting a final note in the mining engineer's file. Hearty laughter sounded through the wall from the office next door. Kim envied John Carlos the time and energy to laugh.

The day proceeded in much the same vein. A steady stream of clients appeared, one after the next. Kim wouldn't have minded the pace had she been able to complete a single tax filing once the music stopped and the face sitting across from her changed. With maddening regularity, her questions elicited frowns of confusion and a rummaging about in memory for utility bills, receipts, sometimes even official tax documents left at home somewhere. Each person promised to deliver the missing paperwork posthaste. From Kim's perspective, the logjam of work only grew deeper.

Sometime past five o'clock, she relaxed, finally alone. Dee, who worked part-time, had left hours ago to go to the historical society, where she volunteered. John was holed up in his office, quiet for once. He had a six o'clock appointment. Kim knew she should take the time to sort the papers scattered on her desk into a semblance of order. Instead she reached for the newspaper. For the third time that day, she read the Trip Garrett story. Garrett's body had been found in Willow Creek, a few miles south of town. Speculation was he went into the creek upstream and was carried down by high water. He was discovered by road workers who spotted a blue jacket caught in the branches of a fallen tree. An investigation was ongoing.

Sheriff Andy Preston was the lead investigator. Kim recalled the man, who stood approximately five-ten and had a broad chest and a curly brown mustache. The sheriff hadn't impressed her when she met him. She couldn't imagine what he had been fishing for from Laurie or why he had needed to do it at eight o'clock at night.

Laurie. Kim spotted the thin file buried beneath the teetering stack. She gave herself a dozen reasons why she didn't need to bother with Laurie's taxes tonight. Then she pulled the file out anyway, opened a new tax sheet on the laptop, and entered Laurie's name and Social Security number. Then she stopped. She had no address for Laurie, no birth date. Hell, she didn't even know her marital status.

Most of the rest came easily. With only a handful of numbers to enter, Kim skipped to the appropriate page to enter stock sale proceeds from the 1099-B form. The software clicked along, calculating tax owed and penalty for underpayment of estimated taxes. Within seconds, the spread of digits flashed on the screen. For her proceeds on the sale of stock, Laurie owed the federal government a whopping thirty grand and change.

Kim heaved a sigh and turned off the machine. She wasn't going to give Laurie that news tonight.

She headed for home via her usual route past the post office. A soft white light inside the building showed a narrow hall fronting a wall of mailboxes. Beyond the unoccupied front counter lay a deeply shadowed central space where the processing and sorting of the town's mail took place. She had meant to stop in today. Now the facility was closed except to private mailbox holders. Kim walked on, wondering whether a letter awaited her behind that ghostly counter. Nothing to be done tonight. Tomorrow she would find out.

She was at the post office in the morning when it opened. An elderly gentleman entered the building ahead of her. When it was her turn, she went to the counter. By now she didn't have to ask, but she did anyway. "Anything for me in General Delivery?" she said to Claudia, the postmistress.

"No, Kim. Sorry. I checked this morning."

And still it came as a shock, the pang of disappointment that struck somewhere behind her chest wall, even though she ought to have known the answer long before she asked the question. She forced a smile. "Okay, thanks." She pushed a thin envelope across the counter, which she easily could have dropped in a box, but this, too, had become part of the ritual. It was a letter to Lena Fallon.

Lena was in Denver. She had been there for the past seven months. Kim had an address and nothing more, exactly the same as Lena had for her, though Kim at least kept Lena regularly apprised of her whereabouts by sending a brief note once a week with her return address printed in the envelope's corner. It was an address, of sorts. All it said was: General Delivery, Creede, Colorado. If Lena ever came looking for her, almost anyone in Creede would be able to say where to find her.

Kim did not expect Lena to come looking for her. But she hadn't given up hope that Lena might yet deign to write. A few scribbles to say she was alive, doing fine. Or not. Kim knew she was alive, and she knew where Lena was, thanks to a friend in Durango. Eight months ago, Kim had lived in Lena's Durango house and worked for her. Their partnership solving the crime that had left Lena, an ex-cop, paralyzed had resulted in severe collateral damage. Lena had been forced to shoot and kill a young woman, but not before the woman shot three people, including Kim and Lena, and set a fire that destroyed Lena's house.

Kim and Lena hadn't spoken since that horrific night. That persistent silence was one of two black holes at the center of her life. The other was that her real name was not Kim Jackson.

She put the past behind her for now and went to work. Through the morning she saw a succession of clients. At noon, after the last person left, Kim slipped out as well. "I need some fresh air. I'll be back by one," she told Dee.

Outside, the day had turned sunny and warm. Kim walked through town to the cross street into Laurie's neighborhood. She meant to leave a note on the door requesting a meeting that night. To her surprise, Laurie was home.

"Cathy—Trip's wife—took time off from work," Laurie said, explaining her presence. "I've been at the house a few times to help with the girls. I'll probably go back to my regular hours on Monday when Cathy goes back to work."

"Oh right," Kim said. Trip Garrett's death. Laurie worked for the family. Somehow she had forgotten the connection in her immersion in other people's taxes. Questions leapt to mind, which she didn't ask. She needed to get back to work. "Is it okay if I come by tonight? I have most of the work finished on your taxes but I need more information."

Laurie said that would be fine.

The early evening air retained a sultry feel when Kim locked the office door shortly before six that night. A light wind blew. Clouds, as usual, hung low over the mountains, parting occasionally for the last rays of the day's sun to shoot through in uncommon brilliance. Near Laurie's house, frothy, milk-colored water continued to race beneath the road that passed over the creek. Up and down the length of town, several residential roads spanned the wash known as Willow Creek. Kim wondered where investigators suspected Trip Garrett went into the water.

In contrast to her demeanor earlier that day, Laurie was agitated when Kim arrived. She paced, expressing no interest in taxes. When pressed for the few details Kim needed to complete the forms, she blew up. "Why do you need to give them my address? Of course I'm single! How could you not know that?"

Kim smiled, trying to think how to diffuse the explosive energy. When she realized Laurie was more pale than usual, she took a different tack. "Hey, never mind. We can get to that later. Do you mind if I get a glass of water?"

"Of course not."

The kitchen counter and sink were as spotless as they were the first time Kim visited. This time no dishes or silverware were set out to dry in the drain. She found a water glass in a cabinet. On a hunch she opened the adjoining door and was startled to find the cupboard bare except for a box of macaroni and cheese and one can of soup. She thought fast. Last Friday Laurie had confronted Trip Garrett over the issue of back pay. He gave her thirty dollars. Three days later he turned up dead. Kim didn't think there was any chance Laurie could have worked out an agreement with her employer for the rest of the money owed her in the interim. That thirty dollars likely had been spent days ago.

"Did you eat today?" Kim asked casually when she returned to the living room.

"I ate a peanut butter sandwich for lunch. Why do you ask?"

Kim assumed that meant Laurie hadn't had anything since then. "I'm starved. Why don't we go into town and get something to eat?"

Laurie shook her head. "I can't. I don't have any money."

Once again, Kim thought this an odd response from someone who obviously *did* have money. She chose to let it go. "Well, I do. You can pay me back when you pay me for your taxes."

"I'm going to have to pay you?" Laurie's eyes were suddenly bright with alarm.

Kim sighed. "Let's go get something to eat. We can discuss money later."

Miner's Haven was doing a bustling business when they arrived. Francie passed by, arms laden with dirty plates, and said she needed two minutes to clean a recently vacated booth. Soon afterward the two women were seated in a large booth along windows fronting the town's main street.

"How is the Garrett family doing?" Kim asked after they ordered.

"The baby is fine. She giggles and chatters and toddles around making everyone laugh. Her sister keeps asking for her daddy."

"What about Cathy?"

"She's holding herself together. Trip's family is around more than usual, his mom and his brother. I think they're trying to help, but they're not."

"What about Cathy's family, are they here?"

"No. She doesn't have one."

Francie dropped off a salad and a bowl of soup at the table, briefly interrupting the conversation. Kim took small sips of soup while she watched Laurie all but inhale the salad.

"That cop's been back to talk to me," Laurie said after scooping the last forkful of greens into her mouth.

"About what?"

"Trip. He asked the same questions as before. When was the last time I saw him? What did we argue about? Valerie told me I shouldn't talk to him. Joan, her partner, is a lawyer, so I guess it's really Joan who says I shouldn't talk to him. But I don't see what difference it makes."

Much as Kim wanted to pursue the subject of Trip Garrett, she didn't. There was a larger topic looming. "Laurie, we need to spend a few minutes talking about your tax situation. The other night I said you might owe as much as $30,000 to the government."

Laurie shrugged.

"It's actually a bit more than that. You owe a little over $32,000 to the federal government and another $7,000 to the state of Colorado. I strongly advise you to pay estimated taxes as well to avoid future scrutiny from the IRS."

"Isn't there some way to make this all go away?"

Kim wondered what a less scrupulous financial advisor would make of that request. Sure, the money could disappear. Right into someone else's pocket.

"No, this isn't going to go away. Once I print the tax forms, you'll need to review and sign them. Then you'll have to write two checks, one to the US Treasury and another to the state of Colorado."

"I don't have any checks! How am I supposed to write a check?" Laurie's eyes blazed anew.

"Laurie, your money has to be sitting in an account somewhere. You must be able to access it. Do you have any idea where it is?"

"No. You'd have to ask David."

"David who?"

"David Sandoval. He works at a bank in Santa Fe."

Francie returned with two heaping plates of roast chicken. Kim busied herself slicing off bites before delving back into the mysteries of Laurie's money. Loath to surface from the simple pleasure of chewing and swallowing, she was startled when Laurie spoke.

"Are you and Paula Rowe friends? Do you model for her?"

"What?"

"I just wondered. I know you live in her cabin. It's not any big deal to me if you do model for her. I'm not a prude, if that's what you're thinking. But I would question whether Paula is a good person for you to associate with."

"Laurie, stop. How do you know I spend time with Paula?"

"I just assumed. Because you're her tenant. Valerie, or maybe Joan, mentioned Paula likes to work with nude models. They've lived here a long time and know all about her. They're curious about you."

Kim smiled uneasily.

"Paula's the problem," Laurie said. "I don't know her, but from what I've heard she's selfish and extremely manipulative, taking what she wants without giving anything back. I don't like to think she's doing that to you."

"Trust me, I can handle Paula," Kim said, eyeing the woman sitting across from her with growing doubt. A plateful of food seemed to have done Laurie a world of good. For the first time, Kim wondered whether she was up to the challenge of handling Laurie Beltran.

CHAPTER 6

When the cell phone rang, the man shrouded in a dark robe looked up from the book in his hands. The last words he'd read fled his memory. It had been so long since the phone rang. He had nearly doubted this moment would come. He answered.

The caller identified herself as Mrs. Dominguez. But he already knew who was calling. Only she had the number to this phone. "Mrs. Dominguez, how wonderful to hear from you. How is your family?"

"Everyone is fine, Father. We have been blessed. I am calling today because I have news."

"Yes?"

"There has been activity in the account."

His heart quickened. For months he had waited for news—any news—concerning Laurie Beltran. "I see."

"It was an internal transfer of funds. A substantial amount of money was moved to a money market account."

"Is there anything else you can tell me?"

There followed a moment's hesitation. "Yes, Father." Another moment passed. "A set of blank checks was mailed to an address in Creede, Colorado."

He knew nothing about the place. No matter. He would learn everything he needed to know soon. Speaking gently, he asked the woman if she had the exact address. She did. Pen poised, he wrote down the address of an accounting services firm in Creede, Colorado.

"Thank you, Mrs. Dominguez. May God's blessing be upon you and your family as you continue to do His work."

He bowed his head and prayed after the call ended. He gave thanks for the work of his faithful servant, Mrs. Dominguez. He meditated on the coincidence of word reaching him today, of all days, Good Friday. No, not a coincidence. It was symbolic.

There were countless ways of doing God's work. Father Brian had been persuaded of this truth for decades. Never once in all that time had he failed to do his duty according to the Church's tenets. But there were limits imposed on him—budgetary limits. How he hated that word. Twice before, he'd been the beneficiary of private funds generously gifted to him as intermediary of God's work. A third opportunity was on the horizon. A young woman had made promises, and though she had strayed from the flock, now she was found again. Finally, after nearly a year, she was found again.

He put the book away and gazed humbly upon a world transformed. He reached for a different phone and rang a man who had been awaiting his call.

CHAPTER 7

The rock wall towering over the entrance to the canyon sparkled with metallic flecks. Shards of gold, silver, copper, and platinum shot out from a darker-hued background of solid browns and blacks, a veritable prism seeming to tilt this way and that, firing off terrestrial messages to some distant universe.

Kim watched the light show from her broken chaise longue. Swaddled in a down sleeping bag, only her face was exposed to the forty-degree air and the almost imperceptible breeze that glanced across her nose and cheeks, a touch that reminded her of an artist's brush dipped in ice water.

It was April 16. She had work to do. And as of today, she had all the time in the world to do it.

Thoughts spun from her mind with the same apparent randomness as light glinting off rock. She was meditating on the utter improbability of being here, precisely here. The thought took her to a different time and place, one that hadn't included rocks and light. One year ago the circumference of her reality had been bounded by daily trips to a high-rise building in downtown Chicago. There, heels clip-clopped across a marble floor and fine clothing rustled as a cadre of soldiers, including her, marched to the beat of numbers.

It was the life she had trained for. It was the life she had thought she wanted, only because she had never imagined any other sort of life, and that, she admitted now, was an error. At the very least she should have entertained other possibilities rather than set an unswerving line for the corporate world once she became a newly minted MBA and CPA.

Or so she thought here, in the presence of rocks and light.

In its own way, that other life had satisfied her. Then one day a good man turned over an ordinary rock and something terrible crawled out. He saw it, and she did too. And before she could fathom the meaning of the discovery, that man was dead and Kim—whose name wasn't Kim then—was swept into a sordid array of circumstances where she learned that not only was the man dead because he had stumbled onto evidence of corporate fraud, but she was supposed to have killed him.

Her boss at the Chicago skyscraper told her this fantastical story.

Her boss had committed those crimes. He laughed when he told her the evidence would land her in prison or worse—on death row—if she didn't do exactly as he said. He promised her that everything would be all right if she kept her mouth shut and went on doing her job.

As if. As if any of it could be right ever again.

What he didn't say, but what she believed, was that he meant to kill her. She was a loose end. He wasn't a man who tolerated loose ends.

A voice cleared softly. Hearing it, Kim reconciled the other sounds she had lately heard of twigs snapping and stones crunching beneath a foot. By the time she finished a rapid run-through of possible visitors, eliminating all but two then winnowing that list to one, knowing Paula would have approached from the opposite direction and not nearly as quietly, she turned to confirm her theory.

"What are you doing out here? Are you okay?" Laurie Beltran said.

"Hey," Kim said, surprised—yet not—to see the other woman standing nearby in the noonday sun. They satisfied each other's inquiries as to why neither one was at work. Cathy had come home to spend an hour with the girls, relieving Laurie temporarily of her duties. Kim explained that her time was her own now that April 15 had come and gone. She was, however, planning to go into the office shortly.

"Oh, that's good. I didn't know how busy you'd be. I have a favor to ask," Laurie said as her glance skittered away before settling on some object at ground level.

Kim hadn't seen Laurie for over a week other than at the Sunday service. The time in between seemed to have vanished in a wisp. It seemed much longer ago when Kim had tracked down David Sandoval at his bank in Santa Fe, requested the transfer of funds to a money market account, and ordered checks for Laurie to use to pay her tax bills. Sandoval had required a faxed letter from Laurie authorizing the actions. Kim had expedited that. When the checks had arrived, she wrote them. Laurie had signed. Kim had sent them off, and since then she had been swamped with work on other tax returns.

Now she watched the outward evidence of Laurie's inner turmoil, amused by a knowing sort of resignation. In the history of their brief acquaintance, she had yet to turn down any request Laurie had made. She assumed this one, whatever it was, would be no different. "What is it?"

"It's huge. I need a ride to Santa Fe."

A number of questions popped to mind, among them: why, and how far away was Santa Fe? She waited for an explanation.

When one was not forthcoming, she asked, "What's in Santa Fe?"

"I'll tell you tomorrow."

Kim laughed at Laurie's brazen assumption that the plan was arranged. In her mind no such thing was certain. Santa Fe was in New Mexico. New Mexico bordered Colorado to the south, but that was the extent of her geographical knowledge. The city was reputed to be beautiful, though she doubted a leisure getaway was what Laurie had in mind.

She resumed her meditation of light and rock. "What time do you want to leave?"

At seven the next morning, Kim backed her baby-blue Cadillac out of its parking place alongside the cabin. She and Laurie drove out of town beneath a sky lit in a soft pinkish glow. The color gradually changed to peach as they crossed a wide river valley. Flanking their right, the Rio Grande flowed from its headwaters in the mountains west of town, beginning a journey that would take it to the Gulf of Mexico.

Traffic on the two-lane road was light. There was a stillness about the morning that led Kim to believe anything was possible, a pleasant thought, however untrue. Laurie, sitting beside her, was wrapped in silence. Kim didn't mind the quiet. Nor, for that matter, did she mind the drive. It felt good to be going somewhere, if only for a day.

On the ascent of Wolf Creek Pass, she gunned the Cadillac's engine and was rewarded with a burst of unbridled power.

"This doesn't seem like your kind of car," Laurie said, breaking her long silence.

"It isn't."

Kim owned a different car. Her real car, as she still thought of it, was a maroon Lexus sedan. She'd driven the Lexus from Chicago when she ran out on her life as an accounting manager at a Fortune 500 company. That car, registered in her real name, was locked inside a self-storage unit in Montrose, Colorado.

The Cadillac had come to her as a gift from a friend and was not a story she wanted to tell.

They crested the summit of the pass and sped down the other side.

"Turn here. This is our turn," Laurie said sharply when they reached the town of Pagosa Springs.

Kim set the signal and made the turn.

"Today is my birthday. I'm twenty-five," Laurie announced a few miles down the new road.

"Happy birthday."

"Today I get my trust fund. All of it. It's from my grandparents. That's why I need to go to Santa Fe. I have to see David Sandoval."

"Did you make an appointment with him?"

"No. Why should I have to do that? It's my money."

Over the next hour, while Kim drove through picturesque rolling hills in northern New Mexico, Laurie, for once, spoke freely. She told an American tale about a fortune made by a scrappy couple who were as lucky as they were smart. During the 1960s, her grandparents had lived in Northern California, where they dabbled in real estate. Their holdings in communities with bucolic names such as Sunnyvale, Los Altos, and Mountain View exploded in value with the birth of computer technology in the last two decades of the twentieth century. More fortuitously, her grandfather correctly read the future in the metallic chips the area became famous for producing; he invested heavily in a slew of new companies, the majority of which went on to boast astronomical profits. Disenchanted with the changes rapidly being wrought on the Silicon Valley landscape, husband and wife left the coast for the interior, settling in Santa Fe while their investments continued to multiply. Laurie had no idea how much her grandparents were worth. All she knew was that their holdings had been sufficient to subsidize their son, her father, in a European lifestyle for the past twenty years. He and Laurie's mother were currently living in the South of France.

When asked about siblings, Laurie said she had a sister.

The landscape grew more beautiful the farther south they drove. Mountains loomed closer, still snowcapped in mid-April. Their dark-green sides stood in stark contrast to the brown earth rippling far and wide, sometimes forming rocky ridgelines and outcroppings chiseled in intricate patterns. Cresting one hill, Kim was startled to see a city laid out below. "Welcome to Santa Fe," Laurie said softly.

She directed Kim onto a wide boulevard that led to narrower streets. Three blocks later, she told her to park. When they got out of the car, Kim got her first good look at Laurie, who was dressed smartly in dark slacks, a nice blouse, leather flats, and a leather jacket. "Whoa, you look nice," she said.

"Thanks. Let's walk for a bit."

They walked along a street dappled in golden sunlight. Intrigued, Kim thought the light seemed something unto itself, subtly different from ordinary light in ways she couldn't describe. Under other circumstances, she would have studied it happily for hours. "Where is the business district?" she said, wandering along at Laurie's side, wondering why they were in a neighborhood of adobe shops.

"We're in it."

"You must be joking." Kim didn't see a single high-rise building or anyone dressed in a suit hurrying along the street.

"What were you expecting, New York?" Laurie said. "Come on. I want to show you something." She grabbed Kim's arm and led the way to a plaza that could have been lifted straight out of Madrid or Mexico City. "I need some time before we go to David's office."

Kim needed more than a few minutes to absorb her impressions of the adobe buildings flanking the square on all sides. Shops, art galleries, museums, and restaurants were knitted together in four long walls surrounding an open area of tall, shady trees and footpaths. In front of one long building with a low-beam roof, Native American artists sat shoulder to shoulder in front of trays of silver and turquoise jewelry, pottery, and weavings. Laurie said it was the Palace of the Governors. She said the women and men were there every day of the year.

Kim craned her neck for a look at the handcrafted pieces as Laurie marched them past. When they turned at the next corner, she stopped and stared. Two blocks away, a massive cathedral loomed over the narrow Old World street.

"St. Francis Cathedral," Laurie said.

The silence that followed grew long.

"Is that where you attended church?" Kim asked.

"No. Well, sometimes."

Another minute passed. With sudden determination, Laurie said, "Let's go."

Before they reached their destination, she said, "Soon I'll be able to repay you for everything you've paid for up to now."

"I'm not worried about the money."

"I appreciate that. But your expenses have to be adding up."

They were. Kim didn't argue the point.

To Kim's surprise, Laurie stopped at a Wells Fargo Bank, where she verified the existence of a checking account with a balance of nearly $1,000. She asked for and received a book of ten blank checks. At the bank manager's insistence, she grudgingly agreed to order more checks and arranged to have them sent to Creede. Kim stood by, listening, surprised by Laurie's familiarity with the account. She thought Laurie had denied having a checking account during one of their tax meetings. They left Wells Fargo and went to Bank of the West, located on an adjacent street. Inside, Laurie led the way up a flight of stairs only to be prevented from proceeding farther by an older woman dressed beautifully in a dark jacket and skirt. She wore an ivory-colored blouse that set off the gold cross around her neck. Her desk sat recessed in an alcove, allowing her full view of bank employees and visitors entering the corridor that led to a suite of private offices. The nameplate on her desk read "Mrs. Herrera."

"Just tell David Laurie Beltran would like to see him," Laurie said, speaking in a strident voice Kim hadn't heard her use before.

"I'll see if Mr. Sandoval is free," the woman said stiffly. She picked up her phone and made a call, face averted to keep the two women from overhearing her conversation. When the call ended, her expression was set primly. "Mr. Sandoval will see you. However, in the future, I advise you to call ahead to arrange an appointment. It is our policy."

Kim sensed movement deep in the corridor. A man approached, smiling broadly. He sidestepped the other woman and moved directly to Laurie, whose hand he clasped in both his own.

"Laurie, it's so good to see you! You look wonderful. Please, come to my office."

Laurie motioned for Kim to follow. Once inside, Laurie introduced Kim. The nicely built man with dark hair and the distinguished look of a Spanish gentleman greeted her less effusively than he had Laurie. Kim thought she saw a trace of suspicion behind his professional guise.

"Happy birthday," he said to Laurie. "I hope this will be a very happy day for you."

"Thank you. I hope so too."

A moment of silence fell.

"How can I help you?" Sandoval said. For the first time Kim read strain in his voice and posture.

"I want to know about the trust fund my grandparents created for me," Laurie said.

"Ah, of course." He hesitated. "I assume I may speak freely?"

Kim caught his questioning glance at her. "Yes. I asked Kim to come to help answer my questions. Anything you have to say to me you can say to her," Laurie said.

"Very good. The details are straightforward. The trust is unchanged from the day your grandparents created it. The portfolio consists of stock holdings in one company. Many years ago, your grandparents purchased thirty shares. That's what you own today."

"One company?" Kim said.

"Yes. The company is Shenandoah Hawthorn. Are you familiar with this company, Ms. Jackson?"

"Of course. It's Roland Bradley's company," she said, startled all the same. The last she knew, the stock was trading at a price above $250,000 per share. Times thirty—she did the math. If the price was still that high, Laurie's trust was worth well over $7 million.

"Thirty shares? Is that all?" Laurie said. "The other stock I had, the one I had to pay taxes on, I owned thousands of shares, didn't I?"

"Yes," Kim said. "But each share of this company is priced extremely high." She looked at Sandoval. "I assume that's still true."

"Yes."

"So where is this stock? I don't understand what this means," Laurie said.

Kim expected Sandoval to explain about a portfolio maintained by the bank, or perhaps at a brokerage firm. She expected him to say that all Laurie needed to do to gain access to her money was to place a phone order to sell one or more shares of stock. The proceeds would then go into a money market account against which she could write checks. That was the path to her money.

"We have the stock certificates here," Sandoval said.

"You do?" Kim said.

"May I see them?" Laurie said.

With obvious reluctance, Sandoval said, "Of course. Excuse me for a few minutes." He left the office.

"Is this what you thought would happen?" Laurie asked when they were alone.

"No. It's uncommon for individuals to hold the actual stock certificates, except in special circumstances. Generally speaking, certificates don't get printed. Brokerage companies keep the records of all purchases and sales of stock."

"But these are still good, right?"

"Oh yes."

Sandoval returned bearing a plain brown envelope. He started to open it, then reconsidered, sliding it across the desk.

Laurie opened the clasp and reached in, removing a thin wad of documents bound with a paperclip. She thumbed through the stack.

Kim watched, awed by the sight. The crisp certificates all but gleamed.

"Both of you are telling me these are worth a lot of money?" Laurie said.

Sandoval and Kim nodded.

"And I can take them with me?"

"No!" Kim cried. Mustering great restraint, she lowered her voice. "That is a very bad idea, Laurie. The certificates need to be kept here, where they're safe."

"Can I take them with me?" Laurie said to David Sandoval.

He closed his eyes heavily. "Of course you may take them. They're yours. But Ms. Jackson is right. It is not a good idea."

Kim tried not to scream. "Please listen to me, Laurie. There is nothing written on those certificates to identify them as yours. Carrying them around is exactly the same as carrying seven-and-a-half million dollars in cash. Anyone could take those certificates from you, take them to any brokerage house in this country and convert them to currency. It is far too dangerous to remove them from this building."

"Believe me, Kim, I'll be careful with them," Laurie said dryly.

"May I ask why you wish to do this?" Sandoval said.

Laurie let out a breath, and with it, something Kim couldn't name. She didn't know the younger woman nearly well enough to make sense of her current musing expression.

"I need to take control of what's mine. I'm not unhappy with the work you've done on my behalf. Not at all. If I'm going to do this, I need to do it."

"What you're doing is not smart," Kim said tightly. "You do have control over every single penny of this money. By removing it from this building you potentially forfeit that control. Please, Laurie."

As though she hadn't heard, Laurie turned to David. "Can you tell me about other accounts I have at this bank?"

He typed in several commands at his computer. "You have two accounts with this institution. One is a brokerage account, presently empty. The other is a money market account with a balance of a bit over $200,000. If you have accounts at other institutions, I'm not aware of them."

Laurie told him she had a checking account at Wells Fargo. "I'd like to have my money moved there as soon as possible. All of it."

David nodded. "We can arrange a wire transfer."

Laurie looked at Kim. "Is that okay?"

"Yes."

Laurie returned the stock certificates to the brown envelope.

"Before you leave, may I ask one question?" David Sandoval said. "I realize I am completely out of line. Please forgive my impudence. As your friend, and as a longtime friend of your grandparents, may I ask whether it is still your intention to enter the convent?"

Laurie stood up. "Not at this time."

It was apparent she meant to leave.

Kim remained sitting. "Please don't do this," she whispered. "I'm begging you."

Laurie touched her shoulder. "It will be fine. Believe me, it will be fine."

Kim felt the coffee she drank hours ago churning in her stomach. She chanced one last imploring look. "Please, Laurie. Leave the certificates here."

Laurie reached for her hand and pulled her out of the chair.

CHAPTER 8

"I'd like to make one more stop before we go home," Laurie said when she and Kim were in the car.

"Fine. Tell me where we're going."

Any delay was welcome, as far as Kim was concerned. She needed time to talk Laurie into returning the stock certificates to David Sandoval for safekeeping in the bank's vault.

"We'll stay on this road for now."

Halfway up the hill leading out of town, Kim followed directions onto a new road. Ten minutes later, at the end of a circuitous route into a country-club-like estate populated with elegant adobe houses only partially visible from the road, she stopped outside a metal gate.

"I've forgotten my grandparents' code. We'll need to call," Laurie said.

Kim found a listing on the display for R. Beltran. She pushed a button and heard a dial tone followed by digits executed in a rapid sequence. A woman answered. Laurie leaned across Kim to speak through the open window. "Hello, Sofia. This is Laurie Beltran. Is my grandmother home?"

"Laurie! Yes, she is. Please, one moment." There was a brief silence before the woman's voice again came through the line. "Please, come in." The black gate blocking the entrance began a ponderous swing open.

Kim accelerated into the community of homes. She followed Laurie's directions, at the same time gaping at intricately carved wooden gates fronting exquisitely crafted adobe structures tinted in a variety of earth tones. The colors spanned the spectrum from light beige to deep red. Per instructions, she turned onto a long driveway leading up a hill. Kim smiled at her first glimpse of the home. The sandstone exterior blended perfectly with the landscape, interrupted only by the wood and glass of windows sculpted into it. Its foundation followed the contour of the land. The highest point was at the far right, an alcove set into the hillside. Kim could only imagine the views it afforded.

"Are you ready for this?" Laurie said.

"I'm not sure. Are you?"

"I think so."

They got out and approached the front door. Even though they were expected, Laurie rang the bell. The door swung wide. Behind it, a uniformed woman exclaimed joyously as she pulled Laurie into her arms. Kim was introduced to Sofia, who led them through the tiled entryway to a broad room with vaulted ceilings and tall windows, furnished exquisitely in a Spanish style of woods and leather.

A woman stood as they entered. Laurie rushed to her, though their embrace was less effusive than Sofia's warm reception of the prodigal granddaughter.

"Grandmother, I'd like you to meet my friend Kim Jackson. Kim, please meet my grandmother, Mrs. Janelle Beltran."

Kim stepped forward. Janelle Beltran was dressed beautifully in a suede skirt, ivory blouse, and turquoise belt. Inches shorter than her granddaughter, she held her spine straight, lending an imperious air to her manner. That, and her coolly appraising eyes, combined to create an effect Kim had no doubt was intended to be intimidating.

Laurie allowed her grandmother to lead her to a sofa and hold her hand as they sat together. Kim sat down on an adjacent chair.

"Happy birthday, Laurie. Had I known you were coming today, I would have had something for you," Janelle Beltran said.

"But you did, Grandmother. We've just been to see David Sandoval. Thank you for all you and Granddad have done for me. Is he home?"

"No, dear. He's out for a round of golf. Will you be able to stay until he returns?"

"I'm afraid not. Kim and I need to return to—" She didn't finish the sentence.

An awkward silence ensued. It already had grown long when Kim broke it. "Mrs. Beltran, would you mind terribly if I explored outside? I can't seem to get enough of the sunshine and mountain views in Santa Fe."

Laurie started to object. Then relief showed in her eyes, and Kim knew she had made the right call. On the way out, escorted by Sofia, she saw a framed photo in an out-of-the-way spot on a corner table. It sat next to a lamp, currently unlit. The photo showed a family of five: a handsome, dark-haired man; a blond woman; and three children, two girls and a boy. Kim could have sworn one of the girls was Laurie at a much younger age. On reflection she decided she was wrong. Laurie had said she had only one sister.

Happy to be moving after so many hours spent in the car, Kim walked down the driveway. At its end she turned and continued walking along a narrow asphalt road. Forty-five minutes later she returned to the house. With no wish to announce herself, she opened the car door and sat inside. Waiting, she grew warmer by the minute. The brown envelope lay innocuously on the floor below the passenger seat. Kim reached for it, unable to resist the temptation of peeking inside. For a split second she hoped the events of this morning had been a figment of her imagination. No. The stock certificates were there.

She was drowsing when she heard voices at the front door. Hurriedly, she roused herself to join the others to say goodbye.

"It's been a pleasure to meet you," Janelle Beltran said. "Thank you for taking the time to stop by."

"It's been nice to meet you," Kim said.

Sofia earned her everlasting gratitude by appearing behind the other two women, bearing two large bottles of water and a bulging paper bag. "Something for both of you," she said.

Kim took the items while Laurie allowed herself to be enfolded in a parting hug from Sofia. Her grandmother kissed her cheek while clasping both hands tightly. It was more emotion than she had shown earlier. Still, Kim wished Janelle Beltran had pulled her granddaughter close.

She and Laurie retraced their route out of the gated neighborhood.

"Good visit?" Kim said once they regained the main highway leading north.

"Yes."

"When did you see your grandmother last?"

"It's been a while. A year. She's upset because I won't tell her where I'm living." Another beat of silence passed. "We called my parents. I talked to them too."

"How was that?"

"Same as always."

Laurie slouched against the passenger door. They put thirty miles behind them before she emerged from whatever fog she'd been drifting in. She sat up straighter and began digging in the bag of food. While she rummaged, Kim dared to ask, "What are you going to do with the stock certificates?"

"I don't know. Put them in the safe deposit box for now."

"So you got a safe deposit box? For the church money?"

"Yes," Laurie said.

"Do other people have keys to that box?"

"Yes. I guess that wouldn't work." Laurie broke off from her search for food to consider the problem. "Do you have a safe deposit box?"

"Yes."

"Could we put the certificates there? Temporarily?" Before Kim had a chance to reply, Laurie said, "Why do you have a box? What do you keep in it?"

Taken aback, Kim was instantly angry. "Personal stuff." It was extremely personal stuff and nothing she had any intention of discussing.

"Sorry." Laurie resumed her search through the bag of food. On finding a sandwich, she removed the wrapping and offered half to Kim. "There's a lot of food here. You can always count on Sofia for great food."

Kim took a bite of the sandwich. It was turkey, cheese, avocado, and another flavor she couldn't identify. Laurie said it was green chile, a New Mexico specialty.

"I have to say, you make me kind of crazy," Laurie said while they both ate.

Kim choked. After a coughing fit, she said, "I make you crazy? That's priceless."

"Why?"

"I'm not the one walking around with $7 million in convertible stock certificates! I'm not the one living in a house with a door that won't lock."

Laurie didn't comment. For the moment, Kim didn't care. Driving fast on a two-lane road with almost no traffic, she saw the vista opening up ahead. A rock wall in endless shades of reds and browns lay dazzling beneath the blue sky. Her breath caught at the beauty. "Why do I make you crazy?" she asked, despite telling herself not to.

"Because I want to get to know you and I can't. You seem so incredibly transparent, as if you're completely present. But when I try to see into you, all I find is this hard shell of clear coat. I want to smash it and know who you really are. But I can't do that. No one should ever do that to another person."

Kim tried to smile. "Who I am. That's not an easy question to answer."

"You must know the answer."

Kim closed her eyes briefly. The winding road compelled her to open them. "Not completely. Not anymore." She steeled herself and searched for some way to give Laurie a better reply. She settled for a vague version of the truth. "What I know is that I started out living my life one way. Some things happened and it wasn't possible to go on living that way. What I haven't figured out is how I'm supposed to live now."

"Huh."

"What?"

"That's not so different from what happened to me."

They sped across the open landscape. When they reached the outskirts of a town called Chama, the speed limit dropped. Kim slowed. The car behind her did as well. A second glance in the rearview mirror and she knew that the car, an American sedan, had been there for a while. The other driver could have passed her anytime in the last half hour. Not especially worried about it, Kim signaled and pulled into a gas station. The other car, a dark-gray Ford Fusion, sped past.

"May I ask a question?" she said after she had topped off the gas tank and they were driving again. The Ford was nowhere in sight.

"It depends. What is it?"

"I gather at one time you intended to enter the Catholic Church. As a—sister." Kim couldn't bring herself to say the word "nun." It didn't fit. She didn't know why.

"That's not a question."

"No. It's really none of my business, but what is your current standing with the Church? Are you on a sort of sabbatical?"

"No. Or if I am, it's one of my own design."

Laurie had told David Sandoval it was not her intention to enter the convent *at this time.* That was one heck of a qualifier, considering her wealth. Kim assumed if Laurie entered the Church, she would be expected to take a vow of poverty and gift her assets to the Catholic community.

"Could you be a little more specific?" Kim said.

"Last June, I left the convent without telling anyone. I shouldn't have, but I did. I wanted time to think, and to sort things out."

Kim made a leap. "You said earlier that your grandparents don't know where you're living. Is that also true of your—" Kim hesitated. She didn't know how to phrase the question. "Your sisters at the convent?"

"Yes."

The subject catapulted Laurie into a remote interior space. Kim let her go. Another hour and they would be home, she thought wearily. She set her eyes to the road, hungry for the solitude of her cabin. Then, curious about gaps in the story, she spoke up. "So you left the convent in June last year. Where did you go?"

"To Oregon."

"Do you have friends there?"

"Yes. Good friends from college. I went to college at UC Santa Barbara. I loved it." Her voice sounded calm again. The convent, apparently, was the touchy subject.

"Did you work while you were in Oregon?"

"Yes, but not at a paying job. My friends were living on a commune. They grew most of their own food. Some were woodworkers. Some of the guys worked construction and went off to jobsites. Others of us contributed financially for the supplies we needed to buy."

Laurie laughed. "I showed up with hardly more than the clothes I was wearing. My college roommate took me around to some great secondhand shops. I found the most amazing clothes, including these." She pointed at the outfit she was wearing. "I loved living there," she added wistfully.

Kim waited a minute before asking the obvious. "Why did you leave?"

Laurie exhaled a sigh. "I stayed longer than I had planned to. I only meant to be away from the convent for a few weeks. I just needed . . . I don't know. Time." She was quiet for a long moment. "For many years I traveled a path I thought I meant to embrace throughout my life. My faith is not in question. All I want to do is live simply. I want to serve others. That hasn't changed."

Kim bit her bottom lip until she feared she would draw blood. "Then what has?"

"Nothing's changed!" Laurie shouted. "I've been blessed to have the love and support of my community. And in my weakness I should be able to go to them to talk about this but I can't. Don't you see? They would draw me back in, and for a time I would feel content. But if I return to the Church, I want to do so in strength, not in weakness. That means waging my struggle in the world, however hard that is and however long it takes. I made promises and I will keep them! Just . . . not yet."

Kim drew a troubled breath. The car's engine hummed on the ascent of Wolf Creek Pass. Two cars roared by at a high speed, prompting her to glance behind to see if others were following. Instead she spotted a familiar sedan trailing at a distance. Suddenly worried, she pressed the accelerator. At the summit she steered into the overlook's parking area.

"Why are we stopping here?" Laurie said.

Kim didn't answer. She got out of the car and pretended to admire the sweeping ski valley. A gray Ford Fusion accelerated past the overlook.

"Is something wrong?" Laurie said.

"No."

It might not have been the same car. Its presence behind them may have been a coincidence. It likely meant nothing. Kim wasn't inclined to believe that.

Laurie didn't talk when they resumed their drive. Kim didn't see the Ford again nor did she try to draw Laurie into a conversation. As they drew closer to Creede, Laurie emerged from her silence. She talked about suggestions people had made regarding changing the format of the Sunday service. She mentioned several newcomers to the group, including a couple by the name of Channing. Kim replied in monosyllables when necessary. Otherwise she kept her eyes on the road ahead and behind them. Despite no further sightings of the gray sedan, she was unable to shake the feeling that they had been followed from Santa Fe.

"Sorry. What did you say?" she said when she realized Laurie had asked a question.

"Nell and Tucker—the Channings—have you met them?"

Kim hadn't.

"Oh well. You should. They're very nice."

Greatly relieved to be home, Kim negotiated the turns through town. Her relief was cut short by the sight of a sheriff's car parked outside Laurie's house. A uniformed deputy got out of the vehicle when Laurie opened the passenger door and stepped out.

"Laurie Beltran, Sheriff Preston wants to talk to you," the man said.

Laurie shot a panicked look at Kim. "Do I have to go with him?" She answered her own question. "Never mind. I'll go. Take these, please." She thrust the brown envelope containing the stock certificates into Kim's hand.

CHAPTER 9

Kim found a note pinned to the cabin door when she arrived home. She dropped it on the sofa and set about starting a fire in the woodstove. The room hadn't lost its chill when she emerged from the bathroom, freshly showered, hair washed and dried. While the wood crackled and spat sparks behind the cast-iron door, she bundled in the down sleeping bag and read the note.

Paula wanted her to come to the house tonight.

Her first thought was that she was much too tired.

Her second thought was that it didn't matter. She would go.

At the appointed hour, she arrived. Paula answered her knock without a word of greeting. It was apparent she was edgy and off-balance. Had Kim not known better, she would have said Paula's nerves were wrought. Instead she registered Paula's intensity as a driving need to work.

She went directly to the bathroom. She kicked off shoes, removed socks, and stripped off upper layers, leaving them to fall in a hapless pile. She reached for the oversized men's shirt.

Paula was at the front window when Kim emerged. The room was ablaze in light. The windows were bare of coverings. Anyone standing outside could see clearly into the interior, assuming he or she breached the fence line on the property and crossed thirty yards from the road. Kim went to the bar-stool and took off the shirt. The sudden rush of air against her bare skin shocked her into strained awareness of what she was about to do. She took the position she was meant to hold, head up, turned slightly to the right, shoulders squared and back.

In the beginning she hadn't understood why Paula, a suc-cessful artist, required a model. Her work was shown in gal-leries from New York to San Francisco. She had honed her technique decades ago in studios and classrooms. Initially, Kim had speculated that Paula sought practice. Later she thought perhaps the sessions passed for social engagement.

Her breath caught when she realized Paula was standing directly in front of her. She steadied herself with a long, fluid breath. Her chest rose and fell. Her breasts moved with the easy rhythm of breathing. She didn't know what Paula was seeing, or what had moved her tonight to gaze with probing interest. One thing Kim knew: *she* was invisible. Paula might devour her outward form, or attempt to. But she could never get to anything that constituted her essence. Such a thing no longer existed, if it ever had.

She didn't notice when Paula moved behind her. Eventually she heard the scrabble of charcoal against paper. The sound became a river, carrying her downstream, and as she floated, she saw a scene unfolding inside a barren room where a naive young woman and a gruff older man—Laurie and Sheriff Preston—clashed wills. She tripped mentally.

"Hold still," Paula barked.

Kim breathed through the arrows of accusation that she ought to have done something different when the deputy took Laurie away. She thought of the plain brown envelope inside the backpack on the bathroom floor, draped with blouse and bra, and thought she had done enough. Then she didn't think anything. Images streamed through her mind. She let each go, as if in a dream.

"I'm done," Paula said much later.

Automatically, Kim reached for the too-large men's shirt. For one instant she thought her muscles, called so suddenly back to life, might snap. She slid one arm in, then the other, and without buttoning the shirt, went to the bathroom to dress.

Paula was waiting in the kitchen when she emerged. The sketchpad was open on a stand. After she had gone to work for John Carlos and had internet access, Kim had researched Paula Rowe online. At the house she had observed a couple of works in progress. Only once before had she seen the fruits of Paula's efforts in sketching her. She knew Paula aimed for a central focus in her work and achieved a discernible energy through the creation of static images. She also knew that when Paula sketched her, all bets were off on what she was seeing. "Everything isn't personal," Paula had said the day Kim glimpsed a drawing that depicted strands of shaggy ends of hair, hers, woven into a rainforest of hanging moss.

But this sketch was personal.

A hollowed-out feeling in the pit of Kim's stomach plummeted. It left a void between her vital organs and her brain.

"It's a black hole one nanosecond after it was struck by a piñata stick," Paula said, volunteering a rare remark.

A bottle of whiskey and a glass were on the counter. Kim poured a shot and downed it in one gulp. Instantly her senses overpowered her mind, which was the point, after all. Wispy fumes of fragrance and fire curled through her brain, stinging her eyes. She steadied herself by taking an inventory of the countertop: plates, glasses, cutlery, napkins. There was a salad bowl brimming with greens, a loaf of crusty bread.

"Tell me a story," Paula said.

Kim laughed. "You want me to tell you a story?" She shouldn't have been surprised. It was a regular request. But this day had sapped her store of creative reserves.

"Yes. Any old story will do."

Kim poured a second shot, half as tall as the first. She reattached the cap to the bottle and pushed it away. Once settled, she cupped her chin in the palm of her hand, elbow braced on the countertop. She didn't know any stories. Tonight she was much too tired for Paula's games.

Her eyes tracked the familiar contours of granite counter, stove, refrigerator, wood floor. She let herself become a will-o'-the-wisp, slipping out the window on the far wall, out into the night, where she blended into the rock wall that was waiting as if it had always been there for her, waiting to absorb her, transform her into something substantial, enduring, beautiful. Her breath faltered. It frightened her, this wanting.

She had forgotten Paula.

To her surprise, a story opening popped to mind. She went with it. "Once upon a time, a long time ago, there were three princesses. Each princess was born to parents who loved her. All of the parents wanted their daughters to live in a princess dream world, but it didn't work out that way. One of the princesses grew up and chose to serve God. Another princess grew up and chose to serve the people. The third grew up and chose to serve numbers."

She stopped. She thought she had already said too much.

"Okay, I give. What happened to the princesses in your story?" Paula said.

"It's your story."

Silence fell, less pleasant than before.

Kim said, "Since you asked, I have to tell you. None of the princesses grew up to live in a princess dream world. It simply didn't turn out that way. One nearly died, literally. Another died figuratively. The third never learned to live at all."

"What is this, a princess shell game? Match the princess to her fate and win a prize?"

"I don't know."

"Tell me about the princess who almost died."

Kim thought of Lena, formerly of Durango, now in Denver, and came up empty. Lena-in-Denver was as fantastical a notion as Santa Claus's workshop at the North Pole. More so. At least there were elves in the workshop and presents wrapped with fancy ribbon and delivered on Christmas Eve.

"Her name was Elle. She made those who knew her better people. She never knew that."

Paula reached for the whiskey bottle. "That's all?"

Kim nodded.

Paula laughed. "When I'm awake tonight, if I'm awake . . ." She waited until Kim looked over. "I'll be wondering what I would have heard had I asked about your other princesses."

But it was Kim who lay awake long after returning home and crawling into bed. She couldn't escape the image she had glimpsed on Paula's sketchpad. Energy and matter cast as dots spewed in perfect symmetry from the silhouette of the bullet scar on her back.

CHAPTER 10

At noon the next day, Kim tapped on the front door of a small wooden house situated on a corner lot on the southern end of Creede. The exterior of the Garrett house appeared to be in better shape than most of the homes around it. It sported a fresh coat of paint and new windows. All of the gutters were attached. The grass had a worn, faded look. Yellow tips sprouted on a forsythia bush. Near the front door, curvy tulip leaves nestled against brown earth, blossoms nowhere in sight.

Kim hoped she had the right address. A listing for Trip Garrett in the phone book had led her here. So far she had heard no sounds from inside. She was prepared to knock harder, when the door opened.

"Oh hi," Laurie said, standing there with a toddler on her hip. A little girl with straight brown hair clung to Laurie's leg, hiding and at the same time peering out curiously.

"Hi. Is this a bad time?"

"We're eating lunch. Come on in."

Kim collected impressions of a young family's home while she followed Laurie to the kitchen. The rooms were uniformly small and nicely kept. The living room was furnished with a floral print sofa and matching chair. A dark wood table and four chairs were in the dining room. The kitchen was messier. Three plates on the table each held a partly eaten sandwich. Opened jars and a loaf of bread were on the counter, along with a carton of milk.

Laurie strapped the younger girl in her booster seat to cries of complaint. "Sit down, Grace, please," she said to the other child.

"I guess this is a bad time," Kim said.

"We're almost finished eating. Then it's a story and nap time. So no, it's actually a good time."

Kim's first impulse was to say she would come back later. Then she remembered she was in the home of a dead man, the circumstances of whose death were, to say the least, curious. While Laurie coaxed the girls to finish eating, Kim put away the lunch makings. She scrubbed the counter and loaded the dishwasher. She took stock of a compact kitchen whose only excess was the abundance of casserole dishes in the refrigerator and two large plastic bins filled with cookies.

"I'll be back soon," Laurie said when lunch was over. "You don't have to do that." She nodded at the lunch plates stacked in Kim's hand.

"I don't mind. There's hardly anything left to do."

Kim put the kitchen to rights with a final sweep of crumbs off the table. She returned to the living room to the sound of Laurie's voice echoing from behind a closed bedroom door. She knew good manners dictated sitting quietly and waiting. Without a second thought, she took herself on a self-guided tour of the premises.

She started in the bedroom adjacent to the living room. It was a child's room, fitted with a single bed and chest of drawers, bookcase, and toy chest. The space had a disturbingly vacant air. Kim puzzled over the feeling until she remembered Cody Garrett had died last autumn. This must have been his room.

She expected the elder girl would have it in a few years.

Without dwelling on the tragedy of a little boy's life lost, she crossed the living room to a hallway on the opposite side of the house. The first door, still closed, belonged to the two girls. Adjacent was a bathroom, and beyond, the master bedroom. In the master bedroom she opened the closet and saw women's clothes on hangers—blouses, slacks, skirts, sweaters, a couple of coats. Shoes were arranged on a floor rack. There was a purse and a pillow on the shelf. Nothing was out of the ordinary. Nothing struck her as especially interesting.

The room itself was cramped, with a computer desk wedged into a corner next to the chest of drawers. Kim congratulated herself on her restraint in not opening any drawers.

She moved on to the bathroom. Tub, toilet, floor, and countertop were squeaky clean. Personal care products were in the medicine cabinet and on shelves, bottles forming neat rows, all products designed for women.

Down the hall, Laurie continued to read. The baby cried out, obviously not asleep.

Back in the living room, Kim mulled over her impressions, troubled by the feeling of something missing. There were no family photos. There was no evidence that a man had ever lived here. Or a little boy. She was about to drop onto the sofa but decided to make a second pass around the house. She told herself to look at the home the way a cop would. The way Lena Fallon would.

The problem was she had no idea how Lena would do that. They had never worked a crime scene together. They had shared ideas, proposed theories, and spun webs of motives and opportunities, all from the sanctity of the house where Lena remained a virtual recluse. Until the place burned down.

Kim brushed off the memories and went to work.

She made a quick pass over the unoccupied third bedroom, living room, and adjacent dining room. In the hall, she opened a linen closet. Sheets and towels lay folded on shelves. Higher, out of reach of children, were bottles of household cleaning products, one each of toilet bowl cleaner, sink and countertop cleaner, liquid soap, and carpet cleaner.

Kim noted the bottles' precise placement on the shelf, then returned to the master bedroom. This time she opened drawers on the computer desk, observing tablets, pens, and file folders neatly arranged. She stopped short of removing anything. Itchy to probe deeper, she opened the top dresser drawer and found lingerie folded into precise stacks.

For the sake of completing the exercise, she went to the kitchen. The pantry yielded no surprises, only cans and bottles lined evenly in rows. She opened an accordion door and found a laundry room fitted with a washer and dryer. A bottle of stain remover and a clear plastic jar with what appeared to be premeasured packets of detergent were on a shelf. On the floor, stacked behind a mop, broom, and dustpan, were three boxes of powdered laundry detergent. She looked at the boxes and again at the jar of premeasured packets, understanding the latter's function but not why someone would go to the trouble of creating the packets. The plastic scoop that came inside each box was perfectly sufficient for measuring detergent to add to a laundry load. Regardless, why not avoid the fuss and muss altogether and use the prepackaged pods readily available in stores?

"Why does Cathy—" she said. At the same time, she heard a click.

She turned, expecting to see Laurie.

"Why does Cathy what?" a woman, who was obviously Cathy Garrett, said.

She was taller than Kim, standing at five-eight or five-nine. Long, dark hair tumbled below her shoulders. Her face was oval, her cheek bones high, her eyes bright with anger. Kim's first thought was that Cathy Garrett belonged somewhere else.

On a runway, maybe, with the raw power and subtle beauty she exuded. She was nothing like what Kim had expected, not a broken, grieving widow. Not at this moment, anyway. Kim wished she had done a more thorough job inspecting the house.

More than that, she wished she hadn't been caught snooping. Assuming a breezy air, she strode forward, offering her hand, which the other woman pointedly ignored. "Hello. My name is Kim Jackson. I'm a friend of Laurie's."

"Get out," Cathy Garrett said. "Get out of my house right now."

Laurie walked in. "Oh! Have you two met?"

Kim flashed an apologetic smile. "Goodbye," she said, not caring whom she spoke to. She made a beeline for the front door and was out before anyone said another word.

—

Late that afternoon Kim went in search of Laurie for the second time that day. As she unlatched the gate leading to Laurie's tiny house, she noticed that the main residence facing the street was as absent of activity as it had been every other time she'd been here. One light shone through a curtained window. Peering closer, she saw a small lamp on a table in a hallway.

Laurie didn't answer her knock. Kim gave up after a few raps. She was leaving when she saw a runner approaching in the distance. Surprised, she recognized Laurie. Dressed in full runner's kit—tights, jacket, and running shoes that had to have cost at least one hundred dollars—Laurie was breathing hard when she stopped at the gate.

"I didn't know you were a runner," Kim said.

"I ran cross-country in high school. I've always loved it." Laurie ran the back of her hand across her forehead, wiping away traces of a light sweat.

"How far do you usually run?"

"I'm not sure. Today I probably ran seven or eight miles."

Kim was impressed. This marked the second time in two days that she'd seen a side of Laurie she wouldn't have guessed was there.

Together, they entered the property. Kim thrust a thumb toward the big house. "Does anyone live here? I never see anyone around."

"The people I rent from live there. Part-time. Definitely not in winter. They only drop by occasionally to check on the place. Why?"

"Just curious."

They entered the tiny house.

"Sorry about earlier today. I hope Cathy wasn't angry at you," Kim said.

"What were you doing in the laundry room anyway?" Laurie said, closing the door behind her.

"Looking for dishwashing detergent."

"It's under the sink, where most people keep it. Why did you need it?"

"I looked in the laundry room by mistake," Kim said, fabricating an excuse. "Then I couldn't stop looking at all those little plastic bags of laundry detergent. Why does Cathy do that? I mean, I get it that she's a little OCD, but that seems extreme."

"She's very particular about how much detergent is used per load. I'm not supposed to touch the boxes, ever. Anyway, yes, she was seriously angry. Don't ever do that again. Come to the house, I mean. She said if I ever let anyone in again, she'll fire me. Why were you there anyway?"

"I wanted to ask what the sheriff wanted last night."

Laurie turned away and sat down. "He had more questions. Mostly they were the same questions. Why did I go to the bar to find Trip? What did each of us say? How much money did Trip give me? Was I angry? Was Trip? He kept going around and around." She paused briefly. "He wanted to know whether

Trip came to see me the night he went missing. I said he had. He wanted to know why I hadn't seen fit to mention that detail. I told him no one had asked."

Kim felt a stabbing pain in her stomach. She might have thought it was indigestion except she had eaten her last meal hours ago. "You saw Trip the night he disappeared?" At the other woman's nod, she said, "Laurie, don't you see why it matters? You may have been the last person to see Trip alive. Had he ever been to your house before?"

"No."

"Why was he there that night?"

"He came to apologize. About the money."

By degrees, the story emerged. Laurie said she couldn't have been more surprised when Trip knocked on her door late Friday night. He was noticeably unsteady on his feet. He occasionally slurred his words. She thought he'd had too much to drink, but he wasn't threatening. He was more like a floppy dog, the way he sprawled across a chair.

"Trip felt bad about the money he owed me. He said there'd been a mix-up. He gave Cathy the cash to pay me. Cathy misunderstood and used the money for something else. He promised to make up the difference soon."

"So then he left?"

"You're as bad as that sheriff! No, he didn't leave right away. He hung around."

Laurie said it seemed like Trip had wanted to talk. He said it was clear both of his little girls loved her. Grace, especially, was always talking about her. Laurie wasn't thinking of quitting, was she? Cathy was worried she would. Because of the money. He still didn't know where the mix-up had come from.

"He checked his watch every few minutes. I kept expecting him to leave. But he stayed, kind of for a long time."

"What else did you talk about?"

"He asked about my books." She nodded at the bookcase near Kim's chair. "He wanted to know if I'd read them all. I said yes. I said I kept them because I often reread certain passages, especially when I was preparing for a Sunday service. He said he'd like to come to the service sometime, but weekend mornings at home were a special time for his family."

"Do you think he was interested in you? Was he flirting?"

"No! He loved Cathy. He did say he wished he knew her better. He admitted they'd both been having a hard time since their son died." She averted her glance. "He did mention one odd thing. He said Cathy loved to play video games. Well, not plural. She played this one game every night before bed. He said it was a violent one, and that was probably what she was doing right now. Then—"

"Then what?"

"He checked his watch again. I don't know. Maybe Cathy told him not to come home until a certain time."

"Huh," Kim said, remembering the icy, hard look in Cathy Garrett's eyes earlier that day. She could easily imagine the woman immersed in a violent video game. She recalled the perfect arrangements of bottles and cans in the house. There was no doubt Cathy Garrett had control issues. Still, she gave the woman the benefit of the doubt. "Maybe it's Cathy's way of dealing with grief. Do you know what happened to their little boy?"

"It wasn't theirs. It was hers. She had Cody before she married Trip. He got sick. Some awful disease, I'm not sure what. Cody died before I started working for Cathy."

"Laurie, did you have any sense that Trip might be suicidal the night he came to talk to you?"

"No!"

"How can you be so sure?"

"Because he talked about how much he loved his girls, how he had to take care of them and make sure they were always safe."

"His girls—meaning his daughters?"

"I thought he meant the whole family."

"Did you tell Sheriff Preston everything you told me?"

"Well, most everything. I didn't tell him about the video game. I didn't see how that was relevant."

Kim thought every single detail from that night was potentially relevant, but she let the omission go. "Did the sheriff give you any idea why he thinks Trip's death is suspicious?"

"I'm not sure he does. I don't know what that man thinks."

Kim didn't either. Given everything Laurie had just told her, it was easy to imagine that Trip's death had been either accident or suicide.

"The sheriff did want to know if I noticed any injuries on Trip while he was here. Any blood, especially on his head."

"Did you?"

"No! I would have said so. Same as I would have said if he'd fallen coming in or leaving the house."

"The sheriff asked you that?"

"Yes. I think he was trying to be funny when he asked if I'd ever fantasized about whacking Trip over the head with something."

"Like what?"

"I don't know. A hammer or a piece of pipe. But I don't think anyone ended up hitting him after he left. I think he must have fallen in the creek by accident!"

Doubts over having left Laurie to deal with Preston alone last night assailed Kim while she tried to piece together the details. Trip must have had some head injury or bruising consistent with having been struck by an object before he went into the water. She didn't know how a pathologist could make that determination. The creek bed was lined with boulders of all shapes and sizes. Trip could have hit his head on any of them, and probably had. Her thoughts spun around what the Mineral County sheriff imagined had happened to Trip—that a young woman, for reasons known only to herself, had followed him out of her house into a pitch-black night, and as he was crossing the creek, hit him over the head, and watched him fall into the rushing water.

Laurie sighed. "Listen, I'm glad you're here. I wanted to tell you there's a gathering tonight at Nell and Tucker Channing's house. It's the big one on the hill, I'm sure you've seen it. You know most of the people who will be there. I thought you might want to come."

Kim had no idea what Laurie was talking about. Her thoughts swirled around the need to talk to Sheriff Preston and learn what she could about Trip Garrett's death. Laurie was obviously a suspect. Kim wished she had searched the Garrett house better while she had the chance. "What? No, I'm not going," she said absently.

"You really should think about it," Laurie said, smiling strangely. "The Channings are wonderful people."

CHAPTER 11

BANK OF THE WEST
SANTA FE, NEW MEXICO

Teresa Dominguez stopped short of reaching for the phone. Her elbows were on her desk, her hands drawn to her chin in a prayerful pose. Surreptitiously, she glanced right and left to see if anyone was watching. No one was. But if she lingered unnecessarily, she would draw attention. There was too much work to be done, always too much work for her to be caught sitting idle. The last thing she wanted was anyone asking whether something was wrong.

She reached for the phone. She punched in seven numbers, silently praying for guidance.

"Mrs. Dominguez, how good to hear from you. How may I help you?"

The soothing tone of Father Brian's voice calmed her. It heightened her resolve. "I have news for you, Father." She coughed, then cleared her throat. She struggled to keep her voice low. "There has been activity."

"Please, tell me more," he said when she paused.

"Yesterday. The accounts were closed. Both accounts. I didn't learn of this until today."

The silence emanating from the other end of the line frightened her.

"Is there anything else you can tell me? Anything pertaining to—a destination, perhaps?"

She told Father Brian what she knew. "The accounts were liquidated. The funds in one were wire-transferred to another bank. Wells Fargo."

Silence followed, no less frightening than before.

"Mrs. Dominguez, I am not a man of the world. I don't know how such things work. I understand vaguely the meaning of the words 'wire transfer.' It is the other that confuses me. If an account is purely liquidated with no corollary trail of a transfer to another account in the same or a different institution, what does this suggest to you? In my limited understanding, it strikes me as, how would you say it? That someone has perhaps 'cashed out'?"

"It would be a highly unusual action, Father. Especially given the account's value." She blushed. It was a betrayal to say so much. Yet it was not a betrayal, she reminded herself, when she allied herself with a higher power. Steeled in her faith, she said what she had promised herself she would not. "The other account was held in stock certificates. They were kept in the vault at this institution."

There was no immediate response. The woman glanced around nervously.

"And you are telling me the certificates are no longer there?"

"Yes, they are gone." She wanted him to say thank you. She wanted this call to end. She didn't want to say what came next. "There is something else," she blurted. "She was here yesterday, the young woman."

"Really."

"I didn't see her. I happened to hear something about it. She was here with a friend," she said. She hadn't told him Laurie Beltran took the certificates with her. But there was no other conclusion to draw.

A moment passed before Father Brian spoke. "Mrs. Dominguez, you have been a most trusted and faithful servant. I will hold you close in my prayers. I will celebrate your name to our Savior. Please call anytime you have need of me or the services of the Church."

She quivered as she disconnected, relieved that he hadn't been angry she hadn't called sooner.

CHAPTER 12

Kim was halfway home before she realized she hadn't asked Laurie the one question she had gone there specifically to ask: what did she want to do about the stock certificates? At the moment, the certificates were locked inside Kim's safe deposit box, safe enough by ordinary standards. Their safety wasn't the issue. Kim wanted to be rid of them. She told herself she didn't care what Laurie did with them, but that wasn't true. She wanted the certificates returned to David Sandoval until Laurie came to her senses, grew up, or gained a clue as to how the real world worked. Kim was in the process of acknowledging that none of the above was likely to happen soon when she saw the car.

It was a gray Ford Fusion with a New Mexico license plate. It was parked near enough to John Carlos's office for her to believe its presence was no coincidence. She jotted down the tag number. The first two letters she recalled from the previous night. Fear tore through her at the possibility that she was being tailed. She held the emotion at bay and forced herself to think. No one from her past could have spotted her in Santa Fe and mounted a surveillance effort so quickly. Which left one possibility. Whoever was driving this car was looking for Laurie.

She crossed the street and sat down on a bench with clear visual access to the sedan.

Thirty minutes passed with no sign of its owner. Kim left her post and took a slow walk past the Ford. A leather satchel lay on the passenger seat; sunglasses were on the dashboard. She tried the door handle and found it locked. She hurried on.

Too agitated to go home, she went to Miner's Haven. As she slid into a booth, she realized she'd had nothing to eat since breakfast. "Hey, Francie." She greeted her regular waitress. "I'll have the special."

"Coming right up, Kim."

The place was filling up with a dinner crowd. Kim glanced around, looking for someone who didn't belong. Rather, she decided, she was looking for a man dining alone. A guy wearing a nice cut of clothes, a man who had a decent haircut and carried his important papers in a leather satchel.

No one fit the description.

Francie delivered a plate of pot roast but was too harried by the crowd to stop and chat. Kim sliced chunks of carrot and ate slowly. By the time she finished eating, she had no more inclination to go home than she had before coming in. And though she had no desire to meet the Channings, Laurie's new friends, when she left the restaurant, she climbed the hill that led to the grand house overlooking town.

Lights were ablaze outside and inside when she arrived. The front door stood open despite the early evening chill. A crowd of mostly familiar faces was visible through the storm door. Kim tapped politely and let herself in.

Heads turned when she entered. She nodded at Valerie and Joan, the couple she knew from Sunday morning services. She smiled at Marla, a woman who owned a coffee shop in Creede. She was sorting out her impressions of the large, well-appointed living room, decorated in a fashionable Western style, when a man emerged from an adjacent room and greeted her warmly.

"Welcome. Good evening. So glad you could join us. My name is Tucker Channing."

"Kim Jackson," she said, shaking his outstretched hand. He had short gray hair. Of a stocky build, he appeared to be fit. He wore a cashmere vest over a designer oxford shirt, nice-looking khakis, and leather shoes scuffed enough to suggest years of wear. For reasons she made no attempt to defend, she immediately disliked him.

"Please, come in. Join us," he said, indicating the living room with a sweep of his hand. "Laurie has told us so much about you."

Kim sincerely hoped this wasn't true. It reminded her of why she was there. She took a second glance around the room and confirmed what she already knew. Laurie wasn't among those gathered. "Is Laurie here?"

"Oh yes. She's with Nell. They're a couple of regular chatterboxes when they're together. I'm sure they'll join us shortly."

Kim took one reluctant step toward the open end of a sofa, where Marla had made a place for her to sit. "Can I get you something to drink?" Tucker said. "Soda, juice, coffee, or tea? Sorry, we don't have anything harder."

"Yes, I'd love something." She moved away from the couch and the feeling of being shepherded there. "Is the kitchen this way?" she said, pointing down the hallway. Without waiting for an answer, she strode deeper into the house. She hadn't gone far when she was rewarded by the sound of lively voices. One belonged to Laurie. She entered the kitchen to the sight of Laurie and a woman standing close. The woman had her hand on Laurie's arm.

In her late forties or early fifties, the woman was trim, her skin smooth and tanned. She was drop-dead gorgeous but looked every inch as fake as her husband.

"Kim!" Laurie exclaimed, breaking contact and rushing over. "I'm so glad you came!"

Kim had a moment of grudging relief at Laurie's warm reception. It ended with the woman joining them, smiling beatifically as though she were witnessing the return of a long-lost daughter. "Hello, Kim. I'm Nell. It's so nice to meet you."

For a split second, Kim thought the woman meant to embrace her. She settled for a lingering handshake. Kim forced a smile. She resisted a fierce desire to pull her hand away. "Welcome to Creede. What brings you and Tucker to our fair city?" she asked.

Nell waved one perfectly manicured hand. "Tucker and I adore Colorado. We make our home in Texas but spend every winter itching to get back to the mountains."

Kim couldn't fault the woman for that explanation. The mountains had the same effect on her.

"Nell and Tucker do missionary work in south Texas with the immigrant population," Laurie said.

"Oh my, don't be telling tales on us," Nell said, seizing Laurie's hand. "Tucker and I have been very blessed, and any little thing we can do to help others is only the smallest of repayment."

Laurie started to argue. Nell cut her off by suggesting they join the others. Tucker, Kim noticed, was nowhere in sight when the three women took seats in the living room.

Several conversations were going at once. Kim made no effort to join in, only listened and watched as everyone's attention gradually pivoted to Nell. She was like a magnet to the others. Kim might have trailed in that wake as well, had her suspicions not been on high alert, especially as she continued to witness Nell's grip on Laurie.

Sometime later Tucker Channing returned to the room. Several times through the evening Kim caught him looking at her. The group broke up late. Even after all the others had left, Laurie dallied at the door, talking. By the time she said her goodbyes, Kim felt irrationally angry.

"I'm so glad you came tonight," Laurie repeated as they walked down the long hill together.

"How long have you known the Channings?" Kim said, wishing she had paid more attention when Laurie first mentioned the couple's presence in town.

"It seems like I've known them my whole life. Aren't they wonderful?"

"Please, Laurie, answer my question."

Laurie didn't answer immediately. When she did, she spoke with heat. "I can feel your judgment and I don't care for it. I don't know why you are so unwilling to give people a chance— good people! Maybe it's the part of you that's turned away from God that makes you act this way."

Kim suppressed a groan. "Laurie, it seems to me that you've gone to a great deal of trouble to separate yourself from people in your past. I'd think you might want to be cautious regarding who you go rushing toward in the present." Kim thought about the Ford Fusion she suspected had followed them from Santa Fe.

Laurie laughed. "Thank you. You've made my point for me. The Channings aren't from my past, and I'm hardly rushing toward them."

Kim wondered whether Laurie was wrong on both counts.

CHAPTER 13

Early the next morning, Kim opened her eyes to gray light illuminating the rock wall that towered over where she lay on the broken chaise longue. She pulled the sleeping bag tighter around her shoulders, feeling both chilled and bruised. The ache on her hip had started sometime since she exchanged the comfort of her bed for a night beneath the stars on a wobbly aluminum frame and tattered nylon straps. All was quiet in the world she awoke to. The sun's rays were still an hour away from reaching the canyon floor.

She stretched and discovered a second ache—this one in her shoulder, not quite as piercing as the one in her hip. She remembered peering at the sky last night, unable to sleep. Once settled on the chaise longue, she'd felt a sudden longing to talk to Laurie. She wanted to point to the boundless array of stars and planets etched in white across the sky and ask: *Where is your God, Laurie? Is He—or She—secreted away in a distant galaxy watching Earth through a mighty telescope? Is your God ethereal, wafting through the atmosphere, everywhere all at once? Is your God a being entirely separate from material reality, and if so, please explain how that might work.*

The only answer she had was Laurie's voice, in her imagination, muttering, "It's not my God."

With effort, Kim extracted herself from the sleeping bag and chaise longue and went inside. She made a pot of coffee and took a hot shower. Feeling marginally restored, she sat down on the sofa. Staring back at her from the low table was a white envelope addressed to Lena Fallon. The envelope had been there for three days. She'd forgotten to take it on recent trips to town, or at least that's what she told herself. Looking at it now, she wondered whether she was on the brink of deciding to stop sending Lena a weekly letter.

She took the envelope when she left for work.

"Hey, Kim. Good morning," Claudia, the postmistress, said. "Sorry to report there's nothing here for you."

"Thanks, Claudia. That's not a big surprise."

Because it was her custom, Kim slid the envelope across the counter. The other woman picked it up and tapped its long end on the wooden surface. "Anything does come in," she said, winking, "I'll come and deliver it straightaway."

It wasn't the first time Kim had wondered whether Claudia, a fiftysomething woman with gray hair and knowing blue eyes, had done enough poking around on the internet to learn whom Kim sent a letter to once a week and what the story—at least part of the story—was between them. Lena Fallon was a legend in southern Colorado. Maybe working in a small-town post office lent itself to an attitude of discretion. Claudia had never once hinted at curiosity about Kim's unanswered correspondence.

After leaving the post office, Kim took a walking tour up and down Creede's main street. She wasn't the least bit surprised to find the gray Ford Fusion parked several blocks south of the central area. As much as she wanted to shortcut the process of discovering its owner by leaving a note on the windshield requesting a face-to-face meeting, she couldn't afford to do that. She assumed whoever drove the car was looking for Laurie; she further assumed the driver was male and had been sent by Janelle Beltran, the person best positioned to put a tail on Laurie when she left Santa Fe. By now the driver certainly had Laurie's address. Which meant there was something more in play than the simple matter of discovering where Laurie was living.

With the winding down of tax season, Kim had ended her temporary employment in John Carlos's accounting firm. Instead, she had arranged to rent the spare office. Officially a freelancer now, she had additionally agreed to do an occasional bit of research for John as part of the lease deal. An unexpected meeting with her former boss kept her in the office late that afternoon. John begged a few minutes of her time shortly before five. Kim didn't leave the building until after six, and only after promising John she would do the research he wanted. John, an athletic man in his forties, was sporting a deeper tan than he'd had the last time Kim saw him. It was no secret he preferred spending his days golfing or fishing—anything that got him out of the office.

A wave of weariness hit her the moment she reached the sidewalk. She turned and headed for home.

"Ms. Jackson," an unfamiliar voice said, stopping her in her tracks.

She glanced sideways and saw a man sitting on a metal bench that was bolted onto the building. In an instant, she knew he was the driver of the gray Ford Fusion.

He stood up and handed her a business card. "My name is Fred Barnes. I'm a private investigator from Santa Fe. Do you have a few minutes?"

Barnes was an inch or two under six feet and had a trim build and short gray hair. Dressed in jeans and a leather jacket, he was a good-looking guy bearing a whimsical smile.

They went to a nearby café, where Barnes ordered coffee and Kim had iced tea. "You followed Laurie and me the other day from Santa Fe," she said flatly, unsure what to think of the PI.

"My bad that you spotted me. You're quite the observer," he said, still smiling. "I've seen you watching my car. I figured I'd answer your questions before I left town."

Kim recoiled against the knowledge that her "surveillance" had been surveilled. "Let me guess. You were supposed to find out where Laurie is living."

"That was my first order of business."

"And the rest of it?"

"I was hired to investigate you."

Betraying nothing, Kim rapidly assessed why Barnes had been tasked with the assignment and what he might have learned. "Laurie's grandmother was afraid of my intentions regarding Laurie. Rather, her money."

Barnes shrugged. "Janelle is naturally mistrustful."

"I've only known Laurie for a few weeks."

"I know that."

"I helped her with her taxes."

"I know that too."

Barnes told the story his own way. He said he'd received a call from Laurie's grandmother a few days ago with an urgent request to come to her house and be prepared to follow an older model Cadillac wherever it went. Janelle Beltran wanted to know where her granddaughter was living. She also wanted a background check run on her granddaughter's friend. "Naturally I started my search for information on you here in town," Barnes said.

He reported that Kim, to her credit, had engendered a great deal of loyalty during the short time she'd lived in Creede. No one had a bad word to say about her, and plenty were effusive in their appreciation of the work she'd done for them. The one person he'd especially wanted to interview had turned him away at the door. Paula Rowe had flat-out refused to talk to him.

No one seemed to know where she hailed from or what had brought her to Creede. All anyone knew was that she recently had lived in Durango.

Kim's brow tightened.

"I went poking around on the internet. Turns out there are many women named Kim Jackson. Wasn't hard to find the most famous one in this part of Colorado. Nor was it difficult to determine that one was you."

"Now don't get all hissy on me," he said, watching the expression on her face darken. "I made a few phone calls. I talked to a Durango cop by the name of Sheila Moss. I explained who had hired me and why. Officer Moss wasn't inclined to chattiness. However, she did make it clear that, in her opinion, anyone whom you chose to befriend was a lucky person."

Kim wanted to curse the man for digging into her past. Instead she studied him through her mask of anger, trying to discern if he knew more than he'd said. "Is that everything?"

"Everything pertinent. I suppose it's worth mentioning that I've read the newspaper accounts of the fire at Lena Fallon's house."

Kim breathed shallowly.

"Ms. Jackson—Kim—I don't doubt you keep your life enormously private, and that is certainly your prerogative. By the time I completed my research I felt confident in my report to the Beltrans that you have no predatory financial interest in their granddaughter nor are you working for anyone who does. Now I have one last question before I start my drive back to Santa Fe. Do you have any questions for me?"

Kim knew she would probably think of a dozen questions the moment Barnes drove away. "I can't think of any."

"It's been a pleasure meeting you." Barnes stood up, shook her hand, and said goodbye.

CHAPTER 14

In want of solitude and a break from what had come to feel like the confines of Creede, Kim drove to Pagosa Springs the next day. She bought a day pass to the hot springs pool. In a bathing suit borrowed from Paula, she passed the day moving from one of the interlinked pools to another until she reached the bottom of a steep hill and the river flowing by. Other people were around. Occasionally someone spoke to her. She resisted being drawn into conversation and eventually found a shaded spot, where she laid out her towel and reclined, soothed by the sound of moving water.

There were too many thoughts in her head. She wanted them all to quit, if only for a few hours. She was far too preoccupied with Laurie. Since first becoming acquainted with Laurie, Kim had sensed many peculiar things about her. She had known from the outset that Laurie had a seriously dysfunctional relationship with money. With thousands of dollars at her fingertips, Laurie seemed to consider it a point of honor to live on the pennies she made from her childcare job. At the same time, she splurged on quality footwear and outerwear for her long-distance runs. Kim didn't generally quibble with the choices other people made. In Laurie's case, she thought her choices more than irresponsible. She thought Laurie was courting disaster, especially when it came to taking $7 million in convertible stock certificates out of the secure location in the bank.

As the afternoon wore on, Kim's thoughts turned to herself. She replayed every word she could remember of her conversation with Fred Barnes. She wondered what Barnes would have found out if he had pressed his background search harder. It was a chilling question. It was the reason she had counseled herself to maintain a low profile since she had started using a new identity in Colorado—and it was something she had done none too well. She didn't want anyone finding out that her real name was not Kim Jackson.

—

Sunday morning, Kim was in her usual seat in Creede's town hall basement.

Nell and Tucker Channing were there. It was the first time Kim had noticed the couple attending services. They sat in the first row. Valerie Crane sat next to them, and her partner, Joan, sat alongside her.

Kim closed her eyes and leaned her head against the wall. The first half of the service proceeded as it ordinarily did for her. Her thoughts drifted. She hadn't managed to put to rest the nagging questions that had started yesterday while she soaked in a hot springs pool. What was she doing in Creede? Did she still want to be here? And if not, where did she want to go?

She didn't know what snagged her attention. It might have been something in Laurie's voice. Kim listened to the sermon.

"Everyone has doubts. Everyone faces temptation, especially the temptation to turn away from God and seek worldly gain," Laurie said. "Even Jesus was tested when he went into the desert. Three times Satan came to him, and three times Jesus resisted the temptation dangled in front of him. I can hear some of you saying, 'Yes, but that was Jesus. He is the son of God. I'm not that strong!'"

Laurie paced across the front of the room more animatedly than usual. Her face shone. It was as though a fire was lit within her. It illuminated her beauty, despite the simplicity of her dress.

"The question is what to do about doubt. We all know ways to escape ours. Sometimes it's easy to bury doubt beneath a daily routine. Or alternatively to attribute uncertainty and restlessness to a unique situation that you expect to resolve.

"Talking can help. Sometimes it's helpful to write thoughts down, however chaotically they emerge on paper. One thing I know from personal experience is that patience is always required. Like Jesus in the desert, sometimes, for reasons beyond our understanding, we are tested. And we can pray. I believe this is always at least part of the answer. God hears *us*, even when we can't hear Him."

Laurie continued in the same vein before inviting the congregation to join her in prayer.

Because the Channings were there, Kim stayed for the post-service discussion. Talk was lively for the next half hour. Laurie's message had struck a chord with many of the regulars. The Channings didn't participate. Kim saw them watching Laurie like hawks. Exactly as if she were their prey.

When the group discussion ended, after exchanging a goodbye smile with Laurie, Kim walked home. She found Paula outdoors, pacing the fence line near the cabin. They greeted each other.

"Checking for loose posts," the artist said. "A guy's coming to do some work. I want to make sure he does everything." She took a closer look at Kim. "Coming from church? Are you feeling spiritually cleansed?"

"Cleansed? I wouldn't say that. I'm pondering temptation."

"That sounds interesting. Any particular one? Maybe I can help."

"Thanks, but no," Kim said with a laugh.

This wasn't the first time she had felt Paula flirting with her. She didn't know how serious the artist was in her teasing or where their relationship might have gone had Kim been tempted by a physical connection. She wasn't interested. She could have told Paula that she liked her better for her mind than her body, but she suspected that message wouldn't have gone over well. "I'm not much of a student of the Bible. I didn't know the story of Jesus's temptation in the desert," she said.

"Oh well. The Bible has one version. I prefer the one in *The Brothers Karamazov*. I assume you've read it. Wait—don't tell me you haven't."

Kim admitted she had not read the book.

"Dostoyevsky! One of the greatest novelists of all time! Jesus. Come with me." Paula turned and marched to the house. "Wait here," she said at the door. She returned with a paperback. "Here. Read this. When you've read Ivan's story of the Grand Inquisitor, we can talk. I have to go to work." She went inside and closed the door.

Kim thumped the thick book against her hand, hoping two things: first, that she would enjoy the book, and second, that whoever this Grand Inquisitor character was, he would show up near the beginning.

At home, she read five pages of her new book but found the text dense and the Russian names impossible to pronounce. She surveyed her pantry and refrigerator for something for lunch but came up empty. With no appealing food options available, she grabbed her wallet and headed back into town.

She stopped at Laurie's in hopes of persuading Laurie to join her for lunch. No one answered her knock, though Kim did encounter a sheriff's deputy parked at the residence. "Seen your friend lately?" the man asked.

"At church this morning. Not since. She's probably out running."

"Doesn't matter. I'm here 'til she shows up."

Kim didn't ask why. She didn't expect the deputy would answer, and in any case, she thought she knew. Sheriff Preston probably had new questions.

Laurie could be anywhere. Kim didn't have a clue how she spent her time when she wasn't at work, at church, or out running. For all she knew, Laurie was with friends, such as Valerie and Joan or any of the others who flocked around her at Sunday service. Irrationally, Kim worried that she was with the Channings. The thought bothered her enough to motivate her to walk up the hill.

The front door of the residence was closed when she arrived. A full minute passed after she knocked. Then the massive wooden door swung open. Tucker Channing stood there, frowning. "Ah, how convenient," he said. He stepped back, inviting her to enter.

Kim walked in and saw Laurie and Nell sitting on the sofa. Nell's smile seemed forced, Laurie's tremulous. They both appeared frozen, as though caught in an illicit act. Kim was still waiting for someone to break the tension when she felt Tucker standing much too close.

"Sorry, I didn't mean to interrupt," she said, aware the door behind her had closed.

"No, no, that's quite all right," Tucker said, taking her by the arm and leading—attempting to lead—her into the room. She tried to shake him off. His grip tightened.

"Let go of me," she ordered.

"Miss Jackson—Kim—sit down. It seems we have a great deal to discuss," Tucker said. He released Kim's arm and she moved a step away but didn't sit down.

Nell said, "Laurie, dear, why don't you tell your friend about the work Tucker and I do. I'm sure this will make sense once she hears it from you." She reached over and touched Laurie's face in an intimate gesture, tucking a stray strand of hair behind Laurie's ear.

Laurie didn't answer. She stared with her glance slightly lowered. She seemed to have withdrawn into a private state that brooked no intrusion. Kim had seen her like this before, but she'd been able to pull Laurie out of the grip of her fears, whatever they were. This time she didn't try. "I guess you're going to have to tell me yourself," she said.

The older woman folded her hands into one another. She smiled and glanced at Tucker, as though seeking guidance. The pause gave Kim a moment to wonder how much trouble she and Laurie were in.

"I'm sorry, I've forgotten my manners. Would you like something to drink? A soda, or a cup of tea?" Nell said.

"No, thank you. I really can't stay."

"All right then. This would be easier if Laurie could explain. I feel a bit awkward telling it. Tucker and I are involved in mission work in Mexico. We've spearheaded a group to raise funds to build a clinic in the community. We only left a few weeks ago after we had reached our goal. We've just learned that one of our largest donors had an emergency and won't be able to contribute her share until the end of the year. The timing is awful. If we can't come up with the money, the entire project will collapse. I told Laurie the story a few days ago. You can't imagine my shock when she said she could loan us the difference until our other donor is able to free up the cash."

Kim tried not to laugh. "How much?"

"Pardon me?" Nell looked affronted.

"How much do you need from Laurie?"

"Oh well, that's a private matter." Nell glanced at Laurie, who gave no sign of having heard or understood a single word. Kim hoped that was true. It might be their only advantage in getting out of the house.

Nell looked from Laurie to Kim. "I've never seen her like this. Do you know what's wrong with her?"

"She's mentally ill. She lapses into catatonia. She says it's where she converses with God. I'm sorry to have to tell you this, but Laurie doesn't have any money."

Tucker Channing struck Kim across the face. "You goddamned liar," he said.

She recoiled from the blow, reflexively raising a hand to her injured flesh. She gaped at him. His eyes burned, revealing the demon in the man.

At that moment, Kim knew her instincts about the Channings had been correct.

"Laurie, dear," Nell said, once again touching the younger woman's face. "You're really going to need to pay attention before Tucker does something we all regret and hurts your friend."

Laurie blinked several times.

Tucker, meanwhile, seized Kim by the arm, which he bent and turned behind her back, elevating the limb until she cried out in pain.

"Oh you see. This isn't going well," Nell said.

Tucker lowered his head and spoke in Kim's ear. "She told us she would have to talk to you to get the money. Where is it?"

"I have no idea."

Tucker jerked her arm higher. She cried out again.

"Laurie!" Nell spoke authoritatively, at the same time grabbing Laurie's chin and forcing her head up. The ploy worked. Laurie looked from Nell to Kim, who remained in Tucker's grasp.

"Why are you—?" Laurie said weakly.

Kim had no idea what question Laurie meant to ask. Tucker steadily increased the pressure on her bent arm. Pain shot from her elbow to her shoulder in waves that would have caused her to collapse had she not been trapped in his embrace.

"Tucker!"

There followed unexpected movement and a brief, welcome release from the pain. A split second later, Kim felt a searing pinprick in her neck and then, nothing.

CHAPTER 15

Kim awoke cold.

She shivered against a hard mattress, disconcerted by the strange bedding and the paralyzing cold. It seeped in from every corner. Her pair of down sleeping bags had kept her warm during the most severe winter nights. Something was horribly wrong.

She sat up in a dark room. She fumbled at the bedside for a table and lamp. Her hand struck a flat wood surface. There was no lamp. Soreness in her neck reminded her of something. Without warning, her memory came tumbling back. She recalled her last conscious moment, standing in the Channings' house with Tucker holding her much too tightly. He'd stabbed her with a needle. She knew then: She'd been drugged. And kidnapped.

Where Laurie was, she didn't know.

Loath as she was to move, Kim forced herself to stand. A blind drawn over the single window cast the room in shadowy darkness. She found her way to the door and opened it into a kitchen illuminated by gray daylight. She seemed to be in a small cabin. To the right was a dining area furnished with a table and chairs. A den was adjacent, with a sofa and several chairs facing a fireplace built into the far wall. A closed door was next to the door of the bedroom she'd awakened in.

There was no sign of the Channings.

An exterior door was built into the wall between the dining area and den. Kim found it fitted with a dead bolt, locked, the key nowhere in sight. Through a curtained window she saw a larger cabin across the way with lights on inside. Snow lay on the ground between the two cabins, hardpacked and bearing tire tread marks, indicating it had fallen some time ago and refused to melt. That told her two things: her captors were likely in that cabin, and they were in high country. Snow hadn't stuck to the ground in Creede for weeks.

She found Laurie in the second bedroom.

"Hey, wake up," she said softly, sitting on the edge of the bed. Laurie was covered with a slightly thicker blanket than Kim had had. Kim nudged her. By the lack of response, she assumed Laurie, too, had been drugged.

Minutes passed before Laurie started to come around. "What are you doing here?" she demanded when her eyes shot open. She pulled away roughly.

"It's nice to see you too," Kim said in a dry tease. "We're in trouble, Laurie. The Channings have us locked up somewhere."

"I'm freezing."

"I'm cold too."

She waited, hoping Laurie's memories would reassemble themselves and she wouldn't have to explain what must have happened. Without having gone to too much trouble to work it out, Kim thought Tucker had drugged her and Laurie and brought them here. Wherever here was. Somewhere in the backcountry. Somewhere where friends or neighbors wouldn't be stopping by.

Prompted, Laurie finally told what she remembered. "Tucker pulled a needle out of his pocket and stabbed you with it. You kind of collapsed. Then—" She started to shake. "Nell held me. Tucker had another needle. He injected something in my arm. Nell kept saying everything was going to be all right." Tears filled Laurie's eyes. Kim could have told her that crying was a bad idea. The tears might freeze halfway down her cheeks. "Why did they do that?"

"I think I know the answer."

Laurie hung her head. After a few moments, she brushed her face roughly. "Then I guess you should tell me."

"I will."

The initial surge of adrenaline had abated, leaving Kim colder than she had been before. She was dressed in the same clothes she had worn when she arrived at the Channings' house in Creede, minus shoes. Having lived in a cabin lacking central heat for the last few months, she guessed the air temperature in the room was in the midfifties, tops.

"First, can I please get under the covers with you? I only have one blanket and it's half as thick as yours. I'm really cold, Laurie."

"Okay."

They made themselves as comfortable as they could.

"Nell and Tucker want your money."

"I know."

"You know that?"

"Well, I didn't know right away. Unless they're just naturally perverts, it's the only thing that makes sense."

Despite everything, Kim laughed. "How did they know about your money?"

"I don't know. Maybe they guessed. When they talked about needing funds to support their mission work, I may have said something about being able to help."

Kim congratulated herself on not berating Laurie for the careless admission. She must have betrayed some reaction because Laurie said defensively, "It was only going to be a six-month loan!"

Kim kept her sarcastic retort to herself. She couldn't imagine how Laurie could still believe any part of the Channings' story.

"How long have you known the Channings?"

"I don't know. Maybe a month. They started coming to Sunday services and stayed after for the group talk. They were so friendly and seemed to fit right in with the community."

Kim racked her brain trying to remember the first time she had seen the couple. She couldn't. She pushed back further to the one time she had stayed for the group talk. It was the morning Laurie had asked her to stay. She was certain the couple hadn't been there then. Which meant their appearance in Creede had occurred after Laurie had engaged Kim to do her taxes.

But before this past week. Before the trip to Santa Fe.

Kim's mind tumbled around two dark possibilities: the first was that David Sandoval was responsible for the leak regarding Laurie's Creede address. Distressing as the thought was, it paled against the second: that the Channings knew about the stock certificates. If the latter was true, she and Laurie were in much worse trouble than Kim had dared to imagine.

"It seems like you and Nell hit it off," Kim said, trying to keep Laurie talking.

"We did."

Kim chose her next questions carefully, less interested in the answers than she was in encouraging Laurie to speak freely. She asked if the Channings had kids. They didn't. Laurie said the couple had devoted their lives to missionary work after Tucker retired from a career spent working in the oil business. Kim said he seemed young to be retired. Laurie said he'd been very successful and when they'd saved enough to live on, they'd turned to doing the work they loved. Kim admired the script. It was the perfect lure for Laurie.

"Laurie, you didn't tell Nell about the stock certificates, did you?"

"Of course not!"

"Good."

Which was no guarantee that the Channings didn't know about them from another source.

They were both quiet after that. Kim concentrated on trying to stop shivering. She tried to think what she could tell Laurie to reassure her. Nothing came to mind.

The minutes dragged on.

"I don't know where we are, Laurie," Kim said after assessing their situation. "I think we're likely in a wilderness area, maybe far from Creede. Nell and Tucker probably planned to bring you here. They may mean to keep you here, wearing you down until you agree to give them what they want. What they need is your cooperation. I don't think they'll hurt you. But they may hurt or threaten to hurt me to get what they want from you."

"I won't let them hurt you. If that's their plan, it won't work."

As much as Kim admired Laurie's confidence, she didn't for a minute underestimate the lengths Tucker Channing would go to, to get what he wanted.

Sounds at the cabin door startled them. Kim jumped out of bed and went to the main room. She was waiting when Nell and Tucker entered.

"Good afternoon. Brisk, isn't it?" Tucker said with false good cheer. "I believe it's as cold in here as it is out there." He opened his leather jacket and showed her a gun, jammed at his waist.

Nell carried a tray of food and a thermos. When the first smells of the cooked food reached her, Kim's stomach lurched in hunger.

While Nell set the food on the kitchen table, Kim watched. The place setting was for one. She knew it wasn't for her.

Laurie emerged from the bedroom and started toward Kim.

"No, no. Sit down. Eat your lunch," Nell said.

"Go ahead, Laurie. Eat," Kim said.

"Will you eat something too?" Laurie said.

"I'm afraid there's no food for Kim," Tucker said. "Only for you. Come on now."

Laurie refused. She took another step toward Kim.

"Sit down, now," Tucker roared. He pulled out the gun and pointed it at her.

Persuaded, Laurie sat down. She didn't touch the food.

"There's vegetable soup and a turkey sandwich," Nell said. "You must be hungry."

Laurie ignored her. Kim sensed the Channings' frustration escalating. They had thought Laurie would be a pushover. They probably had never anticipated the situation devolving to this. She tried to fathom how to use that information.

"Fine. Don't eat it," Nell said. She took the bowl of soup and the sandwich and dumped them in a garbage can.

Tucker handed the gun to Nell and turned to Kim. "Take off that sweatshirt," he ordered.

Kim felt her insides liquefy. She thought her legs wouldn't hold her.

"Take it off," he demanded a second time, and as he drew near to rip it from her body, she complied. "Sit. Down." He kicked a high-backed kitchen chair toward her. She lowered herself onto it. Laurie, sitting only feet away, went white.

Tucker jerked Kim's hands roughly through the slats and bound them with duct tape. He bound each foot to the chair leg. When she was restrained, he drew close, unfastening the top buttons of her flannel shirt.

Only then did Kim see the knife. It was lying on the kitchen table. Nell must have had it.

When Tucker picked up the knife, a scream exploded from Laurie.

"No!"

It was a cry riddled with a terror Kim had never heard before. Laurie's eyes were wide, her features strained as she seemed to be about to rush at the man holding the knife.

"Take one step and I'll stab her," Tucker said evenly.

"He's not going to cut me, Laurie," Kim said, though she was sure of no such thing.

"Shut up!" Tucker yelled. He backhanded her violently across the face, and she knew she was right.

She spat at him.

He dropped the knife and lunged at her. The chair toppled over. Kim's head smacked the floor. Tucker, still on his feet, began kicking her.

"Stop!" Laurie screamed.

Nell yelled.

Kim felt one blow after another, at her ribs and higher, even after Nell intervened, trying to pull Tucker away.

She didn't know when the beating ended. Eventually the cabin went quiet. The next thing Kim knew, Laurie was frantically tugging at the ends of the duct tape. When she had removed the bindings, she disappeared into another room. Released, Kim curled into a ball on the rough floor. She lay there, wishing for an abyss to tumble into, anything to take her away from there. After a moment spent gathering her strength, she pulled herself to her knees. She braced her weight on an edge of the knocked-over chair and stood up. She found Laurie huddled on the bed.

Determined to ignore the pain in her head and ribs, she sat down. Laurie didn't move. Kim reached for the blanket and pulled it over both of them. It was too damn cold in the cabin.

She had to reach Laurie somehow. They needed each other if they were going to get through this.

"I have a story I want to tell you," Kim said.

CHAPTER 16

"It's about a woman named Lena. She was a police detective in Durango, Colorado," Kim said.

Laurie gave no sign of listening.

Kim took advantage of her indifferent audience. She told a rambling tale about the ambush that resulted in Lena Fallon being shot multiple times. One bullet lodged in her back and left her paralyzed. Another shot at close range all but destroyed her elbow.

"Before the shooting Lena was a proud, strong woman. Afterward she needed help for something as simple as buttoning her shirt. I worked for her."

Laurie's head jerked up.

Kim drew a satisfied breath at having elicited a reaction. "In the beginning, Lena hated me as much as she hated the rest of the world. In the beginning, I didn't care. To her, I was some lowlife who couldn't qualify for a better job. To me, she was a nasty piece of work in a wheelchair. I needed a job and a place to live. So I put up with her."

It was a long story. Kim skipped ahead.

"One day it started to be different between us. Lena and I still weren't friends, but we both began edging away from our hallowed ground. We began to find a way to talk to each other."

"What was your hallowed ground?"

Immersed in the story, Kim hadn't realized Laurie was listening so closely. She saw it now in a sideways glance. "Lena's hallowed ground was her pain. Mine was my secrets."

Kim skittered over the admission. She told how she and the ex-cop forged an alliance, how, working together, they solved the crime of who shot Lena and why. Kim told the convoluted tale through to its heartbreaking end, including the part where she'd been shot.

"Wait—you were shot too?" Laurie said.

"In my upper arm. The bullet went through to my back."

Neither spoke for a moment.

"Were you in love with her?" Laurie asked.

"Not 'in love.' Not as a lover."

"But you love her."

Kim let the simple statement stand. Long minutes passed while she waited to feel regret for having told the story. She waited to feel Lena's memory diminished by the casual disregard of someone who hadn't known her. Laurie's silence carried no such signal.

"I don't suppose you'll tell me your secrets," Laurie finally said.

Kim laughed at the hopelessness of the situation. "Only that I have them."

Laurie shrugged. "Doesn't everyone?"

Kim thought she ought to congratulate herself. She had succeeded in drawing Laurie out. The harder problem was where to go next.

Days ago, Laurie had said she hadn't been in contact with anyone from the convent since she'd left last June. She'd cut herself off from both her religious community and her family, for reasons she hadn't explained very well.

It took some coaxing, but eventually Laurie answered most of Kim's questions. She said it had always been her plan to enter the convent after she graduated from college. She said not everyone who wants to join a religious order gets admitted. You have to have an education first. You have to have skills.

Or a trust fund, Kim thought.

"Have you always known about your trust fund?" Kim asked.

Laurie spoke dismissively about the money. "Since I was in my teens. My grandparents structured the trust in three parts. I received the first installment when I turned eighteen and graduated from high school. I got the second when I graduated from college. The third, you know about."

"Laurie, is there anyone affiliated with the convent who you're afraid of?"

"Afraid of? No!"

Kim thought the former novitiate protested a bit too much. Still, it was clear that avenue would get no results. The Channings had orchestrated a complicated kidnapping plot, something Kim doubted they could have pulled off on their own. They had to be working with someone—someone who had prior knowledge of Laurie's wealth. Two possibilities came to mind. Kim's first thought was of someone connected to the Church. Her second was of someone at David Sandoval's bank. Then she realized there was a third possibility. Laurie could have told someone about the money.

"Laurie, you said you had mentioned loaning money to Nell and Tucker. Have you discussed your finances with any-one else? Anyone in Creede? Or anywhere?"

"No. I wouldn't."

Kim made a strategic leap. Laurie had left the convent and kept her whereabouts secret for nearly a year. She became highly agitated each time the convent was mentioned. Yet she had shown no hesitation discussing David Sandoval, nor had she appeared to be the least bit nervous when she met with him.

Kim concluded that the Channings were working with someone from Laurie's Santa Fe church in hopes of getting her money, though to what end? If Laurie took her vows, her assets would go straight to the Catholic Church and not into anyone's personal bank account—presumably.

But that was the problem with stock certificates. They could go anywhere.

Kim changed tactics. She asked Laurie who she had felt closest to at the convent. Laurie said that was easy. It was Sister Iris and Sister Abigail. After a moment, she divulged another name. "I've felt close to Father Brian since I was in high school." With sudden vehemence, she said, "I owe Father Brian my life, but don't even ask me why because I'm not going to tell you!"

The silence afterward grew long. Kim's stomach rumbled. Her body ached. Tucker Channing hadn't done her any lasting harm. Still, she knew she would feel the effects of his boots for several days. If she lived that long.

With no safe place to put her thoughts, she tried to understand what had happened that afternoon. She couldn't imagine anything had gone according to plan. Nell and Tucker must have been hoping Laurie would become unglued at the prospect of Kim's murder. They must have wanted her to make a panicked promise that she would do anything to save her friend.

But Kim had interrupted their script. She had left Tucker unable to improvise other than with a few well-placed kicks. She laughed.

"What?" Laurie said.

"Nothing. Or nothing much. I was thinking that Nell and Tucker aren't very good at their jobs. I don't think they expected you to hold out this long."

Sounds at the door startled her. She leapt from the bed and met Nell and Tucker in the outer room.

"Sit down," Tucker ordered. He set right the overturned chair.

Kim thought about refusing. She didn't.

The duct tape was applied as before. Her arms were bound behind her back, her legs secured to the chair. Worse, this time the Channings took Laurie to the other cabin.

Time slowed. Kim fought against her restraints, but cold and hunger sapped her resolve. She felt defeated, and angry. After everything she'd been through, she couldn't believe she'd lose everything—her life—to a puppet of a man named Tucker Channing.

She didn't know how much time passed before he came back.

"The girls wanted to have a private chat," he said when he opened the cabin door and let in an icy blast of air. "Nell can be very persuasive when she wants to be. I'm sure you have no idea."

The last thing Kim wanted to do was look at him. Even less did she want to give him the satisfaction of knowing she was frightened. Hoping to disguise the fact of her chattering teeth, she made scornful eye contact.

He smirked. "You don't know how easy this could be for you. All Laurie needs to do is follow through on the promises she made."

Her promise to enter the Church, Kim assumed. "Last I heard, it's still a free country. Laurie gets to do what she wants to do," she said.

"Well, ultimately, that may be true for her. It will not, however, be true for you. Rather than being part of the problem, you could become part of the solution."

"And do what? Tell Laurie she should go running back into the arms of an institution that resorts to kidnapping and torture? Don't count on it."

"Well, I did think I should ask."

That answered one question. Their abduction *was* tied to someone in the Church.

Tucker paced behind her. He seemed more dangerous out of sight, a psychological ploy, she suspected, that he counted on. She wondered if he meant to rape her. Almost immediately she decided the answer was no. With her face equally protected from his view, she smiled. Tucker was afraid of her. He'd ensured she was restrained before daring to talk to her.

"I want to talk about the money," he said. He drew up behind her, putting his hands on her shoulders.

Kim swallowed back her revulsion. She steeled herself against flinching. He started to move his hands forward, onto her breasts, but didn't. When he moved away altogether, she decided it was because he didn't want to touch her.

"Tell me about the money," he said.

"There's nothing to tell."

Tucker Channing—or whatever his real name was—became enraged. He picked up an iron prong from its stand adjacent to the fireplace and flung it violently at her feet. It bounced loudly, if harmlessly, across the floor. "The hell you will discuss this with me." He strode over and picked up the tool.

Kim tried to contain her withering look. She decided to launch a bluff of her own. "Laurie's money is an investment portfolio. I'm sure you already know that."

"Oh really. Where is it?"

"It's managed by someone in the Charles Schwab office in Santa Fe."

"What's in it?"

"I don't remember."

He loomed closer. "Tell me what you remember."

She lied. "It's high-tech stuff. Microsoft and Dell, Intel, and I don't know what else. Companies I've never heard of."

"What else?"

"Retail companies, Walmart, Walgreens, drug stocks. It's a whole bloody portfolio. I saw the list of its contents for less than a minute."

"Cash?"

"There was some. A couple hundred thousand, I think."

He drew much too close. With one sweep, he raised his hand and raked the back of it across her face. "Don't lie to me!"

More hurt than she wanted to show, Kim kept frightened eyes on him.

"The stock certificates—where are they?" he shouted.

She knew the truth then. Someone in Sandoval's office *had* violated professional ethics and revealed Laurie's private financial details. "I didn't lie to you," she said, clinging to the vestiges of her former bravado. "Yes, Laurie took the certificates. She went directly to the Santa Fe Schwab office. How stupid do you think she is? She wasn't going to walk around holding on to those. The stocks I told you about, that's where her money is now. She met with an investment advisor and handed over the certificates. She has a new account, one more diversified and more liquid."

Tucker Channing glared at her. "You know, I really don't like you."

Kim didn't tell him the feeling was entirely mutual.

Tucker started to turn away. He stopped, reversing direction with sudden speed. Holding the iron rod fully extended, he took aim at her knee. At the last moment he lowered the rod and struck her on the shin. Kim shrieked. She gasped. Bound, and at his mercy, she could do nothing but suffer the blinding pain. She choked for breath.

He looked at her with pure hate. "You think you can play me? We'll see who plays who." He stepped back. He pretended to turn away but instead whirled around. A split second before he swung the bar again, Kim knew what he meant to do.

"No!" she screamed.

He struck her other shin, harder than before. She screamed and screamed again, helpless against the pain shattering her body.

Everything became a blur. She struggled violently against her bound hands, unwilling to put any pressure against the restraints at her legs. She thrashed until the chair fell over. She heard voices but neither saw nor cared who it was until the tape binding her limbs came off and she reached for her damaged legs.

The voices belonged to Nell and Laurie. Kim fought whoever was trying to help. She tasted blood where she bit her lip. Overpowered, she was half carried, half dragged into the bedroom.

CHAPTER 17

Pain was all she knew.

It radiated in deep swells from the center of her legs, as if a red-hot poker were pressed against her bone.

She begged whoever was torturing her to stop.

They wouldn't.

Later, she opened her eyes to shadows. Hazy light filled the room. She knew where she was before she wanted to.

Laurie came into the room. Laurie seemed taller. Kim wondered if the whole world would always seem taller if she never walked again.

Like Lena.

Weak as she was, she felt charged with wariness. It was that caged-animal feeling. Only her eyes communicated the feeble warning: *Don't touch me.* She refused to look Laurie in the eye.

Laurie sat down next to her and touched her forehead. "I think you might have a fever."

"I need to use the bathroom."

Her legs, as she found out, weren't broken. Clutching Laurie with one hand and using the other to brace against the wall, she hobbled to the bathroom. She cried when she sat down on the cold toilet seat.

She bit back a scream when she tried to stand. By the time Laurie opened the door to lend assistance, Kim felt on the verge of passing out.

Cold nausea continued to seep through her when she returned to bed.

"Please, drink a little water," Laurie said. She offered the cup. Kim pushed it away. When she brought the cup near a second time, Kim leaned her head against the wall and allowed a few drops into her mouth.

Immediately she choked. Laurie apologized. They both managed better on the second try.

"There's some food here. Not much. Crackers and a thermos of vegetable soup."

Kim shook her head.

Laurie waited a moment before opening a package of saltines. When she offered one, Kim took it, consuming it in small nibbles.

"There's nothing I can give you for the pain. Do you want to take your pants off? Would you be more comfortable?"

Kim shook her head sharply.

"Nell is furious with Tucker. He wasn't supposed to hurt either of us."

Yeah, right, Kim thought.

Laurie reached for the back of her neck. Cradling it gently, she held Kim.

The hours passed in a blur of pain. There was no comfortable position. Kim felt only marginally better after swallowing some of the soup and eating a few crackers. Laurie didn't insist she try to talk.

Laurie had negotiated another blanket for them. When darkness fell, she crawled beneath the pile of covers, carefully giving Kim a wide berth. Sleep came to Kim intermittently, interrupted always by the piercing burn of pain.

"I want you to put your shoes on," Laurie said firmly the next morning. "I'll help you."

"Our shoes aren't here."

"Yes, they are. I'll get yours."

"No."

"It's too cold in here. It's raining. The dampness can't be good for you."

Kim only complied when it was apparent Laurie wouldn't take no for an answer.

Once her shoes were on, Laurie said, "I have to talk to Nell this morning. I need to talk to her alone. That means Tucker will have to come over here."

"No, Laurie, please," Kim begged.

"I promise he won't hurt you. You stay here in the bedroom. I'll make sure he doesn't come in."

Kim knew these were promises Laurie couldn't keep. Neither could she stop Laurie from doing what she was determined to do. She rolled away, clinging to a pillow at her chest.

Soon afterward the Channings made their first appearance of the morning, walking into the bedroom where Kim lay. Whatever their agenda, Laurie rewrote it.

"I want to say my devotional prayers," she said defiantly. "I want to share this time with you, Nell. And then," she added, "I think the three of us should talk."

Kim knew what Laurie was suggesting. She was intimating that she had changed her mind. If Laurie had, Kim knew it was to save her. The knowledge brought a crush of sorrow.

The Channings and Laurie went into the outer room. One of them shut the bedroom door. Apparently some deal was struck. Kim heard the cabin door slammed. She strained to hear sounds from the outer room, then felt terrified when she heard light rustling.

Minutes passed during which Kim felt nothing but an increasing swell of dread. Her mind became paralyzed around one devastating thought—that after everything she had suffered, everything she had lost, her greatest loss was about to be dealt by a brutally weak man who called himself Tucker Channing.

Then she heard more sounds from the outer room. The cabin door burst open. Laurie's voice ripped through the interior.

"Don't move!" she yelled. "Kim! Come out here!"

Kim hobbled to the doorway. Laurie stood poised inside the cabin, holding the gun pointed at Tucker. Nell was nowhere in sight.

Tucker snickered. "Oh right. Like you know how to use that thing."

Laurie answered by firing a round into the wall. Jolted by the sound, Kim limped as quickly as she could toward her.

"Hold this," Laurie said, handing her the gun. "If he moves, shoot him. Shoot him anyway if you feel like it."

With the gun trained on him, Tucker did as Laurie ordered. He sat down on one of the high-backed chairs. She bound his hands behind his back, loop after loop of the thick, strong duct tape securing his wrists. She did the same to his feet.

"Tie him at his knees," Kim said.

Laurie did so. Afterward she taped his mouth. "Come on. Let's get out of here," she said.

They left the cabin. Adrenaline had carried Kim the distance from bedroom to door; it sustained her for several steps across the rain-soaked ground. Then her right leg, injured worse than her left, gave out. She nearly fell.

"Laurie," she called. "I can't."

Laurie came back for her. With one arm around her waist, she bore Kim's weight as they made their way to the car.

Laurie left Kim standing at the open passenger door and raced around to get in behind the wheel. Kim's right leg gave out a second time when she tried to get in. She sprawled across the seat, unable to move.

"Get in," Laurie yelled. She pulled Kim in, then reached across her to close the door. "Put your seat belt on. This could get rough."

The engine roared to life. They headed down a short driveway to a dirt road.

"Where's Nell?" Kim asked, fighting the nausea that arose with the pain.

"She's knocked out. I hit her. I tied her up. We have to hurry."

Laurie spoke tersely, recounting what she'd done. "The gun was on top of the refrigerator. The duct tape was there too. I saw them when I was at the house yesterday. Your keys and mine, our wallets, they were in a bowl on the table. And the car keys. I knew if I could knock Nell out, I could get us out of here."

Kim tried to smile. They hit a deep pothole and the vehicle lurched violently, sending a shower of new pain through her legs. "Do you know how to drive?"

"I used to."

"You don't happen to have a cell phone with you, do you?"

"I don't own one."

Kim didn't either.

The road curved, making an ever-downward track out of the high country. When they went onto two wheels at a hairpin turn, Kim begged Laurie to slow down. She did, briefly. Then she pressed the accelerator harder. Kim closed her eyes. That was worse. She opened them, scanning the distance for a sign of a paved highway.

The rain began falling in sheets. Clouds thickened and darkened the horizon. They had driven only a few miles, perhaps two. Kim guessed it could be twenty before they reached a main road.

"I was not going to let them get away with it," Laurie muttered as she drove. "They had no right. I don't care if I killed her."

Her hands were clenched on the steering wheel. Her forward gaze was rigid. Kim wanted to tell Laurie to slow down, that they were safe now, but she knew that wasn't true. The dirt road penetrated a corridor of pine trees creeping close on both sides. The wheels bounced in and out of ruts. On a rare straightaway, Laurie gathered speed. A dark wall rose at the end. Suddenly there was another hairpin bend, veering and dropping off sharply to the left. This time Laurie failed to negotiate the curve. The wheels of the car locked. They skidded. A tree rushed at them. Kim screamed on impact.

CHAPTER 18

The quiet was eerie when it settled.

"Kim?"

"I'm here, Laurie."

Both airbags had opened. The engine had stalled. Dazed, and jolted anew by the impact, Kim pushed the gauzy material away from her, as though she were trying to swim through it.

"We have to get out of here," Laurie said. She fumbled with the gearshift and after several tries got the vehicle started. She slammed it into reverse only to hear the high-pitched whine of the engine straining. The car didn't move.

Laurie got out of the vehicle. After a brief inspection, she reported that one front wheel was jammed in a ditch. The other was several inches off the ground, suspended over a fallen tree.

She opened the passenger-side door. "Come on. Get out."

"What are you doing?"

"Helping you get out. Are you okay?"

Was she okay? Kim's laugh started out as a chuckle. Less than one day ago, her shin bones had been smashed with an iron poker. For over forty-eight hours, she had suffered expo-sure to the cold, not to mention she'd had almost nothing to eat or drink. Now they'd crashed into a tree. Of course she wasn't okay. She kept laughing.

"Stop it! Come on."

"I can't walk, Laurie."

"You have to. It can't be that much farther to the main road."

It could be that much farther. It could be miles. Their mutual ignorance on the subject wasn't worth arguing about. Knowing that Laurie wouldn't take no for an answer, Kim gingerly got out of the car and started walking.

Their progress was dismally slow. Even with Laurie bracing her, Kim could do no more than shuffle along. Her legs threatened to give out at every step.

They might have put a quarter of a mile behind them. It cost them too many minutes and cost Kim her last reserve of strength. She broke away and sank helplessly into the wet weeds at the side of the road. "Go—just go! You'll make better time without me. I can't do it, Laurie."

Laurie started to argue. She surveyed the forest of pine trees around them and glanced at the cloud-draped sky above. "All right. But I'm not leaving you here. We have to find a better place."

They pressed on. In a wooded area on the side of the road, Kim took shelter at the base of an aspen. There was no better choice. Laurie frowned and reluctantly left her there.

Instantly Kim succumbed to violent shivering. She felt a thousand times worse being alone. She wanted to shout to Laurie to come back, but she waited, and waited longer, until she was sure her shout couldn't be heard. By then there was no point.

Rain fell in intervals, sometimes heavily. Thunder rumbled in the distance. She jumped at every sound, terrified she would look up and see Nell and Tucker.

Both legs throbbed. The first time she felt tempted to lie back and close her eyes, she fought the impulse. She forced herself to calculate a timetable. If it was one mile to the main highway—she assumed there was a main highway at the end of this road. If there wasn't, if this road was part of a maze of mountain roads winding deeper into the back country, Laurie might never find her way out. Or back.

The prospect settled like black bile in the pit of Kim's stomach.

Assuming the dirt road led to the main highway and it was only another mile to the intersection, Laurie might be back in a half hour. If it was two miles, it might take forty-five minutes. If it was five miles . . . Kim leaned her head against the tree and closed her eyes. However long it took, it was too long.

She knew they weren't far from the car. Likewise, she knew Nell and Tucker would eventually free themselves. They would have to walk down this road. Too soon, they would find the car. Kim had no idea what Laurie had done with the keys. Hopefully, she'd kept them. And the gun?

The road was less than twenty yards from where she huddled against the tree. She sank deeper into the ground and pulled a few branches around her. It was slim cover. Nell and Tucker would see her if they looked hard enough.

Rain started falling again. It began as a gentle pattering. When it fell harder, she noticed she wasn't as cold as before. Whenever "before" was. She actually felt pretty good. She decided everything was going to be okay.

It seemed like she was in a dream when Laurie was suddenly there, telling her to get up. Kim tried to tell her she didn't want to get up, that she was fine now and would get up later. Laurie tugged on her arm. A stranger was there, a man who tugged on her other arm. Without knowing how it happened, she was in a car. Someone gave her a blanket. Laurie tucked it around her.

The man was speaking on a cell phone. "Yeah, I'm calling back about that car wreck. We've got both women with us. We'll bring them to the medical center."

He might have been speaking another language. Kim didn't know anything about a car wreck.

She slipped into dreamless sleep.

CHAPTER 19

Against medical advice, Kim checked herself out of Creede's medical center less than eight hours after she was admitted.

It might have been a mistake, she acknowledged later.

She couldn't have done it without help. Valerie Crane and Joan Abbott had provided her with a ride to the cabin and left her with an assortment of prepared foods, including a hearty beef stew and cornbread. Laurie was conspicuously absent. Immediately upon her arrival at the medical center, Laurie had been arrested and charged with Trip Garrett's murder. She was presently incarcerated in the Mineral County jail.

"You're going to have to explain this," Valerie had insisted several times over the past hour. By *this*, she meant everything from Laurie's arrest to what exactly had happened to Kim and Laurie that day. Kim had dodged the latter question and had focused her replies to the former on Sheriff Preston's interest in Laurie as a suspect in recent weeks. With a weary sigh, she had thanked Valerie and Joan for their help and had promised to be in touch tomorrow.

A fire burned in the woodstove. Despite its warmth, fingers of cold crept in around the sleeping bag Kim held snug to her chin. She thought she would give anything never to feel cold again, but that wasn't true. She never wanted to hurt again. Not the way she had when Tucker Channing smashed her shins with an iron poker. For now, the pain meds were doing their job and holding the blistering ache at bay.

But the drugs left her head fuzzy and didn't do anything to ward off the chills.

Her legs weren't broken; that was the good news. Her shin bones and the surrounding tissue were badly bruised from having been whacked with an iron rod. Walking was bound to be painful for days, possibly longer. Her doctor had advised using crutches. Kim had declined the suggestion.

Shortly before noon that morning, she had arrived at the medical center at the hands of a pair of rescuers, a middle-aged husband and wife flagged down by Laurie on the main road linking Creede to its nearest northern neighbor, Lake City. When admitted, she was in the throes of hypothermia and severe dehydration. IVs were inserted and fluids promptly delivered. X-rays were taken. Pain meds relieved the agony she had suffered for longer than a day. She slept for several hours. When she awoke, Sheriff Andy Preston wanted to know about the car wreck.

Thus began an odyssey that hadn't yet ended.

The sheriff's questions revealed to Kim that he thought he was only dealing with a car wreck—this despite the onerous detail that the car in question hadn't been located. He blamed Laurie for both the crash and the vehicle's mysterious disappearance. It was only the evidence of Kim's injuries and the doctor's vehement declaration that such wounds could not have resulted from a car wreck that ultimately persuaded Preston there was more to the story, that Kim was telling him the truth when she said she and Laurie had been kidnapped by Tucker and Nell Channing.

Looked at from that narrow point of view, Kim supposed she had something to thank Tucker Channing for after all.

The Channings were gone. Authorities hadn't yet found either the crash site or the cabin where Kim and Laurie had been held. "Do you know how many cabins are up in those hills?" Preston had demanded, as if it were Kim's fault that he couldn't find the right one.

Kim wondered if it even mattered. The cabin would provide a link either to an owner or to a rental agency, which might be worth something. Except she had no doubt the Channings' names were fake. She suspected the trail back to them, including through their rental house in Creede, would dead-end quickly.

"Give me one good reason why these people would have kidnapped you and Laurie Beltran," Sheriff Preston had asked a few hours ago.

Kim hadn't wanted to get into it. She had no intention of divulging Laurie's private financial details to the sheriff. Not unless it became necessary.

The doctor who had treated her had advised staying off her battered legs for a few days. That wasn't going to happen. Moving gingerly the next morning, Kim managed to brew a pot of coffee and eat a bowl of cereal. She cleared the hurdle of getting dressed and left the cabin, intent on driving to work. She found a parking spot near the building, nosed in, and began the arduous walk to the office.

Her first call of the morning was to Fred Barnes. He was shocked when he heard Kim and Laurie had been kidnapped by a couple affiliated with Laurie's Santa Fe religious community. He was doubly shocked when Kim told him Laurie had been arrested and charged with murder.

"Let me talk to Robert and Janelle. I'll call you back as soon as I can. Is this your cell phone number?" he said.

"No, it's the landline where I work. I don't have a cell phone."

"Well, that's not helpful. Are you going to be at this number for a while?"

Kim said she would stay there until she heard from him.

She was still waiting for a call back when John Carlos tapped at the door and walked in. "Just wanted to know how far along you are on that work we discussed last week."

She looked into John's devilishly handsome eyes, thinking that for a guy in his forties he looked plain good. She wondered if he went to a tanning salon. No one else she'd seen around town had even the beginnings of a tan. She faintly recollected a meeting and something about appraising some property, both real estate and tangible assets—artwork, jewelry, and the like—to determine tax implications if said items were given as gifts. She had notes from the meeting somewhere. "I'm planning to get to it this afternoon," she said, though until then she'd forgotten the assignment.

"Great. I'll look forward to a report in the morning." Smiling, he backed out of the room, pulling the door closed with him.

"John, I may have questions. I'm not making any promises about tomorrow," she shouted after him.

"Text me if I'm not around. Use Dee's phone if you need to. She'll be in later." With a click of the door latching, he was gone.

Kim would have glared at the empty space he'd left behind if it would have done any good. Instead she opened a bottom drawer and found the file with the meeting notes. She dropped it on the desk.

Barnes called within the hour. He said Laurie's arraignment was scheduled for Thursday morning, two days' hence, at which time bail would be set. Robert and Janelle Beltran were willing to post bail. Barnes was planning to drive to Creede tomorrow afternoon and wondered whether Kim would join him for dinner. They agreed to meet at Miner's Haven.

Kim left the office immediately after ending the call and went straight to the county jail. She asked to see Laurie.

"Sheriff's not here, but I 'spose a visit is okay," a deputy said. "Come with me."

He told Kim to wait in a small room sparsely furnished with a white plastic table and two plastic chairs. A minute later, he led Laurie in.

Laurie's face was pale and drawn. She wore a blue prison jumpsuit. Her hair was uncombed, and her eyes were filled with fear. "You came," she said hoarsely. "I knew you would."

"Hey," Kim said softly. For the first time in longer than she could remember, she wanted to hug someone. Not knowing the jailhouse rules, she stayed seated. "I got here as soon as I could. How are you?"

Laurie shook her head. "I'm not—okay." She stumbled as she spoke. "I don't understand . . . anything about what's happened. Why does anyone think I killed Trip? I could never!"

"I know that, Laurie. We're going to get you out of here."

"And that nightmare with Nell and Tucker. Did that really happen?" she asked, eyes pleading, seeming to hope it hadn't.

"It happened. Nell and Tucker weren't who you thought they were." Kim smiled. "You saved us. You got us out of there. You're my hero."

Laurie finally smiled. "How are your legs?"

"They'll heal."

They went on talking until the deputy tapped on the door, telling them their time was up. Kim left with a promise to come back soon.

CHAPTER 20

One positive note emerged the next day. Kim was too distracted by a host of circumstances to dwell on the pain in her legs.

Even Sheriff Preston noticed. He commented on how well she was getting around when she saw him in his office. Kim told the sheriff she had always been a quick healer. He replied with a quip that maybe she hadn't been hurt quite as bad as she'd let on. He was downright evasive when she asked for an update on the search for Tucker and Nell Channing. Her fury spiked when, with one eyebrow cocked suggestively, he speculated that the alleged kidnapping might have been a hoax. He hypothesized that the story had been crafted by Laurie Beltran to distract investigators from pursuing her as a suspect in the death of Trip Garrett.

For once Kim was shocked to silence. The suggestion was so outrageous she didn't trust herself to speak. That didn't stop the sheriff. "Funny thing is, every person I've talked to, including a lot of those people who attend Laurie's so-called church, they all told me the Channings were a real nice couple who opened their home to anyone who came to their door. Nobody had a bad word to say about them."

He further intimated that Laurie Beltran had the means to do just about anything she wanted to, including arranging a fake kidnapping. By then, Kim knew he knew about Laurie's wealth.

She forced herself to stay on point. "What is the evidence against Laurie?"

Preston refused to tell her. He said Laurie's attorney would be given a copy of the state's evidence at arraignment.

Joan Abbott had agreed, albeit reluctantly, to represent Laurie. Joan specialized in civil matters. She had never defended anyone charged with murder and didn't want that responsibility now. Kim sincerely hoped Fred Barnes would arrive that night with a qualified defense attorney in tow.

The room where she and Laurie had met yesterday was in use when Kim requested a visit. A deputy told her she could either wait until it was free or speak to Laurie in her cell. She opted for the latter.

Laurie was in worse shape than she'd been in twenty-four hours ago. Her face was more haggard. She wasn't inclined to talk.

Kim sat on the bed and leaned against the concrete wall. A wave of defeat swept her. Whatever Laurie was up against, Kim feared this time it would win. Without expecting a reply, she began talking. She started with their drive to Santa Fe, recalling the road to the top of Wolf Creek Pass and the snowcapped peaks visible to the west under a cloudless cerulean-blue sky. The sights of northern New Mexico were less clear in her mind. She recalled the colors, the seemingly infinite palette of earth tones in shades of red, orange, and sandstone, but the shape of the land, the undulating valleys rolling up against round-topped hills and mountaintops looming higher still had become a blur. She talked for her own benefit as much as for Laurie's, trying to establish a timeline of recent events.

Her stomach grumbled while she spoke. "And those sandwiches Sofia made for us, turkey, cheese, avocado, and what was the other ingredient?"

"Green chile."

"Right. It was delicious," Kim said, startled by the reply.

She'd run out of things to say. While she racked her brain for the thread of a new monologue, Laurie spoke.

"I keep wondering what I did wrong," she said. "I must have done something wrong. I feel like my whole life is a punishment from God. I get it that I made promises that I didn't keep. But before that, I don't know. I really don't know what I did wrong." She sat with her knees pulled close to her chest, arms wrapped around them. Huddled, as if she needed to protect something at her core. Maybe she did.

Kim thought she understood about the broken promises. She didn't know what else Laurie had to feel guilty about. At the moment that seemed to matter less than her current legal predicament. "I can't imagine why the sheriff thinks you killed Trip," she said. "I think he needed someone to blame, and you were his best choice. I know you didn't kill Trip, and I'm going to do everything I can to prove your innocence."

"What can you do?" Laurie's eyes were bright with the question.

"You might be surprised," Kim said, grinning and drawing a hard-won smile from Laurie.

—

It was past six p.m. when Kim walked into Miner's Haven. She waved at Francie, at the same time spotting Fred Barnes in a booth. She slid in opposite him, enviously eyeing his mug of beer.

"What are you drinking, Kim?" Francie asked.

"I'll have one of those." She pointed at the beer. Moments later, the drink was in front of her.

"I'll give you kids a couple of minutes to catch up before I come back for your food order," Francie said.

"How's it going?" Barnes said.

"Not so good," she said. "The sheriff thinks the kidnapping was a hoax. He thinks Laurie set it up to deflect attention away from a murder investigation."

"I know. Preston told me." Barnes looked at her long enough to cause her to fidget. "Any chance Laurie played a part in Garrett's death?"

"No! How can you suggest that? Do you even know Laurie?"

He didn't address her question. "So what are you going to do to prove her innocence?"

She choked on her beer. "You're the private investigator! I was hoping you'd have some ideas." She chased the aborted swallow with a long pull on the lager. "I haven't seen any of the evidence. I don't even know why anyone believes Garrett was murdered."

"There was a witness. A man saw a woman strike Trip on the head with some object and push him over the bridge. Same witness saw that woman run to Laurie's house."

"Any description of the object? Have they recovered it?"

"Something with a handle. And no, not yet."

"Who's the witness?"

"A local by the name of Gerry Verkamp."

Kim knew the name. She couldn't immediately place the man. "Is there any forensic evidence?"

"Not yet. The sheriff is hoping to get his hands on whatever Garrett's assailant used on him. Kim, how well do you know Laurie?"

Something in Barnes's tone caused her bad feeling to grow worse. "I don't even know how to answer that. Not well enough, apparently."

"I don't think you do." He laughed. "I'm not sure how you entangle yourself in criminal investigations, but here you are again." His blue eyes twinkled in merriment.

She waited him out, unamused. Francie stopped by to check on them. Barnes asked for another round. "Unless you want something stronger," he said.

Kim didn't.

When they were settled with fresh drinks, he launched into a story, parts of which Kim had heard before. It was about a scrappy couple named Robert and Janelle who amassed a fortune while raising their son in the rapidly changing landscape on a California peninsula soon to become known as the Silicon Valley. The son graduated from Stanford, intent on going to medical school. A severe car wreck and a lengthy recovery set him back a year. He never regained his passion to become a physician. In his parents' eyes, he "settled" for becoming a researcher at one of the biotech companies sprouting up in the area. While working there, he met a beautiful young woman who was rapidly making a name for herself in the company's marketing division. His parents didn't like her. They thought she was too superficial, too attached to appearances, her own especially. In a word, they thought she wasn't of their son's caliber. During this period, they continued to hope Peter would regain his sense of self and aspire to loftier intellectual and professional heights. After all, with each passing year it was becoming more apparent he would never want for money. Why not shoot for the stars, wherever that took him?

The couple married. It was a grand affair, held on the estate of a winery in Napa Valley. Two hundred guests were wined and dined on the golden hillside, surrounded by the scent of piñon, sage, and money.

Over the course of the next several years, Peter moved up a few ranks at the growing biotech firm. Marilyn worked until their first child was born. A second daughter was born two years later, and two years after that, right on schedule, a son.

"Wait," Kim said. "A son? Laurie told me about her sister. She never mentioned her brother."

"Daniel. Danny. I'm getting to that."

Frustrations of one sort and another continued to boil over, mainly with Peter's failure to advance in the company. By the time the children were of school age, the Beltran family had decamped for the South of France, where Peter was hired at a French pharmaceutical company and Marilyn swam with the big fish in Nice's populous expat community. They stayed for ten years. On returning, they went to Santa Fe, where the elder Beltrans now lived. The family moved into a newly built, sprawling adobe house atop a hill, paid for by Robert and Janelle. The kids attended private school.

Fred Barnes reached inside his leather satchel and extracted a photograph. He slid it toward Kim. "This was taken around that time."

The photo showed a family of five, father lean, tan, and handsome; mother with wavy blond hair and chin cocked in a becoming if haughty pose. Laurie looked much as she did now: slender, with long dark hair. The sister was a wild beauty. She had her mother's hair in a lighter shade and blue eyes that crinkled with lightning. The boy, only ten or eleven, was tall with narrow shoulders, the young man in him hidden in his puckish smile.

Questions piled up. Kim grew impatient while Barnes related details of the tense relationship between Peter and Marilyn and the elder Beltrans in Santa Fe. The animosity didn't extend to the children, whom Robert and Janelle doted on. The grandparents were keen to provide financial security for Laurie and her siblings. They did so by creating a trust fund for each child.

Kim remained silent while Fred Barnes sipped his second beer. There were probably signs, he said when he set the mug down. Suffice it to say, no one could have predicted what happened.

"You don't know about any of this, do you?" His somber eyes bored into hers.

She shook her head.

"It was the weekend before Laurie's high school graduation. Robert and Janelle had given her a BMW. She also had received the first installment of her trust fund, a stock portfolio worth a couple hundred thousand dollars." He exhaled a long breath. "No one knows exactly what set Natalie off. She had failed a couple of classes that year. She was being kept in Santa Fe to attend summer school while the rest of the family planned to return to France. Laurie would only be there until the fall, when she was slated to begin college. Either some grievance had been brewing for a long time, or Natalie simply snapped. Laurie was in her bedroom, minding her own business, when Natalie burst in and attacked her with a knife."

Kim gasped.

"Laurie suffered two stab wounds in her chest. Natalie probably would have killed her except Danny heard Laurie's screams and charged into the bedroom."

Barnes averted his glance before he looked back at Kim. "Natalie killed him instead."

CHAPTER 21

Barnes drove Kim home that night. The canyon was eerily lit by parallel headlight beams of white, illuminating indistinct shapes, when the Ford Fusion swerved to make a U-turn and stopped outside her door. She refused his offer of help and with a muffled good night, got out, closed the car door, and unlocked the cabin. He waited a full minute once she was inside before driving away.

Barnes had told her about Father Brian, the priest Laurie had turned to in the aftermath of the attack that left her badly injured and her brother dead. According to Barnes, Laurie had been a person of strong religious feeling as a young woman but had never expressed any interest in yoking her life to the Catholic Church. Not until that summer of necessary healing.

The phrase stuck with Kim. Necessary healing. She wondered if that was what Lena was doing in Denver.

She'd asked Barnes what happened to the sister. She'd assumed Natalie was still in prison. Barnes said she never went to prison. Natalie Beltran was deemed unfit to stand trial and was committed to a psychiatric hospital. *Good*, Kim thought. Except then he'd added that Natalie had been released two years ago. After spending time with her parents in France, she had returned to Denver, where she was pursuing graduate studies in neurology.

"Returned to Denver? Graduate studies?" Kim had said.

"The psych hospital Natalie was in was there. She finished high school and earned her undergraduate degree while she was institutionalized. Apparently she has a fascination with the brain. She's proven to be quite a good student."

Barnes had said Natalie saw her grandparents every few months. The senior Beltrans had visited her regularly while she was in the hospital. Her parents likewise had visited, though less often. They saw Natalie twice a year. During those trips they also saw Laurie, whether she was away at college or home in Santa Fe.

The private investigator painted a much different family picture from the one Kim had glimpsed, based on Laurie's report.

"This has been a tough year for Robert and Janelle, and for Laurie's parents too, not knowing where she was living," Barnes had said. "They've been worried."

"Can you tell me anything more about the priest, you said his name is Father Brian? Laurie mentioned him when we were held by the Channings," Kim had said.

Father Brian was still at the same parish church in Santa Fe, according to Barnes. Laurie's grandparents believed that Laurie had given him money in the past.

"To him or to the Church?" Kim had asked, her suspicions about the priest growing sharper.

Barnes had shrugged. "I don't know."

Kim had stared blankly, wondering if the priest had profited privately from Laurie's largesse.

"It was her money," Barnes had said. "She could have done as she pleased with it."

Awake early the next morning, Kim was at the office before Dee or John arrived. She filed two sets of taxes for clients who had requested extensions and was out the door at nine twenty-five for the five-minute walk to the courthouse. As she was entering, Fred Barnes jogged up to join her. "I need to call Robert with a report after the arraignment. Can we meet for coffee later?"

Kim had an appointment scheduled for midmorning. She agreed to meet Barnes for an early lunch.

Of all the scenarios she had imagined, one that had never occurred to her was that she would walk into a packed court-room. At least twenty people who routinely gathered on Sunday mornings in Creede's town hall basement were present, show-ing their support for Laurie.

The formalities were dispensed with quickly. The charges were read. Joan entered Laurie's plea of not guilty. The judge set bail and scheduled a trial date four weeks out. With a smack of the gavel, the hearing ended. Laurie was led away. Kim met briefly with Valerie and Joan to give the latter a signed check from Robert Beltran, delivered and filled in by Fred Barnes, posting bail. Both women's eyes popped wide at the sight of it. Joan said she would handle Laurie's release. "We'll see you later, then?" Valerie said, having indicated she would spend the day with Laurie. Kim nodded, unsure what the day would bring.

She was late for lunch with Fred, who she found eyeing his watch impatiently when she arrived. He wanted to know where things stood with Laurie's attorney. Kim said Joan had told her she had no criminal defense experience and was only acting on Laurie's behalf as a favor for now. Joan insisted she wanted off the case.

Barnes frowned. "Do you know anyone else in town to recommend?"

Kim didn't. Barnes's frown deepened. He said the senior Beltrans hadn't committed to footing the entire bill for Laurie's legal fees. They were waiting to hear from Laurie. They also intended to speak to her parents.

"What is your role going to be in the investigation?" Kim asked.

"Hard to say." He sat back while their waitress lowered two plates of food onto the table. Barnes picked up his burger and took a bite. The waitress returned to top off their coffee cups. "I'd like to get copies of all the documents the prosecution has turned over. I especially want to see the autopsy report."

Kim did too. Barnes said Joan should have those by now.

They rehashed what they knew: that it was a circumstantial case. "All they have is Laurie's argument with Trip in the bar on Friday afternoon and his visit to her house that night," Kim said. "The injury to Trip's head seems to be the crucial piece of forensic evidence, but no murder weapon has been found. I wonder if a different pathologist would make a different assessment about the source of that blow."

"Possibly. Don't forget about the sheriff's star witness. According to this man, he saw a woman on the bridge with Trip, pushing him into the water. Afterward, she ran to Laurie's house. Have you learned anything about the guy?"

"Not much. Gerry Verkamp is Creede's version of a town drunk. He works odd jobs for people. He has two brothers, lives in a back room with one until the brother kicks him out, then he goes to live with the other."

"You're sure about the drinking?"

"That's what I've heard."

Having learned that much from Valerie Crane, Kim realized she had seen Verkamp around town on occasion without knowing his name.

Before lunch ended, Barnes pulled a cell phone from his jacket pocket and slid it across the table. "Keep this for now," he said, adding that his number was in the contacts list, as was a number she could use to reach Robert and Janelle, if necessary. The pronounced inflection in his voice told her all she needed to know. The Beltrans really didn't want to hear from her. Her impulse was to decline the gift. Except it wasn't a gift. It was a tool, and he was right, she needed it. She thanked him.

Back at her office, Kim took out a fresh notepad. She wrote Trip Garrett's name at the top, followed by her first question: How did he die?

She stared at the words for a long moment. Then she added another question: Why did he die?

Having no other place to start, she stuck with the sheriff's version of Garrett's death and jotted down questions that would need to be answered in an investigation. By the time she finished, she knew she had to find out who was in Garrett's circle of family and friends and who among them might be willing to talk to her. She needed to find out the state of his business and his marriage. She flashed to the memory of the look on Cathy Garrett's face the one time they'd met—when she'd come face to face with Trip's widow from the open door of the laundry room. She laughed, except it wasn't funny. Cathy had materialized as if from thin air, furious to find a stranger poking through her house.

Because she would never get another chance to search the house, Kim closed her eyes and mentally walked through it. She made notes as she reviewed what she'd seen, or had not seen, in each room: No photos. A dead child's bedroom, untouched. Contents of closets and drawers kept ramrod straight, no wrinkle in any towel, no shoe out of place. It was something about the closets, she thought, tugging at a thread. In the couple's bedroom, all of Trip's clothes were gone. Not even a favorite shirt or jacket left for Cathy to hold close, clinging to the last remnant of her husband's unique scent.

Kim hadn't seen anything interesting in the bathroom medicine cabinet or cupboard. Only the meticulous ordering of bottles and boxes: lotion, shampoo, sunscreen, bandages, Band-Aids, and the like. In the hall linen closet, towels were neatly folded and stacked along with sheets and pillowcases. Bottles of cleaning products lined the top shelf, one of each, well out of reach of a child's hands.

A similar arrangement of supplies occupied the laundry room where Kim had been caught. Cleaning cloths, sponges, and floor cleaner on a shelf; mops in a bucket, handles neatly aligned. That odd tub of premeasured detergent packets, one sandwich bag per load. And three boxes of powdered detergent on the floor, not to be touched under any circumstances, per Cathy's orders.

Kim wrote down everything she could remember.

She jumped when she heard the knock on her door, guilty, as though caught again. Dee announced the arrival of a client.

Forty-five minutes later, Kim escorted her latest potential client through the outer office, having discussed at length the accounting requirements for setting up an internet business. Flustered and overwhelmed by the volume of information, the woman promised to call soon to set up a second appointment. Kim said goodbye and turned to see Dee, who was smiling sympathetically. "Not a paying customer, I expect," the recep-tionist said.

"We'll see. When I talked to her on the phone, I had the idea she was further along in her business plan than she is."

"Business plan in this town—ha!" After a moment Dee said, "You look beat."

"Long night. Long day." Kim was two steps from her office when a thought occurred to her. "Dee, is there anyone in Creede who knows everything about everybody?" She flushed when she realized how silly the question sounded.

"You mean someone who qualifies as the official town gossip?"

"Something like that."

"Only a couple dozen or so. What kind of information are you looking for?"

"I told you my friend Laurie has been arrested for Trip Garrett's murder. I'm trying to help her. I know it's a hard time for Trip's family and friends, but I'm trying to find someone who might talk to me, tell me something about him." Kim didn't get any further. Dee cut her off.

"The person you want is Trip's aunt Sue. Sue Zachary. Her boy is—was—Trip's partner in their construction business. Sue's a talker. Get her started on something and she'll keep going. That's not to promise she'll tell you what you want to know, but she'll tell you something."

"Any idea where I can find her?"

Dee glanced at her watch. "Unless Sue's reformed, she'll likely be heading into Checkers Bar anytime now."

"Thanks, Dee."

Twenty minutes later, Kim found the locals' tavern two streets over from the main thoroughfare through town. The wood plank exterior could have used a fresh coat of varnish, not to mention a sign with its letters intact. Kim walked in, expecting to find the place empty. To her surprise, nearly all of the barstools were taken, and quite a few tables as well. It took a moment for her eyes to adjust to the dimly lit interior. It took another moment to spot the woman with long blond hair going to gray sitting at a table, talking to a man. She walked over.

"Can I help you with something?" the woman said.

"I apologize for interrupting. Are you Sue Zachary?"

"Who's asking?"

"My name is Kim Jackson. I've been working at John Carlos's office for the last few months. Dee, his receptionist, thought I might find you here."

The man pushed his chair away and stood up. "I need to be moving on anyway, Sue. Ma'am," he said to Kim, tipping his cap.

"Might as well sit down then." She shouted at the bartender, "Billy, my friend needs a drink."

Kim started to object. Thinking better of it, she said she would have what Sue was drinking, which turned out to be a pint of beer from a brewery in Pagosa Springs. The bartender set a glass brimming with amber liquid in front of her and left without asking her to pay for it.

"Now that we got that straightened out, what can I do for you?" Sue said.

Sue Zachary, in her fifties, had soft, unlined skin. She had a medium build and a capable look about her, highlighted by a direct gaze. With strong cheek bones, she was a nice-looking woman, though she had long since lost the bloom of youth.

"I'd like to ask you a couple of questions about Trip Garrett. First of all, I want to say how sorry I am for the loss of your nephew. I didn't know Trip, but from everything I've heard, I know he was a truly decent man."

Sue fixed her gaze and stared. Kim held eye contact for as long as she could. When she broke off, she reached for the beer mug.

"What's your interest?" Sue said.

"I don't trust Sheriff Andy Preston to do a thorough investigation into Trip's death. I'd like to talk to some people who knew Trip. I'd like to get a better sense of who he was."

"A good man, that's who he was." Sue gave a sharp nod of her head and put one hand on her glass but didn't raise it. "Andy Preston," she said disparagingly, providing Kim a first glimmer of hope that Sue Zachary wasn't going to boot her out of the bar.

Sue did take a drink after that and embarked on a long-winded tale about what great friends Trip and her son, Jason, had been as boys and how pleased she was when they became business partners as grown men, doing damn fine work in their construction business. In the course of the monologue, Sue said she expected her boy, Jason, knew Trip better than anyone had, including his own wife. "Have you talked to Cathy yet?" she said.

"No," Kim said, not quite a lie. Cathy had done all the talking the one time they had come face to face.

"Don't waste your time. She's the most tight-lipped little thing I've ever seen." Sue drained her beer and signaled for two more.

It took another hour before Kim was able to make a polite exit from the bar. By then she had the names of four people, including Sue's son, to talk to. The others were Tom, Trip's brother; Esther, their mother; and Hallie Kerr, Trip's ex-girlfriend. Toward the end of the conversation, Sue said, "Hallie thought she was as good as engaged to Trip before Cathy came along. 'Course she never had a ring. I expect she thought she didn't need one. Funny thing is, Trip and Hallie were perfect for each other. Cathy? She's a looker, all right, but she's not the outdoorsy type. I wouldn't have thought Trip would put up with that." Sue flung her shoulders in a hapless gesture. "Guess I was wrong."

CHAPTER 22

Kim left Checkers Bar feeling a mite unsteady on her feet. She'd drunk more than she should have and learned less than she'd hoped to. Maybe it was disappointment, but she had the feeling Sue Zachary knew more than she'd revealed.

Half a block shy of reaching Laurie's house, she crossed paths with Valerie Crane, who confessed to having been waiting for her.

"I called your office. I heard you left over an hour ago. I need to talk to you. Actually, Joan does. Neither of us has been able to make sense of anything that's happened this week. Yours and Laurie's kidnapping by the Channings? That doesn't make a bit of sense!"

Kim agreed that Valerie and Joan deserved a better explanation for the kidnapping but she wasn't about to give it to them. "You're right," she said. "It doesn't make sense. But it's not my story to tell, Valerie. I have to leave that to Laurie. Right now I think we need to focus on the charges against her."

Valerie reluctantly agreed. They went in the house where, for the second time in less than three minutes, Kim was greeted petulantly.

"Where have you been?" Laurie demanded.

The first thing Kim noticed, besides Joan's presence, was a newly installed dead bolt on the door. "Nice lock," she said, pleased, patting the burnished bronze fixture.

"Kate Hicks did that. Without asking whether I wanted it," Laurie said.

"Joan and I need to leave. It's been a long day," Valerie said.

"Did you have a chance to make copies of the state's case file?" Kim asked Joan.

"Yes." Still dressed in the jacket and slacks she'd worn to court, Joan took a brown envelope from her briefcase and handed it over before turning to Laurie. "I can't represent you, Laurie. I've told you this. I don't have the experience. Second-degree murder is a serious charge. You could end up in the women's prison in Cañon City for twenty years. I can't have that on my conscience. You have to find another attorney."

"If it's about the money, I can pay you," Laurie said hoarsely.

"It's about much more than that."

Joan and Valerie said goodbye and left. When Kim looked over, her eyes were drawn to Laurie's chest and the scars concealed beneath her shirt. She flashed to the moment when Tucker Channing had raised a knife and threatened to stab her, exactly as Laurie had been stabbed by her sister seven years ago. The flagrant cruelty of the charade infuriated Kim anew. She softened her glance and wanted to tell Laurie that she knew what had happened and understood so much more now than she had before, but the truth was she didn't understand. She doubted she could ever understand the brutality of the attack Laurie had suffered or her unending grief at having lost her brother. And her sister.

"How are you?" she said.

Laurie gave a hopeless swing of the shoulders.

They went into the living room.

"This feels like a nightmare," Laurie said. There were large bags under her eyes. She looked more wan than she had earlier. Possibly thinner.

"Have you had anything to eat today?"

Laurie waved at the kitchen. "Yes. There's food in the refrigerator. People from the Sunday group dropped off food. Valerie organized some kind of schedule."

Kim resisted the urge to laugh. Valerie had it all organized. Except for the part about getting Laurie sprung from the tyrannical wheels of Creede's justice system.

"Marla offered me a job at her coffee shop," Laurie said. "She said business is picking up now that the weather is better and tourists are starting to trickle in. Obviously I can't go back to work for Cathy."

They talked of the job, the café, Marla, and Kate—the two other women whom Kim thought of as members of Laurie's "inner circle" of supporters. All the while she felt a mounting pressure to broach a different subject. Noticing Laurie repeatedly raise her hand to her mouth to cover a yawn, Kim chose her moment. "Laurie, your grandparents want you to call them. They're worried about you."

"They know where I am?"

"I didn't tell them. But yes, they do. They had someone follow us when we left Santa Fe. He's a friend of theirs. I've met him. He's—"

Some veil of dark energy closed over Laurie.

"They care about you. They love you," Kim said, trying to keep a channel open.

"They had us followed? I can't believe it!"

A tap at the door interrupted them. Marla let herself in with a cheery hello. Kim stayed a few minutes longer before she said good night and departed into the early evening twilight.

—

She rushed home clutching the brown envelope. Once settled on the sofa, she opened the envelope and removed the documents representing the state of Colorado's case against Laurie Beltran. She thumbed through legal documents specifying the charges. She skipped the police reports related to Trip's disappearance and the subsequent discovery of his body in Willow Creek. She leafed through the stack until she found the autopsy report. Embedded in dense medical verbiage, two clear statements sent chills down the back of her neck: Trip's cause of death was drowning. The manner of his death was homicide.

She expelled a short, sharp breath. She shouldn't have been surprised. Had the manner of death been declared anything other than homicide, Laurie wouldn't have been charged with murder.

Kim dug further in the text until she found the description of Trip's head injury. The wound, just below his right temple, had been delivered with sufficient force to crack his skull. The fracture measured two centimeters. Bone fragments were visible. The coroner had noted the likely cause as "blunt-force trauma suffered as a result of being struck with a smooth-sided heavy object."

A hammer, Kim thought.

She imagined what had happened. Someone had struck Trip on the head and pushed him in the creek while he was still breathing.

Gerry Verkamp's witness statement confirmed that scenario. According to Verkamp, a woman came up behind Trip, struck him on the head, and pushed him off the bridge. The woman then ran to Laurie Beltran's house. Verkamp didn't see her again. He was quoted as saying: "Trip tripped. But he had some help."

Kim saw it now. If Verkamp's statement could be believed, someone had taken great pains to ensure Trip was incapacitated when he went into the water. She, assuming it was a she, then had set up the trail of evidence pointing to Laurie. Kim reached again for the autopsy report. Nowhere in the document itself nor anywhere else in the case file could she find a page of medical abbreviations in fine print with accompanying numbers reporting bloodwork results. She wasn't sure she could have deciphered the hieroglyphics anyway, but the toxicology report should have been there.

The next morning, she wasted no time calling the sheriff, who grudgingly agreed to provide a copy of Trip Garrett's toxicology results. "Just out of curiosity," she said before Sheriff Preston disconnected, "did Trip have a life insurance policy?"

With another grumble, Preston said, "Haven't found one." The line went dead.

Kim puzzled over the information. The Garretts probably owned their house and had a mortgage. Most young families in their situation would have taken out an insurance policy on the primary wage earner in the event of death. She doubted Cathy Garrett's job as a classroom assistant would pay the family's bills.

Through the morning she set aside thoughts of the investigation and focused on work. She returned phone calls and prepared for two appointments. At noon, after concluding the first, she spared time for a visit to the post office to mail her latest letter to Lena and to receive the unsurprising news that no letter awaited her.

She went to the police station to pick up a copy of Trip Garrett's toxicology report. Ignoring her own best advice to return directly to work, she slit open the envelope while still inside the building and removed the pair of stapled pages. Skimming quickly, she saw what she expected to see: abbreviated medical terms and corresponding numerical values. She was walking to the door when she stopped and turned.

"Can I ask you something?" she said to the dispatch operator. She showed him the tox report and asked whether he knew how to read it.

"What about it?" he said.

She didn't care a thing about Trip Garrett's white blood cell count or liver function. "Anything stand out to you? Anything that shouldn't be there?"

The man scanned the sheet. "Trip had had a few before he went in the creek. Blood alcohol was .14." He pointed out the notation. "Probably nothing he wasn't used to." He started to hand the report back. "Hmm, there is something." Pointing again, he told her Trip had a controlled substance in his system when he died. Lorazepam.

She didn't have to ask what that was. She had taken the antianxiety drug in the past. It was meant to help even out the rough spots, her therapist had said when she prescribed it. The last time Kim took it was ages ago, before she knew the true meaning of the phrase "rough spots."

The phone rang. The man reached to answer it. She thanked him and was out the door before she thought to stick around to ask his opinion of what the combination of alcohol and lorazepam would do to a guy like Trip Garrett.

Much as Kim wanted to talk to Fred Barnes, she didn't have time. Back at the office, she spared five minutes to fax copies of the case file to his machine in Santa Fe. She had an appointment in Del Norte, less than an hour's drive away. One of her Creede clients had begged her to make the trip to consult with the owners of a dry-cleaning business who were in legal trouble with the state over some tax issue. Kim had scheduled a midafternoon appointment, hoping to wrap up the session in time to find Jason Zachary at his jobsite on the way home.

A white van was parked outside Paula's house when Kim picked up her car at the cabin. Occasionally, a brown UPS truck pulled up to the house. Otherwise, Kim had never seen a visitor on the premises. She left without checking on her landlady.

Del Norte proved to be a bustling metropolis compared to the sleepy hamlet of Creede. Kim found the dry-cleaning business without difficulty. A woman working at the counter greeted her. When she asked for Mr. or Mrs. Kirsch, the woman retreated behind racks of plastic-sheathed clothes, returning a moment later with a man in the process of removing thick glasses as he approached. "Some problem?" he said.

Kim identified herself. He gave a deep frown, communicating that he had better things to do than spend precious time with a so-called tax expert sent by his sister. "S'long as you're here," he grumbled. He waved for her to follow. His employee stepped toward the end of the counter and unlatched and raised a panel for Kim to step through.

The meeting went downhill from there. George Kirsch produced the letter that had caused his wife grief. Kim's heart sank when she read the message. According to the state government, four years earlier, the business had failed to pay income tax. Between tax owed, interest, and penalties, the Kirsches' bill came to nearly $15,000. While George Kirsch fumed and said that couldn't possibly be right, his wife wrung her fingers and said that must have been when they had that new girl doing their books. She had stayed just about a year, hadn't she? Could she have done this? Kim delivered the bad news that it was entirely possible the bookkeeper had bilked the Kirsches out of their money.

She agreed to contact the state representative to discuss the matter. She urged the Kirsches to review their bank records from that period to see what checks had cleared and to whom they were made payable. She listened to husband and wife arguing about how this could have happened. George Kirsch insisted he was going to find that swindler, get his money back, and make sure she was arrested while he was at it. Kim silently wished him good luck. She promised to be in touch when she knew more, and with copies of the relevant documents in hand, said goodbye and left.

Twenty minutes later she reached the town of South Fork. Following directions provided by Sue Zachary, she pulled off the road near a three-unit strip mall undergoing renovation. Her eyes were on a blue pickup truck parked at the jobsite. Fifteen minutes later, a man dressed in faded jeans and an unbuttoned flannel shirt flapping over a stained T-shirt emerged from the building. Kim got out of her car and walked down a short driveway. She met the man at the truck. "Jason Zachary?" she said. "My name is Kim Jackson. I spoke to your mother the other day. She told me I could find you here."

His eyes warily met hers. Sue Zachary's son had shaggy brown hair; nicely set, even features; and the solid build of a man who spent his time engaged in manual labor. There was no invitation in his glance. It was all suspicion. "Yeah?" he said.

"I'd like to ask you a few questions about Trip Garrett." She pointed at her car. "I brought a couple of beers. If you have a few minutes, I'd be happy to grab them while we talk."

Something darker flashed in his eyes. "You writing some shit story?"

"No. It's worse than that." She let the silence settle. "I'm a friend of Laurie Beltran. I don't think she killed Trip. I'm trying to figure out why anyone thinks she did."

Jason Zachary spent a long moment studying Kim. "What kind of beer?"

"Avalanche."

The hard set of his features eased slightly. Kim wasted no time getting the cooler with the six-pack and joining Jason on a grassy patch on the hillside. He popped the caps on two bottles and handed her one. "My ma must have liked you." He nodded at the beer and took a long swallow.

Kim tested the brew with a more tentative taste. Sue Zachary had liked her well enough to tell her what kind of beer her son drank. Her fledgling hopes for a conversation were dashed when he said, "To tell you the truth, I don't feel much like talking about Trip. I've been here working since six this morning. I'll be back tomorrow and the next day and the next. Every day's the same. I'll be lucky if I can finish this job. Know any decent electricians?"

She didn't. She expected he was better acquainted with the available pool of craftsmen in the area than she was. "Actually I do," she said, remembering something Valerie had said. "There's a woman named Kate who does handiwork and odd jobs. I don't know her last name, but I can find out."

His eyes crinkled in interest. "Katie Hicks? I forgot about her." He finished his beer. In better spirits, either from the alcohol or something to do with Katie Hicks, he sat back, resting his weight on his palms. "What do you want to know about Trip?"

Kim knew from Jason's mother that he and Trip had been friends all their lives. They both had tried college. Trip lasted one year, Jason two. They fell out of touch for several years, only to run into each other in a bar in Del Norte. By then they were both working in the construction trade. A few years later, they started their own company and had been at it ever since, earning a good reputation in the southern Colorado region.

"Had you noticed any changes in Trip recently?" Kim said.

Jason reached inside the cooler for a second beer. "Nah. Trip was rock solid."

Kim didn't like the answer. It left her no opening. She decided the problem was the question. "I've only lived in Creede a few months. Seems to me it takes a certain sort of person to be happy living here. What kinds of things did Trip like to do for fun?"

"Oh well." Jason took a moment. "He loved being outdoors. He loved hiking and camping. And mountain biking. We rode when we were kids. Man, we were all over those mountains." He paused to smile. The smile lit up his face, displacing the grief Kim suspected had been there since Trip died.

"You quit riding?" Kim said, thinking of guys she knew in Durango who spent every free moment on two wheels in the high country.

"We didn't quit exactly. More like we stopped gradually. I should get my old bike out. Well, if I ever have time to ride."

Kim asked about Trip's wife, Cathy, if she liked the outdoors. Jason said not so much, and having little kids made it hard getting out. "He wanted to buy a camper. Pull it behind his truck." He laughed. "Cathy wasn't thrilled. She told him maybe they could rent first, give it a try."

Kim came at the subject of Trip's marriage from a different direction. "The other day your mom mentioned Trip's ex-girlfriend, Hallie. She said she always expected those two would get married."

"Yeah. We all did."

"But then he met Cathy. Had she recently moved here?"

"I don't remember how long she'd been here. But yeah. Trip kind of lost it for Cathy when they met."

Kim's other questions about Cathy Garrett would have to wait. "Jason, I hate to ask this. Do you know if Trip ever took any prescription meds? Antianxiety drugs? Anything to take the edge off something he was worried about?"

"No! He hated pills. His brother got messed up on pain meds for a while. Tommy kicked it pretty fast."

Kim told him about the toxicology report and the presence of lorazepam in Trip's system.

"Well, that's just plain wrong. He wouldn't have taken anything."

Jason finished his beer. By the agitation in his voice, Kim sensed he was getting ready to call an end to the conversation. "Were you with Trip at the bar the afternoon Laurie Beltran came in looking for her wages?"

"Yeah. Let me tell you, that girl was batshit crazy that day. She looked bad, like she was close to the edge or already over it."

"Did she say or do anything that explained her state?"

"She was mad 'cause she hadn't been paid in a long time. She said she hadn't eaten in two days, but that's nuts. Who doesn't eat? And here's the thing. Trip was really upset about it. He gave her all the cash he could spare, thirty bucks or something."

Kim was about to say something, but Jason didn't give her the chance. "After she left, Trip couldn't shake it off. He said Cathy always paid Laurie on Fridays. Now it was two weeks in a row she hadn't. I didn't want to ask if they were short on cash."

"I heard the family went through hard times last fall with their little boy," Kim said. "With his illness they must have racked up a lot of expenses."

"Trip never missed getting his paycheck. I made sure of that." Jason shot the words at her. More subdued, he added, "But yeah, that's when things changed. Because of Cody." He rubbed a hand through his hair, then spent a long moment studying a narrow cut on his index finger. "You wanted to know if Trip changed. Trouble is, it gets to the point where you can't remember how someone was before."

—

Kim drove back to Creede in a somber mood. She replayed every word Jason Zachary had said to her and came up with nothing. Nothing that would get her closer to understanding why Trip Garrett had died.

The sun was still high in the western sky when she parked at the cabin. Without bothering to enter her own home, she trudged the seventy-five yards to Paula's front door.

The white van was gone. For a moment, Kim thought Paula might be as well. Finally Paula answered her knock, looking as annoyed as Kim had expected her to be, with a dash of something else knitting her deeply creased brow. It was distraction bordering on mania. "Did I ever tell you—" Paula said. She didn't finish the question.

Kim walked past her. "No. You didn't."

She braced herself against hearing the announcement that Paula was leaving. Moving. Going somewhere that didn't include her. As she looked around, she noticed no change in the expansive interior that encompassed kitchen, sitting room, and art studio. A bottle of whiskey was on the counter. She walked over and poured herself a shot.

"Help yourself," Paula said after the fact.

"I saw the van earlier," Kim said. A dozen reasonable explanations for the vehicle's presence occurred to her. It could have been a delivery. It could have been at the house to pick up a shipment.

"I have a show opening in Austin," Paula said. "The van was here to pick up canvases. I have to leave in the morning."

She was wired more tightly than Kim had ever seen her. "What's the worst thing about going?" Kim said.

"The people. Everyone cooing, 'Dahling this' and 'Ooh, dahling that.'" Paula poured herself a drink and tossed it back in one swallow. "I'll eat too much, drink too much, and probably sleep with all the wrong people." When she looked up, her eyes cleared momentarily. "Any chance you could drop every-thing and come with me?"

Kim threw her head back and laughed. It was the best feel-ing she'd had in ages.

CHAPTER 23

Willow Creek surged along the canyon wall at the base of the rock outcropping Kim had come to think of as hers. Upstream, around a bend where she hadn't yet ventured, she knew two creeks—East Willow and West Willow—merged to form the raging stream she was presently mesmerized by. Somewhere up there also lay the remains of mining camps and ghost towns with the names of Weaver, Stringtown, and North Creede, which became Creede until Jimtown, the site of present-day Creede, was officially renamed. Bachelor City, farther up the mountain, had been christened "Teller" by the post office due to a conflict with a town of the same name in California. Local residents never did make the switch.

A dirt road called Bachelor Loop ran seventeen miles into the rugged, ore-rich terrain due north. The discovery of silver in 1889 made Creede the last boom town in Colorado and would have kept the ten thousand miners and their entourage of support personnel who flocked to the region, including saloon and gambling hall owners, gainfully employed for decades if not for the 1893 repeal of the Sherman Silver Purchase Act. Silver immediately suffered a cataclysmic devaluation. Though the mines didn't immediately close up shop, the writing was on those mineral-rich subterranean walls.

"Really, Kim, you have to go. You won't believe what's up there," Dee, John Carlos's receptionist, had told her when she had described the sites along Bachelor Loop. Dee made no secret of the fact that her true passion was local history and not fielding phone calls and greeting clients at the accounting services firm.

Dee spoke fondly of the town's founders and legends, even though she admitted "they were a rough bunch." Nicholas Creede made the first silver strike and gave the boom town its name. Soapy Smith, saloon owner and confidence man, set up shop in Creede after being run out of Denver. Bat Masterson found his way to the lawless mining camps, as did the always fashionably dressed Poker Alice and the less elegantly attired Calamity Jane. Robert Ford, who gained infamy as the man who shot Jesse James, was shot dead in his own saloon and buried in Creede Cemetery.

Dee rattled off the names of mines as if they were a private litany: Holy Moses, Commodore, Kentucky Belle, Amethyst, Bulldog, Last Chance. Her voice sometimes grew wistful when she talked about people still living who'd worked in the mines until the last one shut down in the mid-1980s.

Kim yearned to explore the high country around that bend. But Bachelor Loop remained closed for the season. Dee had warned her that she needed better footwear than sneakers if she wanted to set out on foot.

Going anywhere except to the office was not an option today.

She cast a wistful glance upstream and walked on.

As it was Saturday, she had the office to herself. She spent a couple of hours catching up on work, including making notes about calls she needed to make on Monday. Midmorning, she took a break and went to Marla's café.

The café was busy when she arrived. Laurie barely glanced up from the three salads she was constructing to tell Kim to come back at two. Valerie and Joan were coming then. They were going to have a meeting.

Miffed because she hadn't been told about the meeting until now, Kim went back to the office. She worked for a while longer, then spent a fruitless hour trying to think how to rebrand her accounting expertise into marketable skills. May 1 was around the corner. She had told Paula she meant to stay on through the summer. She needed a steady stream of clients in order to cover rent on the cabin.

She returned to the café in time to order a bowl of vegetable soup before the kitchen closed. At five minutes past two, Marla informed a guy with a laptop and a woman reading a book that the shop was closed. The man walked out the door with a look over his shoulder at Kim, who remained seated. Kate Hicks passed him on the way in. "What's the deal, ladies only?" he said.

"Board meeting," Marla said, closing and locking the door behind him.

Valerie and Joan arrived through a rear entrance. Laurie emerged from the kitchen, wiping her hands on a towel. Appearing embarrassed and uncomfortable, she said, "I really can't stay. I have to work on tomorrow's service."

"This is more important," Valerie said.

Marla pushed two tables together. The women sat down. "Have you come up with anything?" Valerie said without preamble to Kim.

Unsure what she had been tasked with, Kim didn't reply. The list of needs was high, beginning with competent counsel to replace Joan, followed closely by exculpatory evidence or an alternate theory of the crime. She didn't have either, but she did have a new piece of information. "I was able to get a copy of Trip Garrett's toxicology report. For some reason, it wasn't included with the autopsy report the prosecutor handed over at arraignment."

"Anything interesting?" Joan said.

"Trip's blood alcohol level was .14. In addition to being legally drunk, he had lorazepam in his system."

"What's that?" Laurie said.

"An antianxiety medication," Kate said.

There followed lengthy speculation on what the combination of the drug and alcohol might have done to Trip. No one present had ever experienced the combo firsthand. Valerie went off on a tangent, describing Trip as an already depressed man who had a bucketload of chemicals in his system, and what were the odds he rolled the dice with gravity while crossing the creek and either lost his balance or ended up exactly where he wanted to be?

Frustrated, Kim said, "I think we can all agree Trip probably wasn't at his best that night. But we need to focus on a defense strategy. As I see it, there are two avenues to pursue. The first is proving there is insufficient evidence to show that Trip was murdered. He could have sustained his head injuries on rocks along the creek bed when he fell in. It's only Gerry Verkamp's word that a woman was out there that night and struck Trip on the head. I've never met Verkamp, but I gather he may not be entirely reliable."

"I wonder what *his* blood alcohol level was," Marla said, eliciting murmurs of agreement.

Kim made a note to take the question to the sheriff. "That leads to the alternate avenue of defense," she said when no one else spoke. "We try to give the jury a different suspect."

"You mean blame it on someone else? Who?" Laurie said.

"Well, hold on. Back up. That's not all the evidence against Laurie," Valerie said. "There are witness statements describing her argument with Trip in the bar. Also, there's the fact, strange as it is, that Trip came to her house that night."

"Do you have another suspect? Who is it?" Laurie said.

Two thoughts ran riot through Kim's mind. One was relief that so far neither Joan nor Valerie had mentioned finding a new lawyer. The other jolted her into a fresh awareness. She saw it now—a day cleverly set up from the beginning: Cathy Garrett sent Laurie to the bar to find Trip. Cathy Garrett sent her husband to Laurie's house late that night, drunk and drugged. "The other suspect is his wife," she said softly.

"You're wrong! Cathy loved Trip. She would never hurt him!" Laurie shouted.

Several people began talking at once.

"What was her motive?" Marla said.

"Spouses always get the finger pointed at them. That's just so typical," Valerie said.

Kim filed away mental notes, including new questions for Laurie. Right now she needed someone else in this room to lead the discussion. She locked eyes with Joan, who alone remained quiet. "Can you think of anything else we can do?" she asked her.

Joan blinked and looked away. "I know a woman, a friend, really. Tara Dawkins. She's a defense attorney in Pueblo. I was thinking of calling her to consult on the case. I have no idea whether she has the time or interest. At least she has the experience." Joan cleared her throat. "I hate to sound greedy, but is there money—somewhere—for legal fees? I doubt my friend will agree to more than a phone call unless she can be paid. And my hours, well, they're adding up."

Kim slapped her forehead, startling the others. She knew someone who lived in Pueblo too, although at the moment she had no idea where on the planet Andrea Sampson was. But she had her phone number. "You'll be paid," she said to Joan. "And your friend too, though we may have to set a limit on her services." Her mind raced. She needed to talk to Andrea.

Joan nodded. "If we're going to attack the evidence, we'll likely need expert witnesses. I have no idea how to find those people. Maybe Tara will. The problem is we don't have much time."

"I agree with everything Kim has said," Kate said. "We need to approach this as a two-pronged endeavor. The evidence is shoddy; we all agree on that. But to be thorough, we have to identify and either rule in or rule out other potential suspects. Someone is involved. It would be remiss to give Cathy Garrett a pass just because she seems like a nice woman."

Steadied by Kate's rational assessment, Kim said, "There is one other thing I should mention. Trip Garrett did not have a life insurance policy. Collecting a fat insurance payout could not have been Cathy Garrett's motive, if in fact she pushed him into the creek."

In the beat of silence that followed, Kim gleaned several things at once. Kate Hicks gave a tiny nod, approving. Something akin to respect showed in the eyes of Valerie, Joan, and Marla.

Laurie alone was dismayed. "What is wrong with you?" she shouted. "Why do you always assume the worst about people? I didn't think you were like that!"

Stung, Kim forced herself to stay seated when she would rather have bolted from the circle. She drew several long breaths and felt immensely grateful when no one else spoke. In as even a voice as she could muster, she said, "I think the best of *you*, Laurie. And unless you tell me to stop right now, I am going to continue to do everything in my power to prove your innocence."

"But I am innocent!"

"That's hardly ever enough," Kim said quietly.

CHAPTER 24

Some good came out of the meeting.

An hour after walking out of the coffee shop, Kim was on a call with Andrea Sampson. Andrea was back at work as an assistant district attorney in Pueblo a year after taking a sabbatical to work at a national park. She and Kim had shared a house in Montrose, Colorado. They had spoken twice since going their separate ways, ending both calls with a promise to keep in touch, which hadn't happened.

Andrea whistled when Kim finished her recap of the events leading up to Laurie's arrest and the women's efforts to get legal help for Laurie. "Who's the consulting attorney?" she asked.

"Her name is Tara Dawkins."

Andrea whistled again. "She's a tiger. I couldn't recommend anyone better."

Kim suppressed a twinge of disappointment on learning Andrea couldn't spare a day or two to come to Creede to review the case. Andrea did have one urgent piece of advice. She said it was imperative for Laurie's lawyer to get a change of venue for the trial. Creede was too small a community to impanel an impartial jury in a murder trial, especially if the deceased was a local and the accused an outsider. "One last question," Kim said before the call ended. "Who controls an incarcerated person's assets?"

She didn't want to think Laurie was going to prison. Still, better to have the hard questions answered ahead of time. Andrea's advice was to have Laurie sign over a POA—power of attorney—to someone she trusted to transact business on her behalf, if that became necessary.

For almost the first time since taking up residence in the cabin, Kim felt lonely in her humble abode as the afternoon wore on into evening. Paula had left that morning. Last night the artist had predicted she would be home early the following week, then she'd cast doubt on the prediction, adding, "You never know." Pressed to explain, she'd said a sometime-friend wanted her to go to Aruba. She asked Kim to keep an eye on the property while she was away.

A light rain started falling around seven. Anxious to escape her own thoughts, Kim called Fred Barnes on the mobile phone he'd given her. Barnes thanked her for faxing the copy of the case file. He asked if she'd learned anything of interest since the arraignment. Briefly, she summarized her interview with Jason Zachary. She held her breath, hoping Barnes would have something substantial to tell her.

"I really don't, Kim," he said, dashing her hopes. "Robert and Janelle are waiting for Laurie to get in touch with them. As you know, they don't have a way of reaching her. They're tired of using me as an intermediary."

"They realize their granddaughter has been accused of murder, don't they?"

Barnes sighed. "Yes. They assume she's innocent, and that the evidence—rather the lack thereof—will be sufficient to guarantee her freedom."

"I agree it would! But only in the hands of a competent defense attorney. Laurie doesn't have one."

In the quiet on the other end of the line, Kim heard a different voice, a woman's. Barnes apparently had company.

"It's really not up to me, Kim. I'm happy to help you any way I can from here." She thought he was going to beg off and say good night. Obviously he had better things to do than talk to her. "What's your next move?" he said.

She told him she had several interviews planned, including with Trip Garrett's mother and brother. His former girlfriend, Hallie Kerr, was off her list. Hallie had married and moved to Wyoming, according to Jason Zachary.

"What are you looking for?" Barnes said.

"A crack in the armor. A dent in the image of Trip and Cathy Garrett's happy marriage."

"So the wife is your primary suspect now?"

Her anger crystallized into something hard and mean. She wanted to yell at Barnes that she didn't have any suspects. This wasn't her case. She wasn't a private investigator. She didn't know enough to be the one in charge of saving Laurie, and why—with all the financial resources at Laurie's disposal and with God presumably on her side—didn't Laurie have someone more capable stepping in to get her out of this mess?

She mumbled something about seeing where things went. Barnes said to call when she had new information.

CHAPTER 25

Sunday morning, Kim slipped into her chair along the wall in the basement of Creede's town hall, minutes after the service began. She closed her eyes and listened to the invocation and opening prayer.

The service proceeded. Fleetingly, Kim thought of Paula and wondered whether she was in Austin or Aruba. A neglected part of her soul hearkened back to another time in this same space, when Laurie's voice was a palliative to the invisible wounds Kim bore. If she had learned one thing in the weeks since then, it was that other people bore marks, too, some invisible, others concealed beneath layers of clothing.

"You didn't hear a word I said today, did you?" Laurie asked after the service ended. Everyone else was gone. Kim had managed a quick word with Joan before she left. She passed on Andrea's suggestion to request a change of venue for Laurie's trial. Joan said her friend Tara had suggested the same. She intended to draw up the motion requesting the change in the morning.

"I've told you before, I like listening to you," Kim said.

"That doesn't seem like a good enough reason to attend a worship service."

"Maybe not. But it's mine."

Despite Laurie's prickliness, Kim thought she was glad to see her. She suggested they go somewhere for lunch. Laurie declined. She said she still had a refrigerator full of food.

At the house they made sandwiches. Laurie talked about her new job at Marla's, what she enjoyed, what she didn't. They ate quickly. When they finished, they moved from the kitchen to the living room. Kim opened a small notepad and took out a pen. Laurie's eyes flashed with suspicion.

Kim covered the basics first. She suggested that Laurie write a check to Joan large enough to cover the lawyer's hours to date and an initial consulting fee for Tara Dawkins.

"How much?" Laurie said.

Kim took a guess. "Five thousand dollars. The amount you'll need to pay eventually will likely be higher."

Laurie didn't argue. She produced a checkbook and handed it to Kim. "Can you write the check?"

A minute later the check was written and signed. Kim tucked it in her pocket. "Laurie," she said, moving on. "You need to talk to your grandparents. They probably want to help but don't know how."

"I wouldn't know what to say! I wouldn't know where to begin. How did this happen?" Laurie said. Her eyes pled for an explanation.

"I think we need to go back to the beginning. I think we need to go over every single thing that's happened and see if we can make sense of this."

They began by rehashing the key events on the last day of Trip Garrett's life. Laurie said that ordinarily Cathy left an envelope with cash for that week's work on the kitchen counter on Friday mornings. The week before, the envelope was there as usual, but inside was an IOU for her wages. Laurie danced around what Kim already knew, that at the time she didn't have access to the money in her Santa Fe accounts. She was relying exclusively on what she earned from the Garretts to pay her rent and buy food.

"On Monday, Cathy apologized. She said some of Trip's customers were behind on their bills. She said everything would be fine, the money would show up, and she would pay me as soon as she could."

"What happened the next Friday?"

"The envelope was in its usual place on the counter. After Cathy left, I opened it. It was another IOU. I started to panic. I was out of food at home, and well, Cathy doesn't want me eating the food at their house. She said it's fine if I bring my own. But I didn't have any."

"Okay. What happened when Cathy came home from work?"

"I told her I really needed the money. She was surprised. She said, 'Trip didn't give it to you? He was supposed to come straight here after he finished for the day and pay you.' She told me to go to Alvie's bar and ask him for it. I didn't want to. But I was really hungry. All I'd had to eat was the corner of Grace's sandwich at lunch even though I'm not supposed—"

Kim interrupted the digression. "What happened at the bar?"

Laurie lowered her head. "Trip was there with some guys. His buddies. They were laughing and drinking. I just wanted to get it over with. I was angry that he had enough money to be out having a good time with his friends but he didn't have enough to pay me. I don't think I handled it very well."

"What happened?"

"I was nervous. I tried to act confident, but I think I just came off loud. Maybe bitchy. I told him I needed the money he owed me. He didn't understand. He said it was up to Cathy to pay me. I said she hadn't. We went back and forth until he pulled out his wallet and gave me thirty dollars. I could see he didn't have that much more in it. By then I was so embarrassed I couldn't stand it. I left as fast as I could."

Kim had abandoned her plan of taking notes. She thought carefully about what she had heard, scoring it into her memory alongside Jason Zachary's recollection of that scene. When they'd talked, she'd asked Jason whether he thought Laurie was upset enough to want to harm Trip over her unpaid wages. "Hell no," he'd said. "Even if she'd wanted to, she couldn't have. She could barely stand on her own two feet. Unless she went out and ate a sixteen-ounce porterhouse, she wouldn't have had the muscle to push a mouse off that bridge."

"Where did you go when you left the bar?" Kim said.

"To the grocery store! I bought a couple of cans of soup, peanut butter, and the cheapest loaf of bread I could find. Do you know how much bread costs?"

Kim did a quick tally and knew that thirty dollars wouldn't go far toward the purchase of a week's supply of food. "After you got home, did you stay there the rest of the day? And night?"

"Yes."

"What time did Trip come to see you?"

"Late. It was past nine. I had been reading. I got up to get a glass of water. I jumped when he knocked on the door."

"Did you consider not letting him in?"

"No. I hoped he had the rest of my money."

"Did he happen to say why he chose that time of night to stop by?"

"He said Cathy was upset. She was afraid I might quit since I hadn't been paid. She was worried she might have to quit her job if that happened. There wouldn't be anyone to take care of the girls."

"So Cathy sent him?"

"That's what he said." Laurie fell into silence. "He was so different than he'd been in the bar earlier. Quieter. I didn't know Trip very well. I hardly ever saw him. When I did, he always seemed upbeat, happy. But not that night. At times he could hardly get his words out. I thought he was drunk."

Kim recalled the lorazepam and alcohol in Trip's system. By Laurie's account, he'd been significantly affected by the combo.

"I was surprised when he wanted to talk about spiritual things. He asked me how I knew what to believe in. I told him I had almost always been able to trust what I found in my own heart. I said I was fortunate because I believed teachings that had been shared by people for thousands of years. He pointed at the books in my bookcase and wanted to know if I ever found answers there. I told him sometimes." Laurie puzzled over something.

"What?" Kim said.

Laurie remained lost in thought. "He asked if I had a favorite book. I thought he wanted to borrow one. I said the Bible, but there was no way I'd let him borrow it. Then he asked if I had people to talk to if I ever felt uncertain about something. I said depending on the question, other people sometimes could help. Then he got this funny look on his face and said, 'What if there's no one you can ask?'"

"About what? Did he say?"

"No. After that he talked about his girls, about how he needed to protect them. He did say something strange. He said no one ever warns you how much you'll love kids. He said it like it was a bad thing. I'm sure he didn't mean it that way."

Laurie went to her bedroom to get a sweater. While she was out of the room, Kim took out her notebook and jotted down a pair of questions. What did Trip want to ask? Of whom?

She thought about the architect of Trip's last day—his wife, coolly wielding an iron grip over the people around her. Had Cathy anticipated being able to overpower Trip, disable him, and push him over the bridge, unseen? Was she a black belt in karate or a ninja? Had she foreseen all contingencies, laying out a path that led to another woman in the unlikely event of a witness to the crime? What secret was she protecting?

And where inside her house did that secret reside?

Kim did another mental walk-through of the residence, ending, where she had before, in the laundry room. She thought of the three laundry-detergent boxes lined up along the back wall. Several things bothered her about the boxes, beginning with why Cathy would go to the trouble of repackaging powdered detergent and ending with the question of why three boxes? Throughout the house, Cathy kept exactly one bottle or box of any cleaning product.

Kim admitted she was clutching at straws. If Cathy was leading a double life that included secrets worth killing her husband to protect, she was sophisticated enough to find a better hiding place than inside a laundry-detergent box.

Laurie returned. Her face was pale, her expression wan. Kim glanced at her chest and wondered whether they all weren't living double lives.

CHAPTER 26

Over the next few days, Kim used what little free time she had looking for Gerry Verkamp. She had questions for him. She also had a gift for him, a small bottle of whiskey, the kind that would fit in a pocket if it lasted that long. She couldn't find Verkamp in any of his usual haunts. Not that she had a wealth of information to go on. All she had were a few suggestions, courtesy of Dee, and one or two volunteered by Francie, her waitress at Miner's Haven.

Laurie's trial was slated to begin in three weeks. Each time she was reminded, Kim fought a sinking spell. No doubt, details of Laurie's finances as well as the trauma she had suffered as an eighteen-year-old were already known to opposing counsel. How was any of this going to look when it came out? That Laurie would willingly choose to live in penury with the sort of wealth most people can only dream of at the tip of her little finger?

Kim could see it now. The prosecutor was going to paint Laurie as a badly damaged woman. She would be revealed as a woman who had suffered extraordinary psychological harm and was perhaps capable of anything. No one needed to know what had propelled her into an act of violence. Given her past, given her irrational choices, the gun likely had been cocked for a long time. Trip Garrett simply became the object of her wrath.

—

A sharp rap on the cabin door surprised Kim late one night midweek. She opened the door, expecting to see Paula. Kate Hicks stood on the porch. "I know it's late. I wouldn't be here if it wasn't important," Kate said, breezing in.

The fire in the woodstove had burned low. Kim coaxed it back to life with a few sticks of kindling while Kate boiled water for tea. They sat down on either end of the sofa, warmed by the mugs and the fire blazing in the stove.

"I've been working with Jason Zachary the last few days. I've known Jason for ages. Never did any work for him before," Kate said. "He said he got the idea of calling me from you."

Kim barely remembered that part of her conversation with Trip's business partner.

"First day or two he didn't talk much, only about what he wanted me to do. He wasn't in a good space. Gloomy. Pissed off. Yesterday he opened up some. Said his problem, besides Trip being dead, was that he was thinking too much. He said he hates thinking. He blames you for getting him started."

"Did he say what was on his mind?"

"Not at first."

Kate told the story that had emerged in fits and starts and was finally told completely over dinner and more than a few beers earlier that night. Jason said that after Trip died, when Laurie was arrested, he had assumed she'd done it. He figured she wouldn't have been arrested if she hadn't. He said he'd been down too low over losing Trip to do more than get up in the morning and go to work. But after talking to Kim, he started thinking. Not because he wanted to help Laurie. He wanted to do right by Trip.

"What did he say?"

"The story has a lot of pieces. Jason said he didn't know how they fit together, or if they even did. According to him, Trip's trouble started when the little boy got sick. Cody was diagnosed with leukemia a year ago. Early treatments showed promise. Then in the summer his condition worsened. His doctor said he needed a bone marrow transplant. Cathy, his biological mother, wasn't a match. His half sisters were too young to be tested. No match was found in the national bone marrow registry. The family's best hope was to find a match from a blood relative.

"That's when the trouble started. Cathy had told Trip she came from Massachusetts. She said she had family there but wasn't on speaking terms with them. Things had happened. She didn't want anything to do with them."

"What about Cody's father?"

"Cathy said she was a widow. She said Cody's father died in a car crash. Trip told Jason he was sure there had to be relatives on one side of the family or the other who might be a match to Cody, someone who would be willing to help, regardless of whatever had happened in the past. But Cathy refused to reach out to anyone."

Kate paused to let the words settle.

"How urgent was the need for the transplant, do you know?" Kim said.

"Cody's condition was deteriorating. His doctor said it was his best hope for recovery. Cathy insisted on sticking to the chemo protocol. Jason said Trip was a wreck. He couldn't understand why a little boy's life wasn't more important than whatever messed-up past Cathy had with her family. The fact that she wouldn't try contacting anyone nearly sent him over the edge. But then it didn't matter anymore. Cody died."

A moment of silence passed.

"Cody's death wasn't the end of the trouble between Cathy and Trip," Kate said. "Jason said they had a blowout fight over whether Cody would be buried or cremated. Trip wouldn't hear of anything except having the little boy laid to rest in the Garrett family plot, right here in Creede. Cathy said she didn't believe in burials for lots of reasons, including how bad a buried body is for the environment. Trip said bullshit. He dug his heels in. Jason doesn't know what Trip ultimately said to persuade Cathy he was absolutely serious, but he said something. He got his way."

"Huh," Kim said, trying to think what, if anything, it meant.

"Hold on. I haven't gotten to the best part."

Crackling sounded from inside the woodstove. The room was toasty warm. "Do you have anything harder to drink?" Kate asked, setting aside the empty teacup.

Normally Kim didn't keep much alcohol around. Tonight she had the whiskey she'd intended to give Gerry Verkamp. She took it from the cabinet and poured two glasses.

Kate said it had taken until tonight for Jason to let her weave together a semicoherent story out of the bits he'd divulged over the course of the week. He said everyone was such a mess when Cody died. He didn't think anything of the fight between the parents over the burial-versus-cremation question. He figured they were venting their grief the best way they knew how. Besides, they patched things up afterward.

"When did Cody die?"

"Last October. Jason said Trip wasn't himself for the longest time, understandably of course. He said he would get teary while they were working and have to take a break, go for a walk, or bust something up. Since they were working construction, they always had spare pieces of lumber or drywall Trip could take his emotions out on. By the holidays he thought Trip had pulled himself together. Then in January, Trip asked a second favor."

"A second? What was the first?"

Kate grinned. "Yeah. Jason said it took him remembering the second before he remembered the first. He said last September Trip asked if he could use Jason's address to receive a package. He said it was nothing he wanted to talk about. He insisted it was nothing illegal, and he wanted Jason basically to forget about it the instant the package arrived. Of course Jason agreed. About a week later, the package showed up and Jason kept his promise, completely forgetting about it until a few days ago. He only remembered any of this after you started asking questions."

"Okay."

"What Jason remembered was Trip coming to his house to use his computer sometime this winter. Trip said he needed to look up something on the internet."

"When was this?"

"January. That first time Trip only spent a few minutes on Jason's laptop. About a month later, he asked another favor. He needed to use the computer again. So he stopped by one night after work and spent a half hour poking around, reading something. When he finished, he left without saying a word. Jason said that's when Trip changed. For the next four or five days, he was in a bear of a mood. Wouldn't talk. Wouldn't say what was wrong. He started smashing stuff again the way he had after Cody died. And that's the part Jason finally remembered, after you asked him if Trip was acting different before he died. He wasn't. But he did have a bad spell a couple of months earlier."

Kim had questions. Kate wasn't finished. She emptied the rest of the whiskey into her glass and tossed back a slug. "You wouldn't believe how hard it was getting Jason to talk about this. He didn't want to see a connection between any of the 'favors' Trip asked. But once he started backtracking, even he couldn't deny there was a pattern. He said each time Trip asked for a favor, he looked him square in the eye and said, 'Thanks, buddy. I'd appreciate it if you didn't mention this to anyone.' Same words. Nothing Trip had ever said to him before."

"What was Trip up to? Did Jason know?"

"I'm getting there. Back in September, when the package showed up in his mailbox, Jason saw the label. It was a genetic testing kit from one of those companies you see advertised on TV."

It had been a long time since Kim had watched TV, but she remembered the ads. "Who did Trip want genetic testing done on? Himself?" As soon as the words were out, the pieces clicked into place. Of course not. "He wanted the test done on Cody," she said, answering her own question. "He was ready to go behind Cathy's back, looking for a relative who might be a bone marrow match to Cody." She shuddered to imagine Cathy Garrett's rage at discovering her husband's duplicity.

"Jason didn't know who he wanted the test done on. Jason said maybe he'd wanted it done on Cody, in the beginning. But then Cody died."

The new information was a bombshell. Kim still had no idea what it meant. What she knew about commercially available genetic testing would fit in the cap lying next to the empty whiskey bottle on the table. She admitted as much to Kate, who said, "I didn't know anything about it either. I called my sister before I came over. She and her husband had genetic testing done before they had kids. This was a couple of years ago. She said nothing's changed in the way material is collected, but a lot has changed in the reporting, especially in the area of familial links."

"Changed how?"

"The submission process is standard. You request a kit. Once you get it, you register the kit number online, spit in a cup, send in the kit, and a couple of weeks later you get an email telling you your report is available. Then you go online to get it."

Kim started to interrupt. "Hang on," Kate said. "When Trip came to Jason's house to use his computer in January, he said whatever he was doing would only take a minute. Jason went to the kitchen and came back with two beers. Trip was engrossed in typing something, so Jason set the bottles down on a side table. Jason said he didn't mean to look at the screen. He didn't even have a good angle to see it, but he caught a glimpse. It was the website for the DNA testing company. At the time he didn't think anything about it. He figured Trip had his reasons and it didn't concern him. Trip finished whatever he was doing, closed the computer, they drank a couple of beers, and everything was great."

"But things weren't great the next time Trip used the computer," Kim said.

"No. Jason said, looking back, he thinks Trip probably found out something he didn't want to know. Then he got over it, so Jason's conclusion is that whatever he learned, it couldn't have been that bad. Still, it's been bugging him."

"Assuming Trip had genetic testing done on someone, who do you think it was?" Kim said.

Kate shrugged. "If he collected the saliva sample from Cody in the fall, the test could only have been done on the little boy."

Kim agreed. Except the results wouldn't have mattered in January. By then Cody had been dead for three months.

Kate finished her whiskey. "Jason said one other interesting thing. When Trip was in the middle of that terrible funk in February, he confided to Jason that Cody had once told him something weird. He said it happened way back, when they first started palling around together. Trip said Cody told him his real name wasn't Cody. It was Connor."

CHAPTER 27

Kim didn't sleep much that night.

The moment she was alone, she wrote down everything she had learned. Time and again she warned herself to keep an open mind. She remembered Kate's words: *there are too many holes in this story to know what it means.* They planned to meet for dinner the next evening to continue the discussion.

Kim started her research into genetic profiling companies as soon as she reached the office in the morning. She didn't know if there was a way to identify the company Trip had used or get a copy of the report he'd received if she did. One thing she believed: that report held the key to his murder.

She found a copy of Trip and Cathy's marriage application on the Colorado public records database. On it, Cathy gave her last name as Henderson. Not for an instant did Kim believe that was her real name. Nor did she think she would find a Cathy Henderson anywhere in Massachusetts who had relocated to Creede, Colorado, approximately five years ago. Cathy had surfaced in this town like a ghost. With a little boy who once had the name Connor. It wasn't much to go on.

At noon she went to the post office to drop off her weekly letter to Lena. Unsurprisingly, the postmistress reported no letter awaited her. Kim wanted to talk to Lena now more than ever. She settled for a call to Fred Barnes, who gave a long, low whistle when she finished.

Barnes confirmed her suspicion that it would require a subpoena to get a genetics profiling lab to turn over the report requested by Trip Garrett. He asked if she thought she could get her hands on the results another way.

"I doubt Trip printed anything. He probably deleted the report after reading it."

"Maybe. Or renamed it under a different file, something no one would think to look at. If we had the computer, there might still be something in the history log. It may be worth talking to Jason Zachary about this, though it sounds like he's skittish on the subject. Never mind the report, for now. You realize there are a dozen or more scenarios to explain this, right?"

She did. She had generated her own list late last night. She let Fred tick off the first that came to mind. "One possibility is that Cathy, or whatever her real name is, kidnapped the boy to keep him away from her husband. Or ex-husband. Or the boy's father. Or an abusive boyfriend. Hell, I don't have to stop there. For whatever reason, valid or not, she kidnapped the boy and is facing criminal charges, if apprehended."

They both agreed it was a motive for murder.

"I wonder who the genetic test was done on," Kim said. "I assume it was either Cathy or Cody. But Cody was dead in January."

"Wouldn't matter. If Trip collected the genetic material when the boy was alive, he could have submitted it anytime." Barnes said he had worked with clients who had resorted to searching for long-lost relatives through commercial genetic testing labs. "Results depend entirely on who is in the database. Cody would have had to match someone who had been tested by the same company Trip used. A sibling, possibly a half sibling. Maybe a grandparent, aunt, uncle, or even a cousin."

"Or a father," Kim said.

"Thought you said the father was dead."

"That's what Cathy told Trip."

Barnes agreed it would be fascinating to know what Trip had discovered. "Any chance you can get your hands on that laptop?"

Kim said she didn't see how. Last night Kate had said Jason probably wouldn't talk to anyone else about this.

Barnes took a different tack. "Whatever Trip found out couldn't have been that bad. He was upset, but he got over it. Isn't that what Jason said?"

"Yes." Kim had considered this too. "Except I keep coming back to something he said the night he died. He asked Laurie if she had people she could talk to when she had questions. She told him she did. Then he said, 'What if there's no one you can ask?'"

Barnes was quick to dismiss the suggestion. "Even you have to admit there's no way of knowing what the ramblings of a man under the influence of alcohol and an antianxiety drug had to do with anything."

Kim conceded the point. After reiterating the need to stay in touch, she and Barnes ended their call.

Late that afternoon Kate called to cancel dinner plans. It was just as well. A note pinned to the door awaited Kim when she returned to the cabin. Paula was home and wanted to see her.

That night Paula wanted to sketch her but not per her usual custom, with Kim partially nude.

"Put the shirt on and leave it on. Sit the way you normally do. Can you manage that? I need to concentrate," Paula said, as if that explained everything.

The session became a sort of meditation for them both. Paula's early agitation gave way to a steady scrabbling of charcoal against paper. Kim's breathing fell into an easy rhythm. Her mind wandered. It went off the rails, far from every thought that had preoccupied her all day. She felt the sun's rays striking blue water, warming a sandy beach. White-capped waves churned, plowing the shoreline with an incessant tug, pulling away, pushing back. Fishing boats roamed the horizon. "Did you go to Aruba?" she said, forgetting the rule.

"Galveston," Paula said. "Shh."

They were both in a better space when Paula finished. Kim left the oversized oxford dress shirt on. She liked the feel of the stiff cotton against her skin.

The sketchpad was open, propped on a chair. Kim walked over to see a split image. On the lower half of the page, an exquisitely drawn neck disappeared into the triangulated folds of a dress shirt collar, both flesh and cloth appearing lifelike in hues of gray. Above, Kim saw her own face in profile. In the drawing her hair wasn't long and shaggy. Rather, it was sculpted into a neat trim, uncannily resembling the style she had once worn.

"You need a haircut. I've been telling you that for months," Paula said.

With effort, Kim averted her gaze from the disturbingly photograph-like image. She joined Paula in the kitchen area, where the aromas of roasted chicken and vegetables filled the air. Paula poured two glasses of wine. "Tell me a story," she said.

Kim should have expected the request. Somehow it always came as a surprise. As usual, she didn't have any stories to tell and said so. As usual, she started one anyway.

"Once upon a time there was a woman who didn't know what to wish for. It wasn't as though she had everything. There was plenty she didn't have. On a daily basis the portals of emptiness would open and threaten to suck her in whole, obliterating her. Or so she feared. So she flitted past them, and managed."

"Managed what?"

"To live another day."

Paula drank her wine and poured another glass. Kim swirled hers and watched the light sparkle in the pale liquid.

"The woman was wise enough to know there is never just one thing. That's not the way life works. Still, she sometimes thought wouldn't it be nice if the leaf bobbing on the river didn't float by. Or if the sinuous line of paint coming off a brush tip didn't vanish on the canvas. She thought how lovely it would be to have one moment to hold, and to whisper the words: this, and only this. But as soon as you say that, it's gone. And then what do you have?" Kim answered her own question. "You still have the river, of course. And the painting."

"I wondered if you were going to go all Heraclitean on me," Paula said.

Kim glanced overhead at the bank of industrial lights affixed to the ceiling. By their strength the room was lit like a movie set. The wood window frames gleamed. The black marble countertop ran like a dark river from the center of the kitchen to the wall and down the length, past the sink, to the far corner. The massive farm table awaited a crowd that would never arrive to share a meal around it.

Kim had lost the thread of her story. Any second she expected Paula to complain and tell her to get on with it. A different thought sprang to mind. With sudden energy, she said, "Why isn't truth like a bubble, rising to the surface of its own essence? Why is truth negotiated? And how can something so pure become so twisted?"

Paula let the words stand for a long moment. "I wondered when we were going to get around to talking about your friend," she finally said.

Kim smiled into her wineglass, baffled at how Paula knew who and what she was talking about. She had never mentioned Laurie's name in this house, yet Paula had known as if she were a mind reader, as if she kept her finger on the pulse of life, Kim's life anyway, a disturbing thought, no matter how she looked at it.

But they didn't talk about Laurie. The oven buzzer sounded. They ate dinner and talked of other things.

CHAPTER 28

Midmorning the next day, Kim drove out of town. Less than an hour later, she cruised into the tiny hub in the sprawling San Luis Valley and found the Del Norte Medical Center without difficulty.

Because the facility was small, she had little trouble identifying the pediatricians on staff, one of whom likely had been Cody Garrett's doctor. She came up with three names. Thirty minutes later she was standing in the reception area of the third on her list. Dr. Henry Yang's office manager, a middle-aged woman, blanched when Kim mentioned Cody's name. "That poor little boy," she said. "And his poor parents."

The woman was less accommodating when Kim asked if she might beg a few minutes of Dr. Yang's time. "I don't think so. He is always too busy. But I will ask him," the woman said reluctantly.

Ninety minutes later, while the doctor was eating what passed for his lunch—a peanut butter and jelly sandwich and carrot sticks—Kim was allowed into his office.

"My wife," he said, catching her glance at his food. "What she makes for the kids she makes for me. You have questions about Cody Garrett. There's probably not much I'm permitted to discuss with you."

She told him about Trip Garrett's death, which he was unaware of. A shadow fell over his face. "Parents lose kids. Some never get over it," he said.

She didn't correct his assumption that Trip had committed suicide. She couldn't waste precious minutes giving collateral information of no use to him. "I know there was no bone marrow donor match for Cody. I also know that Trip hoped Cathy would reach out to her relatives in search of a match. But she never did."

The doctor shrugged.

"How did they seem to you, as a couple?"

"They were distraught, as any loving parents would be. They were losing their little boy."

"And if a bone marrow match had been found, Cody's chances for recovery were good?"

"Better than good, yes. Children with his type of leukemia who receive transplants generally make a full recovery."

"Did it seem odd to you that no other relatives were tested for a possible match?"

The doctor gave a yes-and-no shake of the head. "If Cody's half sisters had been older, they could have been tested." He paused. "Usually there is at least one person in an extended family worth testing, even if it's a grandparent. I don't want to suggest Cody's situation wasn't urgent. But I remained hopeful. I thought there would be time to find a match."

"Did you ever meet with Trip Garrett privately?" Before the doctor could reply, Kim said, "I'm curious to know whether he ever raised the subject of doing genetic testing on Cody in hopes of finding a close familial match."

Dr. Yang's expression knitted into a frown. "No, I never met with him privately. The subject of genetic testing was never discussed in my presence."

Kim wasn't surprised. Trip had gone to great lengths to conceal his activities around the DNA testing kit. She moved on to her next question. "Was there anything unusual about Cody's death?"

For the second time the doctor gave a mixed answer, shrugging no and nodding yes. "Children diagnosed with cancers tend to be ferocious fighters. Cody was a fighter." The doctor released a heavy sigh. "I wouldn't have said Cody was that close to death when he died. Obviously I was wrong."

"Was there an autopsy?"

"No. The parents refused the hospital's request to do one."

CHAPTER 29

It had not been a good few weeks.

Father Brian could count the number of ways fate had prevailed against him, but he preferred not to. He thought of this period much as he thought of the entirety of his life: as a test.

The couple posing as "the Channings" had failed. Fortunately, they were gone, and that debacle was a fading bad memory. Neither had his lieutenant discovered the stock certificates in his search of Laurie Beltran's home. Topping off his conundrum, Laurie had been arrested. The murder charge was ludicrous. Laurie Beltran didn't have it in her to hurt anyone.

Father Brian admitted his options were narrowing. Much as he had hoped to draw Laurie back to Santa Fe for a face-to-face meeting, the possibility existed that he would have to go to Creede for that to happen. One thing he didn't doubt. The moment he and Laurie bowed their heads together in prayer, she would yield her trust to him. She would defer to his wisdom. She would embrace his vision of a life lived in the bounty of God's blessings.

But perhaps it wouldn't come to that. Sufficient time remained. Another way possibly existed. If it did, Father Brian trusted God to reveal the path leading to it.

CHAPTER 30

For three consecutive nights, Kim searched for Gerry Verkamp. She walked through neighborhoods and the commercial district, peering down alleyways and checking rear doors of restaurants. After dark, she drew the line at entering any of the seedier bars in town. She didn't ask around for Verkamp. She didn't want him aware anyone was looking for him. But the man she had seen on the street more times than she could count was suddenly nowhere to be found.

On Saturday morning, she knocked at the door of a house with a pale-green US Forest Service vehicle parked outside. She hoped the vehicle's presence meant Tom Garrett was home. She had heard the younger Garrett brother worked an irregular schedule in the national forest north of town.

"Not sure what you want to talk to Tom about. One thing to know about him is he likes bears better than he likes people," Francie, Kim's waitress at Miner's Haven, had advised her.

A lean man in his early thirties answered her knock. Tom Garrett had the athletic build of an outdoorsman. He had short, fair hair and blue eyes that Kim suspected took in more than they ever let out. Everything in his demeanor suggested he had no intention of giving her the time of day.

"Trip and I were close as kids. Not as grown-ups. I maybe saw him once a month at our mom's," Tom said.

His answer was a flat no to each question she proceeded to ask. Had Trip seemed upset or worried about something back in February? Did Trip ever stop by to use his computer? Could he think of anyone Trip might have talked to besides his business partner, Jason Zachary?

He cut her off before she could alter her line of questioning in hopes of getting him to reply with something other than a monosyllable. "I'm done talking. I have to get to work." He stepped inside and closed the door before she could point out he hadn't actually done any talking.

Kim hadn't planned to go directly to Esther Garrett's house after her meeting with Tom. She didn't know if Tom Garrett was the sort of son to warn his mother off a stranger snooping around. With "the sooner the better" shaping up as her best strategy, she retraced her steps through town to the house with a tall maple looming over the yard. She went to the door and pressed the buzzer. A moment later the door swung open. "Mrs. Garrett?" Kim said.

"Yes?"

Esther Garrett had short, nicely styled hair on its way from brunette to gray. Behind her glasses her eyes bore a cautious look underscored by sadness, a clear reminder she'd recently buried a son.

"My name is Kim Jackson. I'd like to ask you a few questions. I promise not to take up much of your time."

"You're the new tax accountant in town, aren't you? I believe you did my neighbor's taxes, Ruth Quentin."

"Yes, I did," Kim said, remembering the name.

"Well, come on in then. Get out of the cold. That hard rain in the middle of the night left a chill."

Esther Garrett's demeanor changed perceptibly when Kim told her she was there on behalf of Laurie Beltran.

"I liked Laurie, I really did," Esther said. "Several times I stopped over at the house while Cathy and Trip"—she faltered on her son's name—"were working. We had a chance to talk while the girls napped. She seemed to be so kind, so caring. I really can't believe what she did."

"You're convinced she had something to do with your son's death?"

"Well, yes. She's been arrested and is going to stand trial. To be frank, I'm not sure I should be talking to you."

"Mrs. Garrett, Laurie doesn't have a very good lawyer. I'm trying to get answers to a few questions about some of the evidence against her. I promise this won't take long."

It wasn't at all what Kim had intended to say. When Esther raised no objection, she took that as assent. "Did you notice any changes in Trip's mood last winter? Did he ever seem unusually angry or depressed? I'm only asking because, well, sometimes mothers notice things about their kids that other people don't."

Whatever Esther started to say, she changed her mind. Her lips tightened. She exhaled audibly before saying, "Sometimes, not often, Trip stopped in without the girls and Cathy. Sometimes he'd stretch out on that sofa where you're sitting and he'd be like the boy he was growing up. Trip didn't put on airs. You have to understand, he'd been through so much."

Esther seemed to almost squirm while she debated something. "There was that one time when he looked like he had a storm brewing inside him. I tried to get him to lighten up. I said, 'Goodness, you look like you have the weight of the world on your shoulders!' Ordinarily Trip would have laughed. That day he mumbled something about trouble at work. Something wasn't sitting right with him, that's all I know."

"You didn't believe him?"

"The next time I saw him he was fine."

Esther said she didn't remember when that was.

Kim sensed the bereaved mother's patience growing thin. "Did Trip ever keep any papers here? In his old bedroom maybe?"

"Not that I know of."

"Did he ever use your computer?"

"He used my iPad, yes. Everyone does."

By then Kim had spotted the lineup of framed photographs on the mantel. Seizing what little time she had left in the house, she stood and pointed. "May I look at these before I go?"

Esther nodded.

Kim walked over for a closer look. The first photograph showed Trip, Cathy, and the two girls on a Christmas card. *Their most recent*, Kim thought. A photo of their first Christmas without Cody. The smiles on the adults looked forced. The little girls were glowing. Still, there was no arguing they were a beautiful family.

The next photo was the previous year's card. It showed only the kids, the younger girl just a baby, the other a toddler. Cody was a mop-haired little boy, a beautiful little boy. For a long moment Kim couldn't take her eyes off him.

She moved on to a picture of a family of five. Trip was a drop-dead handsome guy, well built with a lean, chiseled face, smiling as if he didn't have a care in the world. Cathy was lithe and gorgeous, though to Kim's eye she had a slithery look that lessened her appeal. She was about to say something about Cathy in hope of eliciting a reaction from Esther when her eyes lighted on the next photo. "Oh," she said softly, stunned to silence. Esther came up behind her. "Oh how beautiful," Kim managed.

The photo was of Trip and Cody. They looked like father and son, both blond with shaggy mops of hair. It was the look of absolute adoration in Trip's eyes that stilled Kim's every thought.

Esther pressed a hankie to her eyes. "Happens every time," she said, frowning at the wadded cloth in her hand as if it were the fabric's fault that she had teared up.

"Cathy doesn't have any pictures in her house," Kim said. Quickly she added, "I was there once."

"No. Cathy says it's too hard. Some days I can see her point. But I wouldn't part with these for any—"

There was a sudden sound from the hallway. A moment later the front door opened. Voices signaled several people entering the house.

"Oh, that will be Cathy now," Esther said, giving Kim a moment's warning.

Having the advantage, Kim was waiting when Cathy followed her elder daughter, who charged into the room exclaiming, "Grandma!" Cathy held her younger daughter at her hip. Initially her expression was fixed and inscrutable. Then she saw Kim. Anything remotely affable shrank behind Cathy's guard rising, and with it the wariness of a woman rapidly reassessing the playing field, seeing more than Kim wanted her to see.

"Esther, I'm sorry. I didn't realize you had company. Grace, come on. Grandma's busy this morning. Let's go home. Hello again," Cathy added coolly to Kim.

"Oh no, no," Esther said, flustered.

Kim felt the force of her mistake in being caught by Cathy a second time without knowing what it meant. "No, no, I'm the one who needs to be going. It's been lovely talking to you, Esther," she said, slipping past the older woman. "It's nice to see you again, Cathy," she said before she reached the door, pretending for Esther's sake that she and Cathy were on cordial terms.

CHAPTER 31

Kim walked without knowing where she was going. Thoughts swirled in her mind. None succeeded in erasing the terrible feeling she'd had since the moment Cathy's eyes met hers. Kim didn't feel guilty for being at the house, except on Esther's behalf. She didn't know how Cathy might punish her mother-in-law for allowing Kim to cross her threshold.

That wasn't what worried her. More troubling was predicting what conclusions Cathy might draw from Kim's visit, as revealed by Esther. The last thing they had talked about was the photographs. Possibly that was all Esther would mention. Kim's other questions—had Trip seemed upset or angry any-time this winter, had he kept papers at the house, had he ever used his mother's electronic devices—if Esther repeated those questions, Cathy would know Kim had been on a fishing expedition. Kim tried to reassure herself that Cathy couldn't possibly know what she had been fishing for.

Unable to shake her anxiety, she went to Marla's café. Marla and Laurie were busy, which was just as well. Kim wasn't in the mood to talk. Fear nagged at her while she sipped a cup of coffee. It was nearly impossible for her to reconcile the image of Cathy Garrett as a devoted mother and classroom assistant with that of a cold-blooded killer. Which she was if she had killed her husband.

"Hey," Marla said sometime later, sliding onto the chair opposite Kim. "Did you see the flyer on the way in?"

Kim hadn't.

"We're staying open for dinner four nights a week now. Tonight's opening night. I'm turning the kitchen over to a professionally trained chef who's scrambling for work while he builds his reputation. There's also going to be music. A local guitarist, a woman."

"That sounds great."

"Anything new going on?" Marla said.

"No." Kim wasn't ready to reveal anything about her interviews with Trip Garrett's brother and mother. "I still haven't talked to Gerry Verkamp. All I ever hear is how that guy is constantly wandering the streets, but I haven't been able to find him. How are things here?" she asked, nodding toward the back, indicating Laurie.

"Fine. The best I can say is this job keeps Laurie busy. I don't think she enjoys it. Go on back if you want to."

Kim did, earning a quick smile as Laurie looked up from the salad she was making. "I saw you here," she said. "I really don't have time to talk."

"Are you coming here for dinner tonight?" Kim asked.

Laurie made a face. "This is the last place I want to be when I finish work. Are you coming?"

"I don't know."

New food orders piled up while they talked. Kim said goodbye and despite it being Saturday went to the office and her neglected work.

The need to make a concentrated effort to find Gerry Verkamp drove her back into town that evening. Wanting to support Marla's new venture, she arrived at the café fashionably late, happy to see a nice crowd filling the place. Marla beamed as she led Kim to a vacant table for two in a corner. "I didn't know what to expect. The turnout has been fabulous. And the food is off the charts. Try the roasted cauliflower soup and bruschetta. Or anything, really. I thought Kate was going to come in, but she hasn't, at least not yet. Is it okay if I seat her with you if she does?"

Kim said that it was. With one table of guests leaving and new arrivals waiting to be seated, Marla rushed off. Kim took her advice and ordered the soup, bruschetta, and a spring veg-etable salad. She spent the next hour swooning over the flavors and tapping her foot to the beat of the music, a soulful blend of jazz and blues. Kate never did show up. By nine thirty it was as if a curtain had fallen on the festivities. The tables emptied. The once lively room took on a hollow feel. Remembering she still had a job to do, Kim settled her bill and reluctantly traded the warm space for a typically cool spring night.

She walked past Laurie's house, where a light shone dimly through a window. She walked on, past the houses she knew belonged to Gerry Verkamp's brothers. Because she didn't have a good idea where to find him, she walked past Esther Garrett's house and then Cathy's. Lights were on in both homes. Other than teenagers hanging out on porches and in cars, she didn't see anyone out and about. Creede didn't boast much of a night-life, a fact that was brought home when she returned to Main Street. The stores were closed. Overhead lights lit the street in a hazy glow. She passed the post office and the hotel, quiet as usual. She could have done cartwheels down the center stripe for lack of traffic on the town's main thoroughfare.

She nixed the temptation to skip the alley behind Willows Bar and Grill and ducked in and out quickly, seeing no sign of Verkamp holing up near the rear entrance. When she returned to the street, there were red lights flashing ahead. Drawing closer, she saw a police car parked nose in to the sidewalk. She detoured across the street to avoid the situation. From there she spotted a deputy standing at the opening of a narrow passageway separating two buildings. He was on the phone. She stopped when she heard him say, "It's Gerry Verkamp. Yeah, I've already called the EMTs."

Her eyes were drawn to the corner of the building. Shrouded in darkness lay an oddly shaped lump. She might have thought it a bundle of old rags if not for the emergence of a man's head, tilted to rest on his shoulder.

She knew the deputy's name from past visits to the police station. When he ended his call, she walked over. "Officer Rowan, hello. It's Kim Jackson. Is Gerry okay?"

"Not one of his better nights," the deputy said in a grim voice. "I'll let the EMTs decide."

A siren was audible. Less than thirty seconds later, the box ambulance rumbled to a stop next to the patrol car. A man and woman got out and ambled over. "Evening, Carl," the male EMT said. "What's up?"

"Looks like Gerry's had a bit too much to drink. I had trouble finding a pulse."

Kim moved away. She slunk against the brick building and watched as the EMTs worked with increasing urgency on the man. She was still there when a large, dark SUV raced to the scene. Sheriff Andy Preston got out of the vehicle. He noted her presence as he strode forward to talk to his deputy.

Time took on a surreal quality of seeming to stretch forever, only to seize in an instant of dread. Kim felt impatient, wishing for the medics to get on with it, to strap Gerry Verkamp onto a stretcher and get him to the ER and the help he obviously needed. She heard low voices. Then she didn't hear anything until the female EMT declared Gerry Verkamp dead.

"Oh jeez, the poor old guy," the woman said. "I can't say I'm surprised. Only surprise is it didn't happen sooner."

Kim leaned harder against the brick. She needed to feel the force of the wall behind her against the sudden upheaval in the pit of her stomach. Incomprehensibly, the other four stood in the darkness, trading stories about Gerry Verkamp and the dire situations they'd found him in in the past.

"He have anything with him?" the sheriff asked.

"There's a bottle next to him," the male EMT said.

"Anyone touch it?" Preston said.

"No," the others murmured.

"You touch anything here?" Preston said, stepping aside and addressing Kim.

She shook her head. "No, I didn't—"

He cut her off. "Bag it," he said to his deputy. "And take some damn pictures."

The deputy did as he was told. The sheriff spent the next few minutes chitchatting with the EMTs. When he was satisfied with the deputy's work, he told the EMTs they could remove the body. Kim watched as Gerry Verkamp was loaded onto a stretcher with a sheet pulled over his head. It wasn't anything she wanted to see. She understood she didn't have a choice.

"Ms. Jackson," the sheriff said when the ambulance drove off. "A bit of a coincidence, you being here. Any particular reason you happened by?"

"I was walking home after having dinner out."

"Kind of late to be eating dinner, isn't it? Where did you go?"

She gave him the name of Marla's café.

"And you just happened by a dead man?"

"Officer Rowan was already here. I didn't know what—" She broke off, unsure what the sheriff was asking or what she wanted to say.

"Stay there," the sheriff said. He stepped away to confer with his deputy. Apparently Rowan confirmed her account.

When the sheriff turned back, he said, "You're not planning on leaving town anytime soon, are you? In case you were thinking about it, don't. I expect I'm going to have more questions for you."

Kim swallowed hard. She disputed the sheriff's authority to issue the order but kept the thought to herself. "This is my home. I'm not going anywhere."

CHAPTER 32

News of Gerry Verkamp's death spread swiftly. It was the main topic of conversation at Miner's Haven the next morning. Nodding while listening to her waitress, Kim said, "I know. I was there last night."

"I heard that too. Let me get your food. Maybe you can tell me anything worth telling when this crowd thins out," Francie said.

Kim took her time working her way through a plate of pancakes and eggs. She drank more coffee than usual. She hadn't slept well. Much as she had looked forward to morning, the gray light, when it came, did little to lift her spirits. She feared worse things were going to happen. She feared this time they would happen to her.

"Okay," Francie said, pausing at the booth with a coffee pot in hand. "I've heard everything from Gerry was hit by a car and dragged into that breezeway to cover up the accident to someone hit him over the head and left him for dead. Now I want to hear it from you."

"He was just there," Kim said weakly, remembering what she would rather not: the sight of a man's body crumpled in a heap. "I was walking home when I saw flashing red lights. Deputy Rowan was talking on the phone. I heard him say Gerry's name. Next thing, I saw Gerry on the ground. It looked like he'd fallen asleep and forgot to wake up."

"Crazy old coot." Francie wiped her eyes. "Gerry took to drink early. Never could kick it. Let me tell you something about Mr. Gerry Verkamp. He could play the saxophone like nobody's business. He went to school with my brother Jed. Growing up, Gerry was just one of the guys. Normal, you know? Jed thought he should have moved to Denver and joined a band. Now look where he ended up." Francie took a hankie from a pocket and wiped her eyes again. "Well, listen to me, going all maudlin. Thanks, Kim. I suppose we were bound to lose Gerry to his demons one day."

Kim drank the last of her coffee and paid her bill. She left an extra-large tip on the table.

Though it was Sunday, she had no intention of attending morning service. She walked past the steps leading to Creede's town hall basement and went on to work. Unsurprisingly, she had the office to herself. The moment she settled in her chair, she reached for the phone. A laugh of disbelief echoed from the other end of the line when Fred Barnes heard the news. "Now there's a game changer. Verkamp was the state's only witness against Laurie, wasn't he?"

Kim affirmed that Verkamp was the primary witness.

"They'll probably have to drop the charges," the private detective speculated. "It was a damn flimsy case to begin with. Without eyewitness testimony, the state doesn't have much left."

Kim thought the same thing.

"Kim? Are you there?"

"I'm here." Her stomach was tied in knots. She regretted having eaten a big breakfast.

"This is good news," Barnes said.

"Maybe."

"I suppose there'll be an autopsy," Barnes said.

Kim had assumed the same. She said she would ask Sheriff Preston about this. The call ended with her promise to let Barnes know of any new developments.

She pushed papers around for an hour before she left the office. Rather than go home, she went to the park bench opposite the post office and sat down. She was still there when a familiar truck pulled to the curb. Kate Hicks got out.

"Saw you sitting here. Waiting for someone?" Kate said.

Kim glanced at the post office façade and imagined a letter that would never arrive. "No."

Neither said anything for a long moment. Kim watched a crow sweep down from a building. The bird took a direct path for a paper bag fluttering in the gutter. It pecked at the bag until a few french fries fell out.

"We all heard what happened last night. About Gerry Verkamp being found dead. And you being there. I assume that's why you weren't at church this morning. Must have been hard," Kate said.

Kim didn't make any effort to compose a response.

"Laurie didn't find out until after the service. Good thing, I think. She was kind of a wreck. But that may have been because you weren't at the service."

Kim didn't know what to make of the statement.

"I wonder if Gerry died of alcohol poisoning," Kate said.

After a lengthy pause, Kim said, "I hope they'll do an autopsy so we'll know what killed him."

They talked about a murder trial that might never happen now, though Trip's murder still hadn't been solved. "Have you found out anything new about why Trip might have been using Jason's computer?" Kate said.

"No. All I can think is that it's possible Trip found out his wife and adopted son weren't who Cathy said they were."

"That's what I've been thinking too."

"I've talked to Trip's mother and brother. His brother wouldn't tell me anything. His mother at least let me in her home." A wave of something she wasn't sure she wanted to know crested and came crashing down on Kim. "Cathy walked in with the girls while I was there. She wasn't happy to see me." Briefly, she described the first time she had met Cathy, in a laundry room where she shouldn't have been.

"You really do want to be an investigator, don't you?" Kate said, laughing.

Kim didn't laugh.

"Hang on. You don't think Cathy had anything to do with Gerry Verkamp's death, do you?" Kate said.

The thought had lurked deep in the recesses of Kim's mind. Now it was out in the open. Before she could say anything, Kate blurted, "Wait. Do you honestly believe Cathy Garrett killed her own husband?"

Kim nodded slowly. It had been an idea before. A theory to debate in the effort to configure a defense strategy for Laurie. Now there was a second dead man.

"This is getting creepy. I thought I wanted to know what was going on. Now I'm not sure I do," Kate said. After a minute, she spoke more assertively. "Let's not get ahead of ourselves. Think about it. It doesn't make any sense. Whatever Cathy had to do with Trip's death—if anything—she had no reason to kill Gerry Verkamp."

Kim agreed. She echoed the reminder that there was possibly nothing suspicious in Verkamp's death at all.

"What are you going to do?" Kate asked.

Kim answered honestly, "I have no idea."

CHAPTER 33

The shocking news of Gerry Verkamp's death continued to ripple through the town. On Monday, Dee was in and out of Kim's office all morning, wanting to say one thing or another about Gerry. John Carlos joined them. John, whom Kim had spent perhaps two full hours with since acquiring the spare office in his suite, couldn't stay away. He and Dee exchanged stories about Gerry, laughing, occasionally wiping away tears. At times they seemed to forget Kim was there. Much as she felt hostage to their reminiscences, her attention rarely wavered. She soaked in the lore of a man who had meant more to the people of his hometown than he could possibly have known.

The sheriff had ordered an autopsy of Gerry Verkamp. Kim heard the news when she went to Marla's café to pick up a sandwich for lunch. Marla had heard it from Joan, who also reported that the request for a change in venue for Laurie's trial had been denied. The request was summarily dismissed due to an error in the application. Kim did a poor job hiding her disappointment. Marla shrugged. "Maybe it won't matter. Maybe there won't be a trial now that the state's star witness is dead."

"Is Laurie working today?" Kim asked.

"She was here. I told her to take the day off when it was clear she was too upset to focus."

"She was upset about Gerry Verkamp?"

"I think so. I couldn't get a read on her mood."

"It's a beautiful day. I hope she's out enjoying it."

Kim went directly to Laurie's house. Not finding her home, she passed the time walking on nearby streets, keeping an eye out for a lone woman running. Fifteen minutes later, her vigil was rewarded. Laurie finished her run in an all-out sprint. She stopped outside the gate, face red and breathing hard. "You didn't come to church yesterday," she said after she'd caught her breath.

"No. I was upset. I spent the morning walking."

"Church might have been the best place to be if you were upset."

"I needed to walk."

They went inside. Laurie drew a glass of water from the tap and drank it. When she turned to get a refill, Kim couldn't help noticing how young she looked. Laurie's face was soft and unlined. Her hair was tied back in a band. She was only twenty-five. Sometimes, especially when she was standing in front of a congregation, she looked older.

"You were upset about that man—Gerry?" Laurie said.

"Yes."

"I am too, and I didn't even know him. Sometimes he came to church in winter. I think he was only looking for a warm place to be inside."

Laurie took her water glass into the living room and sat down. "I think someone was in my house when the Channings took . . . when we were . . . gone," she said, stumbling over the words. "I kept forgetting to tell you. With everything else going on, it didn't seem . . ." Her voice trailed off.

"Was anything taken?"

"No. Things were moved. Books. My Bible."

Kim thought of the stock certificates. Good thing they hadn't been here. At some point, she and Laurie needed to discuss them, but not today. "You have a good lock on your door now. Are you worried about someone coming back?"

"No." A minute passed in silence. Laurie gazed over the top of her water glass at some indistinguishable spot on the floor. Abruptly, she said, "Why do you live in Creede? You could live anywhere. Why are you here?"

Startled and without any idea where this was coming from, Kim thought carefully. "I'm at an in-between place in my life right now, Laurie. I think Creede is beautiful. I like the people I've met here."

"You could go anywhere or do anything! I'm not saying I'm sorry you're here. I just don't understand why you chose to live in this place."

Kim didn't try to answer. She sensed Laurie hadn't finished. She was right.

"Valerie says there's a good chance I won't have to stand trial now because that man who died can't testify. Joan says it's okay to hope, but we have to wait and see what the prosecutor decides. It's strange. I didn't feel afraid before. None of this seemed real. But another man is dead. How much more real can it get?"

"Do you feel afraid now?"

"I don't know what I feel! That's the problem. I feel too many things, really. Mostly I feel like the walls are closing in. The only time it's okay is when I'm out running. Then as soon as I stop, it starts all over again."

The claustrophobia began to feel contagious. Kim felt the breathable air in the room shrinking. There seemed something pent up in Laurie, something that wanted to burst out and flood the atmosphere.

And then it came.

"I don't know if I want to spend my life in a convent. I don't know any longer whether I want to be a nun."

She wasn't finished.

"I want to keep my money," Laurie said in a voice so soft Kim wasn't initially sure she'd heard.

CHAPTER 34

Kim walked home, sorely troubled by everything she'd heard during the past hour.

After Laurie's "confession" that she wanted to keep her money—a perfectly reasonable desire, Kim thought—other, more vitriolic outbursts, had followed.

"I don't mean that! I don't even know why I talk to you! I've never talked to anyone about this!" Laurie had shouted more than once.

"I want to keep my money."

The words were no sooner out than Laurie had insisted it wasn't true. She hated money. Money had destroyed her family. She knew better than to covet money. Its only useful function was to be put in the hands of God's servants.

Kim had a pretty good idea which servant Laurie had in mind. She thought his name was Father Brian.

Laurie had ranted until her emotion was spent. By then Kim had promised to forget what she'd heard, though of course she wouldn't. Because she knew the Beltran family history, Kim thought she could trace the path that had led Laurie to this pivotal moment. Her sister's attack had all but destroyed her. In her own mind, Laurie credited one man with saving her. Deeply grateful, she had made a promise to him, to God, and to herself that she would devote her life to serving Christ as a member of a cloistered religious community. That couldn't happen immediately upon making the promise. There were steps to be taken. Laurie had dutifully marched through the steps, earning her college degree and receiving the second installment of her trust fund. Laurie became a novitiate and was on her way to taking permanent vows when something in her rebelled. She ran away. But a promise was a promise, and the one she had made haunted her. She could neither escape it nor fulfill it. She was stuck in a purgatory of her own making.

"In a way this would be easier if I did go to jail," she had said despondently less than an hour ago.

"You don't mean that!" Kim had exclaimed.

"No. I don't know what I mean."

That, Kim could believe.

Embroiled in her thoughts, Kim jumped at the sound of sharp knocking. She opened the cabin door, expecting to see Laurie. Sheriff Andy Preston and a deputy stood there.

"Ms. Jackson," the sheriff said, pushing past her without waiting for an invitation, "we have a warrant to search the premises. Would you mind waiting outside."

It wasn't a question.

Since the night the sheriff had found her within spitting distance of the deceased Gerry Verkamp, Kim had anticipated this visit. Now that he was here, she fought her escalating panic. She sat outside. She studied the rock wall rising on the other side of the dirt road leading into the canyon. She wondered if Paula saw the pair of law enforcement vehicles parked at the cabin and if so, what she was thinking.

Sooner than she expected, the deputy emerged from inside. He held the key to the Cadillac. "Warrant gives us the right to search your car." He dangled the key.

The deputy returned empty-handed from the car. Not so the sheriff. He joined Kim on the porch, holding an envelope bearing the imprint of the Durango police department. Inside was a letter Sheila Moss had written to her some time ago. Her heart lurched when he removed the contents and photographed both sides of the single page using his phone camera. "Maybe someone I need to talk to," he said, reinserting the letter and handing her the envelope.

The men found nothing and took nothing when they left, other than the digital image of Kim's private correspondence.

She knew she should feel relieved. She didn't.

At work the next morning, she was at her desk when there was a light tap at the door. Dee opened it and looked in. "You have a visitor."

Preston walked in. Dee closed the door behind him. Eschewing pleasantries, he said, "Results from Gerry Verkamp's autopsy are in. Cause of death was alcohol poisoning. Gerry got hold of grain alcohol somewhere. The doc identified a commercial brand. None of the bars in town sell it. It's not illegal, except if you give it to a man who won't know any better and drinks too much. Even then a prosecutor would have a hell of a time proving intent."

Kim kept her breathing slow and even. If Preston was here to arrest her, he was taking his sweet time about it.

"You don't have any credit card purchases or receipts for grain alcohol. Hell, you don't have any credit cards. All you did was wander past a dead man several people, among them your closest friends, say you were looking for. Ordinarily I'd find that plenty suspicious."

Preston spent a moment fiddling with a fingernail. "This morning I had a long talk with a buddy of mine over in Durango, guy by the name of Mark Stankowicz. He works with your girlfriend Sheila Moss. But I guess you know that."

Kim's eyes twitched. There were a dozen ways this could go, and she didn't like any of them.

"Stanky said you're a good investigator. Untrained, but good. He said it wouldn't be the worst mistake I could make to ask what you think is going on in this town." He gave his fingernail another long, considered look. "So I'm asking."

Stung by Mark Stankowicz's words, Kim tried to think fast. If this was a trap, she thought it awfully clever. "I don't know what's going on."

"If you think of anything, I hope you'll tell me." He was halfway to the door when he stopped. "Oh, thought you might want to see this. Save you the trouble of coming to the station." He handed her a collection of pages, stapled and folded. "Toxicology report is only preliminary. Final isn't available yet."

It was a copy of Gerry Verkamp's autopsy results. Kim skimmed the dense narrative on the first page, moving quickly until she found the tox report. The blood alcohol level leapt out at her. "BAC of .32?" she said incredulously.

"That's what grain alcohol can do to you. Damn fast too."

Still skimming, she latched onto another result and another question. "He had fentanyl in him?"

"Trace amounts, as I'm sure you can see. The coroner didn't know what to make of that. Thought it might have been transfer from the bottle. Forensic unit's running more tests."

"But the fentanyl didn't kill him?"

Preston shifted uncomfortably. "It couldn't have helped."

"Do you know where Gerry got whatever he was drinking that night?"

"No, but I sure as hell want to. Neither of his brothers knows either." Preston continued toward the door.

"Were there fingerprints on the bottle?" she asked, stopping him.

Preston grinned. "Wondered if you'd ask. Only Gerry's. Not even a smudge belonging to someone else. In case you haven't figured it out by now, you're not a suspect. Coroner ruled Gerry's death accidental. That's what I'm sticking with until I find out otherwise. If you learn something you consider interesting, let me know. That isn't a polite request." He said good day and left.

A single word stuck with Kim long after Andy Preston walked out the door. *Untrained.* It took no effort to picture the man from Durango, her friend Mark Stankowicz, with his probing brown eyes that didn't miss much. *Untrained.* His word. Now hers. It felt like a professor she admired giving her a D grade in a class. Barely passing. The burn on her face wasn't anger. It was humiliation. Mark was right.

It was over. She was finished. The case against Laurie would be dropped, in all likelihood, and if it wasn't, Kim intended to call Fred Barnes and tell him what she knew. She wouldn't walk out on Laurie, but she sure as hell could demand some help from someone with more investigative experience.

Ignoring the work on her desk, she tapped at her computer until she opened the home page for Western Colorado University in Gunnison. The school had a criminology department chaired by Professor Abraham B. Craft. She had heard the man speak at a community center a year ago. Since then, she had read his books.

She wanted to become his student.

CHAPTER 35

Late that week the second-degree murder charge against Laurie Beltran was dropped. Joan called Kim at her office with the news. She said she and Valerie were hosting a small party that night to celebrate. She hoped Kim would come.

Kim didn't attend. She walked past the couple's home in the twilight and glimpsed laughing faces through the windows. She walked on.

Her reasons for not attending had nothing to do with not feeling relieved at the outcome. She felt enormously relieved knowing Laurie wouldn't have to face a murder trial. There simply were too many unanswered questions. Two men were dead. Although Gerry Verkamp's manner of death was listed as accidental, Kim couldn't shake the feeling that he too had been murdered. She suspected Cathy Garrett was involved in both deaths. Trip may well have learned something Cathy hadn't wanted him to know. But what was her motive for killing Gerry? All Gerry could do was point a finger at Laurie. The only obvious benefit to his death was an end to the proceedings. It meant an end to all questions. For a woman with something to hide, that might be worth something.

Defying her own resolution not to ask a single new question, Kim met with the sheriff in his office late Friday afternoon. She wanted to know if there was any new information on the fentanyl found on the whiskey bottle Gerry Verkamp had when he died.

"Funny you should ask. Got the report this morning." Preston reached for the top page on a stack on his desk. "The forensics lab found trace amounts on the bottle. Heaviest concentration was on the cap and around the top."

"Meaning what? Whoever mixed the cocktail Gerry drank that night had powder residue on his or her hands? It was accidental transfer?"

"Possibly."

"And no fingerprints, other than Gerry's?"

"That's right."

"Could he have had access to fentanyl?" she said.

"Gerry kept a couple of stashes of booze around town. We've confiscated the ones we could find. No sign of grain alcohol, no sign of drugs, prescription or otherwise in any of them. That's not to say he didn't have other stashes we haven't found." The sheriff grimaced. "Folks who knew him best said he always stuck to alcohol. A few also said kids sometimes cruised the streets and handed off bottles to him. Not locals, generally. Out-of-towners. Thought it was funny, seeing a destitute old man with his hand out for any old thing that came in a bottle. In case you wondered, we're following up on a couple of leads."

"Is fentanyl a drug you see often?"

"No. We see plenty of other narcotics, but not that one."

"So if you found it in someone's possession, you'd find that suspicious?"

He looked at her for a long moment. "You have anyone in mind?"

She glanced away. When she looked back, she said, "I assume you looked at Cathy Garrett for her husband's murder."

"We did. No motive. Husband and wife got along. Great kids. No money troubles. Both had decent jobs. There was no motive."

"And Laurie had one?" Kim said, more forcefully than she intended.

Preston shook his head. "She's one strange bird. Maybe she had a thing for Trip. Maybe he made a promise he didn't keep. Ask me, it wouldn't take much to tip her over the crazy edge."

The sheriff didn't have to say it. He had been prepared to convict Laurie on the basis of illogical life choices stemming from having suffered a violent past. But this wasn't news. Kim moved on. "Any idea where Trip got the lorazepam that was in his system?"

Preston frowned and reached for the papers in front of him. "Anyone can get lorazepam."

"Jason Zachary, Trip's business partner, said Trip hated drugs. He said Trip wouldn't have taken it."

"And I suppose you've never noticed that people sometimes do things they say they won't? It's called human behavior."

The sheriff stacked the pages and set them aside. Kim knew it was her cue to leave. She didn't wait for him to throw her out. She wanted his door open in case she wanted to come back.

Which wasn't likely to happen. The case against Laurie had been dropped. That was all Kim had wanted not long ago. It should be enough now, and whatever Cathy Garrett had done, or not done, for whatever reason, was not Kim's concern.

CHAPTER 36

With the murder charge against Laurie dropped, Kim turned her thoughts to the future. At home on Friday night, she laid out the rudiments of a plan. The idea that had been incubating for several days settled firmly in her mind: she was going back to school. By September she intended to be living in Gunnison, enrolled in at least one criminology course. Between now and then she intended to stay in Creede. Day by day the weather was improving. She had mountain trails to explore on foot and on her bicycle, which had been collecting dust in the shed behind the cabin since she'd moved in.

She was at the café the next day at closing time. Laurie, still finishing the last of her tasks, said she didn't have time for a walk. She needed to work on tomorrow's service.

"You have to walk home," Kim said.

Laurie conceded the point. "You didn't come to Valerie and Joan's the other night," she said as they set off.

"You know me and crowds. I really don't like them."

Laurie didn't object when Kim led her on a circuitous path that took them through the neighborhood and several crossings over Willow Creek.

"I think Trip must have fallen in the water by accident," Laurie said during one creek crossing. "That's possible, isn't it? He was so unsteady that night."

Kim agreed it was possible.

"We'll never know what happened now, will we?"

"I don't think we will."

The sound of rushing water faded as they walked on. Kim asked Laurie what she planned to talk about at tomorrow's service.

"I haven't decided."

At the house Laurie said she had something for Kim. She went into her bedroom and returned with an envelope. "Here's $500. I don't know how much I owe you." She handed it over.

Before Kim could say a word, Laurie added, "Joan returned some of the money I gave her. She subtracted her expenses and gave me the rest. Now if you don't mind, I really need to get to work."

—

Sunday dawned overcast and cool. Kim trotted down the steps into Creede's town hall basement moments before the service began. She shook off Kate's wave to join her and took her usual seat along the wall. She bowed her head for the opening prayer. She stood and joined in singing the first hymn. During the scripture reading, her thoughts wandered. The reading was a long one. Listening, Kim recalled times before when it had been enough simply to sit and listen to Laurie without hearing anything she said. Today she rode the sound of Laurie's voice as if it were a wave. It carried her across an imaginary sea, depositing her on a strange and distant shore. Cast off on dry land, she rose unsteadily to her feet. She brushed bits of flotsam from her knees. She pushed straggly ends of damp hair away from her eyes. One phrase stuck in her mind as she trudged across shifting sand: *Who am I to judge?*

She, who would have no one, not one soul, know the truth about her—what right did she have to attempt to unmask another? Her name was not Kim Jackson. She had not committed a crime, but the prospect of being charged and found guilty of not one but two felonies had frightened her badly enough to make her run from everything and everyone she had ever known. She of all people ought to sympathize with a fellow traveler, forced—for whatever reason—to assume a new guise. As Cathy Garrett presumably had done.

But that was the kicker. Were all reasons created equal?

Kim tired of the argument. She took herself back in imagination to the tropical paradise smack in the middle of the deep blue sea. She found a waterfall. Standing beneath it, she felt cleansed of salt and sand, also of weariness and duplicity. She emerged to find herself not alone, as she had imagined. Lena Fallon was there. "I've been waiting for you," Lena said, and Kim staggered under the enormity of feelings she couldn't separate.

She blinked and opened her eyes. She caught Laurie looking at her. Something passed between them. Kim felt a softening in her own features and saw what she thought was a smile flit across Laurie's face.

She closed her eyes. She leaned her head against the wall and began thinking about what she intended to do next.

CHAPTER 37

Creede's cemetery was located on top of the hill above town.

Kim found it without difficulty when she left the office one day midweek to take her customary afternoon stroll. Ordinarily her daily walks took her through a familiar neighborhood, where she sometimes saw Cathy Garrett leaving work to pick up her daughters at their grandmother's house.

Sometimes she waved to Cathy when she saw her.

Sometimes Cathy waved back. It was never a friendly wave.

Kim knew what she was trying to do, and she also knew it probably wasn't a good idea. She was sending a not-so-subtle message: *Don't forget about me.*

The cemetery had an unkempt look about it that, curiously, added to its appeal. Tall grasses moved in the slight breeze. Most of the headstones were a weathered gray, bearing dates from the middle of the last century and earlier. It didn't take long to find a mound of dirt not yet fully settled over the casket that lay beneath. Kim stood over the patch of earth where Trip Garrett lay buried next to the little boy he loved.

She choked up unexpectedly. She tilted her head back to keep the tears welling in her eyes from spilling over. Without forgetting where she was, a part of her felt joy at the sight of sky and clouds, a simple sight, a simple day. Then she looked where a man and a boy lay buried, heedless of the tears rolling down her cheeks. She couldn't help but think that Trip and Cody had their heads turned toward each other and were smiling.

She spoke to the father. "I've done what I could. All that's left to me now is to do exactly what you did."

Almost exactly.

Earlier in the week, she had searched a missing children's database for a boy named Connor. Connor would have been approximately three years old when he was reported missing. No photographs of a tow-headed toddler with a first name "Connor" appeared in the database. Much as she would have liked to run Cathy Garrett's fingerprints through national registries, including AFIS, the FBI's Automated Fingerprint Identification System, she had no authority to do so. Nor could she commandeer Jason Zachary's laptop and turn the machine over to a computer geek who could, with a few nimble keystrokes, backtrack along the path Trip had taken and perhaps discover the same secrets he had found.

Kim was clear on what she wanted. She wanted to know who Cathy Garrett really was. Once she knew, she would decide what to do with the information.

There was more to her commitment. It had come in the form of a promise made to herself. If she succeeded in flushing out Cathy Garrett's true identity, Kim vowed to reveal her own to someone.

Not to just anyone. To Lena Fallon.

Little as the one had to do with the other, Kim had settled on her own version of a quid pro quo with an unflinching determination. She didn't know when she would tell Lena, or under what circumstances. But she would tell her the truth about herself, that much was certain.

The idea of following the path Trip had taken had come to her in church on Sunday. It came out of the blue, after she had considered and eliminated other options, including purchasing three boxes of the powdered laundry detergent favored by Cathy Garrett and somehow—that was the tricky part—slipping into the house to exchange her purchases for the boxes in the laundry room. Those premeasured packets of detergent bothered her. They made no sense.

Her other idea was to casually drop the name "Connor" in Cathy's presence and watch her reaction. Kim couldn't defend her obsessive need to do something, even if that something was on a par with poking a stick at a venomous snake.

Without overthinking her chances of success, she had used some of the cash Laurie gave her to buy a prepaid Visa card and order a DNA testing kit from the same company Trip had used. She wanted to do the test on one of the Garrett daughters. If she was right, the results should match to a brother named Cody. She hoped to learn more. If someone on Cathy's side of the family had had genetic testing done, and if the relative was close enough—a parent or a sibling—it would give Kim a possible path to discovering Cathy Garrett's identity.

It would also prove that Trip Garrett had had genetic testing done on his deceased adopted son, for reasons known only to himself.

It was likely a waste of good money.

One small detail remained. Once Kim received the kit, she needed to persuade a grandmother to let her near a child and persuade that child to spit in a cup.

By virtue of her daily strolls through town, Kim was well versed in the Garrett family schedule. Two days a week, Cathy bundled her daughters up and drove to her mother-in-law's house to drop them off. The other three weekdays, Esther Garrett came to the house to babysit. Often Esther took the girls out for a walk around lunchtime. There was a playground in the neighborhood that elicited a squeal of delight from the elder girl each time she saw it. Esther didn't always lock the door when she left. Not once while Kim had been surveilling the Garrett family had Cathy returned home during the workday. Kim thought it possible that she could outwit Esther Garrett with a brief, unauthorized visit to the house, though there remained the sticky problem of getting a child's saliva sample while she was there. Something told her it was probably not worth it to try and outwit Cathy.

She returned from her cemetery walk in time for a meeting with a new client. A local shop owner by the name of Mason Weld had requested an appointment to discuss a bookkeeping problem. He frittered away the first few minutes by leaping across questions regarding her experience and hourly rate without saying a word about what had brought him there. Her hopes for snagging a paying customer began to fade.

"Hang on," he said after she pressed him a second time for details.

He left her office and returned with two good-sized cardboard boxes. Inside was a collection of invoices, receipts, deposit slips, product orders, and shipment notices among other less easily identifiable slips of paper. The pair of boxes contained three months' worth of accumulated documents that his previous bookkeeper had admitted she hadn't gotten around to filing before Weld had fired her. Kim leafed through the stack and concluded the woman hadn't been doing much of anything except running payroll for Creede Naturals, the holistic vitamins and supplements store, if the letters from collection agencies were anything to go by.

Weld said the documents needed to be sorted and filed and the shop's computer system updated with the information. He wanted to know how long the work would take and what it would cost.

"That's impossible to say until I know what I'm dealing with," Kim said, holding back a laugh.

He insisted on an estimate.

It was getting on toward the end of the day. Despite her misgivings about Weld, Kim wanted the work. She told the shop owner she would have an estimate for him in the morning, after she'd had a chance to review the contents of both boxes. With a frustrated glance at his watch, Weld said that would be fine and left.

By midmorning the next day, her desk was covered with four piles of documents separated by type and a fifth stack composed of handwritten notes and other papers she needed to question Mason Weld about.

"Going for your walk?" Dee asked when Kim emerged from the office.

"Yes. I've never seen such a mess of paperwork. I need fresh air. I'm going to stop at the café after I talk to Mason. Can I bring you anything?"

"No, thanks. I have my sandwich."

At Mason Weld's shop, Kim looked at his business software and assured herself that she was familiar with it. Against her better judgment, she caved in and gave him a price for the work. He argued. She held her ground. After a bit of grumbling, he agreed to pay what she asked. Their tenuous deal nearly unraveled when she said she couldn't start the data entry work until the next day. Weld grumbled a little more, then agreed.

By then, Kim was almost sorry she'd taken the job.

Force of habit drew her to the side streets east of Creede's main thoroughfare when she left Weld's shop. She strolled through a neighborhood she knew well, passing the school where Cathy worked. She went as far as the park and saw Esther Garrett and the girls in the company of other adults and children, enjoying the fine day. The school year would be ending within a few weeks. Kim wondered whether Cathy's work schedule would change, and if it did, would the girls' babysitting schedule change as well? The questions sent her to the post office. The post mistress's eyes lit up when she walked in.

"Kim! I have something for you!" Claudia said.

Kim's heart leapt in hopes of seeing a letter from Lena. But there was no letter, only a package from the genetic testing company.

Claudia laughed as she handed it across the counter. "More and more folks around here are getting these test kits. I hate to think how many are going to find out they're related to each other!"

"Thanks, Claudia." Kim tried to keep herself from asking but did anyway. "Nothing else for me?"

"Not today, Kim."

At the café, Kim said hello to Marla and ordered a salad. "Is Laurie working?"

"Yes. Go on back."

She found Laurie standing over a large stainless steel bowl, using two wooden forks to combine chicken salad. "That looks good," she said.

"It is good. You should know. You've had it before."

"Do you want to have dinner sometime?" Kim said.

"Not tonight. Not tomorrow. Joel and his wife are cooking dinner tomorrow night for some of us from the church. You could probably come if you want to. Everyone wants to see you. I keep telling you that."

"Everyone," Kim knew, meant Valerie, Joan, Marla, and Kate.

"Thanks. Maybe another time. How about a walk up the canyon when you get off work on Saturday?"

Laurie looked up and smiled. "I'd like that."

CHAPTER 38

Friday proved to be a tedious day. Kim spent the morning at Creede Naturals, pinned in at a small desk with room barely enough for a computer and the stack of documents she needed to process. Under the pretext of "getting her started," Mason hovered until she threatened to double their previously agreed upon fee. He took the hint and left her alone. Afterward, she made steady progress. Other than stopping for a short break for lunch, she stayed in the airless room, painstakingly transferring numbers from paper to digital storage. Long before quitting time, she faced the twofold realization that she wasn't going to finish today and she had grossly underestimated her fee.

Mason Weld wasn't happy when she told him she would have to come back next week.

"It's fine by me if you want to finish the job yourself," she said, standing in the showroom, which smelled of lilacs. An array of bottles and packages lined the shelves. The center displays were nicely arranged with soaps and skin-care products.

The arrival of a customer saved her from an argument. "No, no. Monday is fine. Just—be quick," he said. "What I mean is, I hope you don't run into further difficulties."

She would have liked to point out that the origin of the difficulties was all on his end. Given an opportunity to escape, she took it.

An invitation from Paula to come to dinner was tacked to the cabin door that afternoon. With time to spare before she was due at the house, Kim went to the storage shed and wheeled her bicycle out into the bright light of day. Neglect showed in a thick layer of dust on the metal tubes and handlebars. The tires were flat. So much for her fine idea of jumping on the bike for a spin up the canyon.

She set to work.

An hour later it was a new machine. The tires were inflated. The metal bars shone. The chain, newly lubed, gave a satisfying tick-tick-tick when she spun it backward. But an inaugural ride would have to wait. She returned the bike to the shed, took a shower, and presented herself at Paula's door at the appointed hour.

"You didn't even miss me, did you?" the artist said.

"I guess I didn't. Did you go somewhere?" Kim sidled past her into the house.

"Denver. Business crap. I need to work."

Kim went directly to the bathroom. She changed out of her top garments into the man's shirt. In the outer room, she took her usual position on the barstool, naked from the waist up. Suddenly self-conscious, as she hadn't been since her earliest days modeling for Paula, she wondered whether she would be able to pull off the session tonight.

"Stop it," Paula ordered, as if she were a mind reader.

Kim raised her chin. She relaxed her shoulders. She slowed her breathing and sank into a quasi-meditative state. Cool air glanced off her shoulders and neck, as if the air itself were alive and curious about this body it found perched on a stool. She became entranced by a peculiar reflection on the west-facing window that created a double image composed of tree, rock, and sky.

Paula worked intently. Kim felt her frown as she moved back and forth, circling the chair, her charcoal pencil rarely still. A long time seemed to pass. Paula flipped to a new page. The double image in the glass dissolved with the onset of twilight.

They took a short break and went back to work. Much later, Paula closed the tablet and set it aside. She stood for a long moment with her back turned, gazing in the same direction Kim had been looking during the session. Kim studied her, wondering whether Paula could see her gaze boring into her in the glass.

"We're finished," Paula said in a tone that sounded uncommonly ferocious. Kim wondered whether she meant permanently. She moved stiffly off the stool. In the bathroom, she changed into her own clothes.

An open bottle of wine was on the counter when she returned to the outer room. Paula stood at the sink, glass in hand. As she had before, she stared out the window. A crusty loaf of bread sat on a cutting board. There was no sign of other food. If she didn't model for Paula, Kim wondered as she poured a glass of wine, would they have a relationship other than as landlord and tenant?

"It's the spiders in my head," Paula said, with her back still turned. "They're always there after I travel. I haven't been able to get rid of them since Texas. Then I had to go to Denver. Whatever." She opened the refrigerator and took out a plate of cold salads and cheese.

While they ate, Kim waited for Paula to ask for a story. She didn't have a story to tell. Somehow that never seemed to matter. Instead, Paula continued to lapse into long silences that were abruptly suspended when she made one comment or another. Kim tried to imagine the feeling of spiders in her head. It was easier to imagine the feeling of cobwebs.

Late in the meal, Paula set aside her fork. Her eyebrows were knitted closely in concentration as she reached for her wineglass. "When you first came here, I was fascinated by your negative space. It was a veritable force field, dark and intractable and so incredibly lovely. I'd never seen anything quite like it."

Kim, suddenly tense, dug her fingernails into a slice of bread.

"I was surprised when you consented to model for me. I'll confess now my motive in asking was hardly pure. I can sketch a female nude in my sleep and sometimes have. I thought I could dislodge you, propel you out of your comfort zone at least. I thought." Paula gave a funny laugh. "Whatever I thought was wrong."

She muttered a curse. She went to a cabinet and returned with a bottle of whiskey and two glasses. She poured the drinks.

"Because I didn't know where you were, I could go any-where." Paula made a fist and tapped it lightly on the table. "I want the wave of energy that is created when you look out that window." She pointed at the west-facing window. "I want the thing that exists in the space between you and whatever the hell is out there." She pointed again. "Other models I've worked with scream, 'Look at me!' You scream, 'I'm not here!' It's as if you're saying *I don't exist*. And if you don't exist, well, that's a hell of a funny Cartesian inversion." Paula laughed at her own joke.

Kim felt hollowed to the core. A crazy laugh started some-where deep in her soul—at her own smugness in thinking she was so good at fooling people about the secrets she kept, when in truth it was they who were so good at fooling her, letting her keep them.

She drank her whiskey.

Paula continued rambling. Kim barely listened. She ate. She drank. Later, when Paula mentioned an unfamiliar name, Kim checked in. "Who?"

"Wittgenstein. Ever read anything by him?"

Kim shook her head.

"Most people haven't. He's not an easy read. There's a line in his *Tractatus* that makes me think of you. I don't remember the exact quote."

Kim tightened her grip on her whiskey glass.

"It goes something like this: *What we cannot speak about we must relinquish to silence.*"

—

Kim waited until the first rays of sunlight touched the canyon floor the next morning before wheeling her bicycle out from the shed. She filled a water bottle, tied a light jacket around her waist, and fastened the straps of her helmet before mounting the bike and pedaling north. Two vehicles passed her before she reached the first curve. Bachelor Loop had opened for the season. The canyon was crawling with people again, as Paula had mentioned last night, displeased by the emergence of the great outdoors crowd from their winter hibernation.

Around the bend, the dirt road ascended at a deceptive incline. Mountains rose on three sides, suddenly there as they hadn't been before. Kim pedaled on, winded but unable to stop gaping at the remains of a mine shaft jutting out from the hillside. She dug in and pedaled harder.

She had been warned. Several times Dee had described Bachelor Loop as an unrelenting but drivable road, but had she mentioned . . . steep? Kim had shrugged off the warnings. She had ridden up challenging trails before, and after all, this was a road, not a trail. Out of the corner of her eye, she saw decaying wooden structures, other mine entrances or perhaps the remains of shacks or businesses left behind from the time when this stretch of narrow canyon had called itself a town.

Straight ahead, the road rose against a seemingly impenetrable wall. Kim knew she was looking into the teeth of what the earliest residents had called "the Black Pitch." She came within a hairsbreadth of dismounting while ascending the vertical stretch. She doubled down on determination and through sheer grit pedaled to the top of the wall.

Beyond, the road never leveled out. Gasping, she shot quick glances at other buildings, other mine shafts nestled into the hillside, the visible testament to Creede's legacy of having once been a silver-mine boom town.

But she wasn't thinking about Creede.

She was thinking about Paula.

She thought she understood now why she'd been invited to the artist's house. What she had interpreted as generosity was, after all, a transactional arrangement. Each had wanted something from the other. Wasn't that the buried truth in all human relationships?

She dug harder into the pedals, trying to burn off the humiliation of having been caught out. Paula's words rang through her mind: "It's as if you're saying, *I don't exist.*"

That's exactly what she had been saying for the past year, but no one was supposed to hear.

How had Paula heard?

Had anyone else?

Had Lena?

Kim rode fast and far into the high country. She went farther than she had intended. Too late, she wished she had brought more layers. When she turned around to descend, the chilly air cut through her light jacket to the perspiration-dampened jersey underneath. She gritted her teeth. Her fingers stiffened on the handlebars. She was freezing as she rode down the steep road, chilled to the bone by the time she reached home.

—

She was late meeting Laurie.

Laurie was sitting at an outside table when Kim arrived at the café. She hadn't forgotten their plan to go for a walk that afternoon. She had gotten there as fast as she could.

"I really don't have time to go for a walk. I have to work on tomorrow's service. I'm way behind," Laurie said in a put-out voice. She took a second look at Kim. "Why are you dressed that way?"

Kim wore long pants, two shirts, a jacket, and a vest. She was still cold. She explained about the bike ride and the chill she couldn't shake.

"I didn't know you had a bike. Who did you go with?"

"I went by myself. And yes, I do have a bike."

"Oh."

Kim didn't feel like going for a walk either. She wanted to go home and curl up in a down sleeping bag. Something in Laurie's manner made her ask, "Is everything okay?"

"Yes. Why wouldn't it be?"

"No reason."

Laurie asked how she'd gotten so cold when it was a perfectly pleasant sixty-something-degree day. Kim explained, though she was pretty sure Laurie didn't understand, about how much colder it was in the high country. She didn't know why they were still there when they both wanted to be somewhere else.

Laurie fidgeted. She crossed one leg over the other, turned sideways, then turned to sit straight again. For a second time, she mentioned the need to work on tomorrow's service. Kim would have stood up and said goodbye if she could have mustered the energy to walk away.

With a sudden burst of vigor, Laurie said, "I'm going to babysit the Garrett girls next week. I was surprised when Cathy asked me, but I'm happy."

"You're what?"

There followed an uneasy silence. Laurie's eyes darted nervously. "I'm going to babysit the girls. Esther has a doctor's appointment. Cathy needs someone for a couple of hours. She asked me and I said yes." She paused. "I didn't think you'd like it. I almost didn't tell you."

Kim didn't like it. "Laurie, back up. When did you talk to Cathy?"

"She came into the café one day. She said she was in a jam and needed a babysitter, maybe for an hour. Maybe for a little longer. She told me she knew I didn't have a thing to do with Trip's death and she was glad all of that was over. She said the girls miss me." Her voice grew soft. "I miss them too. I really don't like working in a kitchen."

Kim tilted her head back to look at the sky. She heard people talking as they walked by. A car slowed to a stop at the corner. She drank in the sense of normal life surrounding her and urged herself to say nothing. She needed to think about what she'd heard. And if there was a reason why Laurie should never again step foot in the Garrett house, she would have to persuade her of that reason some other time.

More than that, she needed not to dwell on the first thought that had sprung to mind. She needed *not* to see Laurie's gig at the Garrett house as a golden opportunity to collect baby slobber.

"When does Cathy want you to babysit?"

"Next Wednesday."

CHAPTER 39

Kim slipped into her usual spot along the wall in Creede's town hall basement on Sunday morning. While people mingled and Laurie remained ensconced in an alcove, Kim's thoughts remained where they'd been hovering since yesterday—on the latest piece of the Cathy Garrett puzzle. She did not think Laurie should babysit the Garrett girls. Not on Wednesday and not on any other day. Kim suspected Cathy was setting Laurie up for something, though for what, she didn't know. Anyone with a lick of common sense would know to steer clear of the Garrett household. Unfortunately, common sense was one of several life skills Laurie sorely lacked.

The service started. Kim tuned in briefly, then went back to thinking.

Based on the determined set of Laurie's eyes yesterday, Kim knew she had little chance of dissuading her from keeping the babysitting commitment. Which left her wondering how she was going to get inside the Garrett house and leave with a child's genetic material in a tube.

Laurie's voice resonated with strength and clarity this morning. Soothed by the sound, Kim closed her eyes and leaned against the wall, indifferent to what anyone thought of her odd posture.

Her reverie was interrupted by the announcement of the first hymn. She stood with the others and sat down when it ended. In the few moments of shuffling that followed, she noticed a late arrival descending the staircase. It was a woman, no one she knew.

When she looked over again, the woman was still on the staircase, poised a step above floor level.

Laurie segued into a scripture reading.

Shielded by the wall, the woman could neither see Laurie nor be seen by her. She backed up a step and sat down. A woman sitting nearby gave a friendly wave, indicating the array of vacant chairs. The stranger gave a sharp, emphatic shake of her head, *no*.

Kim's interest in her quickened. Something about her looked familiar. It took Kim a moment to realize why. It seemed ages ago when Fred Barnes had slid a photo of the Beltran family across the table and Kim had her first and only look at Natalie Beltran. That photo had been taken seven or eight years ago. Despite the effects of time and something darker— tragedy, to say the least—the woman sitting on the stair was easily recognizable as Laurie's sister.

Natalie's hair was shorter than it had been in the photo; it was blond, straight, touching her shoulders. She was slender, wearing black slacks and a beautiful beige jacket, long and obviously well made. The blouse underneath was a light color patterned with long, triangular swaths. The most striking feature about her was a mature look, absent in the teenage girl. More striking than that was the fact that she was here. Kim kept one eye on her without looking directly at her. Natalie didn't look a bit like Laurie. No one in the congregation would suspect the two were sisters.

Kim didn't hear a word Laurie said through the remainder of the service. She wanted to call Fred Barnes. She wanted to be prepared for whatever was coming next but was savvy enough to realize that no power on earth could prepare her for that. So she did what she could. She braced against a force she couldn't name yet feared.

During the final prayer, Kim bowed her head. When she checked on Natalie next, she was gone.

The service ended. People stood. A small crowd gathered around Laurie, as happened regularly at the conclusion of the weekly hour. Kim stayed where she was, torn between wanting to go after Natalie and sticking close to the elder sister.

"Kim, hello," Kate Hicks said. "I called you this week. I wondered if you wanted to have dinner or get a beer one evening. Are you staying for the discussion?"

Kim glanced at the stairs. "Yes." She followed Kate to the circle of chairs in the process of being arranged. "I didn't check my cell phone. I rarely use it," she said, explaining her failure to return the call. She wished she had the phone with her now. If she did, she wouldn't be here. She would be outside, talking to Fred Barnes.

Marla joined them. Kim smiled hello and sat next to her.

Laurie opened the discussion with a question that bore some relation to the morning's theme. Valerie promptly seized the lead and redirected the conversation. The next half hour dragged interminably. Too late, Kim realized she had made a mistake. She could have left after the service, gone home for her phone, and talked to Barnes before the session wrapped up.

Then she might have had a clue what she wanted to say when, finally, most everyone had left and only Laurie and her closest friends remained. Kim didn't have a good response when Laurie said to her in some surprise, "You're still here."

The women climbed the stairs together. At the sidewalk, Marla broached the subject of planning a dinner. She asked whether Tuesday might work, nothing fancy, maybe everyone could bring a dish. Kim spotted Natalie standing outside a shop several doors down.

"That woman." Kim pointed. "She was at the service. She sat on the steps." She would have said more, something aimless, hapless, a bridge from one unknown port in the universe to another, but she didn't need to. Without taking a step, Laurie seemed to withdraw from the circle. Likewise, Natalie seemed to gain stature against the ordinary backdrop of Creede's main street.

Marla's question went unanswered.

"Who is she?" Kate asked Kim softly.

"She's my sister," Laurie said.

The congenial atmosphere among the six grew strained. Valerie reacted first. She said she and Joan needed to be going. Marla and Kate were slower to take their leave. Kim stayed.

Natalie drew closer after the others left. "Hello, Laurie," she said while still ten feet away.

There was a simple elegance in Natalie's clothes, the cut of her hair, and her composed features, unmistakably beautiful after the fashion of her mother, whose photo Kim had seen once. There was also something of Janelle Beltran's air of self-possession in her.

Kim wondered what the younger Beltran sister was doing here. She wondered whether Laurie was thinking the same.

Watching, Kim saw a remarkable transformation come over Natalie. Her brow creased faintly. An expression fraught with purpose settled over her. At the same time, something else slipped away, all traces of edginess. She erased another few feet of distance. "I—I've come to apologize, Laurie. And to ask your forgiveness."

The words stunned Kim. Laurie, too, apparently.

A long moment of silence followed.

Finally Laurie said, "It's not up to me to forgive you, Natalie. That's between you and God."

No act or words of forgiveness seemed to be forthcoming from the elder sister. Natalie waited, then turned and started to walk away. Looking over her shoulder, she said, "Oh, Mom and Dad really want to hear from you. They miss you. They— please, call them."

Natalie resumed walking.

"Wait! You talk to them? Have you seen them?" Laurie shouted.

Natalie nodded.

Kim felt as if she were watching the shell of Laurie's world collapse. She felt as if she had no right to be there. She spied an open bench across the street. "Why don't you two go over there and sit down?" She pointed. "I'm going to pick up a couple of hot drinks. Natalie, can I get you a coffee or tea?" When the younger sister looked at her, she said, "By the way, my name is Kim Jackson. I'm a friend of Laurie's."

"Very nice to meet you," Natalie said.

Appearing numb, Laurie walked toward the bench. Natalie joined her, not quite at her side. Kim went to the restaurant on the next block, where she ordered three coffees and two sandwiches. She was unsurprised to find the sisters still at opposite ends of the bench when she returned, but at least they were talking.

"Will you be home later?" Laurie said when Kim announced she was leaving.

"Yes."

She said her goodbyes and left. Immediately on arriving home, Kim phoned Fred Barnes. The call went directly to voice mail. She left a message about Natalie's arrival. The private investigator didn't return her call for several hours.

"Well, there's a crazy game changer," the private investigator said. "I spoke to Robert a few minutes ago. Neither he nor

Janelle gave Natalie Laurie's address. Robert confirmed that Natalie has been in Santa Fe for a few days, visiting. When she left, she said she was going to a religious retreat in Colorado. She told her grandparents she would be back in a week. Robert said Natalie is on a break between semesters."

"What retreat? Did she say where she was going?"

"Neither Robert nor Janelle could recall the name of the place."

"So here's the million-dollar question. How did Natalie know where to find Laurie?" Kim said.

The phone line went quiet.

"It's anybody's guess, Kim," Barnes said softly.

"What's yours?"

"I suspect it's the same as yours. I think Natalie talked to the priest. Father Brian. Apparently Natalie has wanted to reconnect with Laurie for some time. Her family has been reluctant to arrange that meeting. No one has been quite sure of Laurie's mental state. And there's the small detail that no one has known where she's been living until quite recently."

The priest. Kim's heart sank.

"You still there?" Barnes said.

"Yes. I'm wondering what new trouble Natalie has brought with her."

"Time will tell."

There wasn't anything more to be said. They said goodbye and hung up.

—

Laurie never showed up at the cabin that afternoon.

Early in the evening, Kim walked into town. Lights were on inside the tiny house set back from the street when she walked past. Uncertain whether Natalie was there, reluctant to interrupt if she was, Kim walked on. On her next circuit, she tapped at the door.

Other than being more subdued than usual, Laurie seemed fine. She said her sister had left hours ago to drive to Crestone, wherever that was. She was attending some religious gathering. "She was never interested in religion before," Laurie said.

"Did she say how long she'd be there?" Kim said.

"No."

"Is she planning to stop here again when the retreat is over?"

"She didn't say. I don't think so. Why?"

"Just wondered."

If Kim could have thought of a way to tell Laurie that she knew her family's history, knew at least the outline of the tragic events, she would have done so. She feared any mention of Natalie's treacherous acts would only drive Laurie deeper into herself.

"Did you have a good visit?"

"I guess so. It was a shock seeing her. She's living in Denver. I didn't know that. I . . . well, you know. I haven't been in touch with my family. I still don't feel ready to talk to them. I don't feel ready for anything."

"But now they know where you are," Kim said, resisting adding that it wasn't only Laurie's family that had discovered her whereabouts.

"Yes."

Kim could think of many things Laurie ought to do to protect herself and her sizable assets, beginning with depositing the stock certificates in either a bank vault or a brokerage account. She thought a letter to her former convent indicating a change in her life plans at this time was in order. She thought Laurie ought to retain legal counsel in the event that Father Brian made another move against her. Those were real-world strategies almost anyone would see value in. Even as she thought these things, Kim knew Laurie would do none of them.

"My family is complicated," Laurie said.

"I'm sure it is," Kim replied.

CHAPTER 40

On Monday morning Kim stopped at the office long enough to say good morning to Dee and to double-check her calendar, which was clear until afternoon. From there she hurried on to Mason Weld's shop. Her hopes to finish quickly were dashed when the shop owner deposited another dusty box on an already cluttered desk. A peek inside revealed a cluster of loose papers piled haphazardly.

"Thought this was extra printer paper when I found it. I figured you'd know what to do with it," he said.

Kim reached inside. The first two pages were dated six months ago. The third was a notice from a collection agency, dated more recently.

"I can't get to this today."

"How much longer do you think you'll need? This really isn't right. I've already paid someone to do this work!"

"We'll have to discuss this work separately," she said, turning decisively toward the computer screen. She opened the file folder of documents. When Weld started to argue, she cut him off. Pointing one finger at the manila folder, she repeated that its contents represented the only work she had committed to doing this morning.

"Plus the reports," he added in a whining tone.

"Plus the reports." She picked up the first document and got to work.

Three hours later, Kim left, promising Mason she would return tomorrow to assess the contents of the newly discovered box. He hadn't paid her yet for the work she'd done. The thought grated. She suspected he was going to argue that the additional work fell under the scope of the project they'd agreed on or perhaps deserved to be prorated at some marginal dollar figure above that.

Her two o'clock appointment that afternoon was late. Twenty minutes past the hour, she was still waiting for her clients to arrive. She waited another ten minutes before the twentysomething couple walked in without a word of apology. The woman announced peremptorily that they were being harassed by the IRS.

The story came out between blistering tirades against the government. The couple hadn't filed an income tax return in the five years they had been married. The woman insisted their income fell below the minimum required to file. Government documents, however, showed otherwise.

"Well, there was that one time when you went to work in the oil fields," the woman said to her husband. To Kim, she explained, "But that was only for six months."

"That doesn't make any difference," Kim said. She was further frustrated by the couple's failure to provide the W-2 forms they had received from their respective employers for the period in question. "You did have taxes withheld, didn't you?" she asked, doubting she would get a straight answer.

The man surprised her. "We ticked off whatever box would get us the most in our paychecks."

She reread the letter from the Internal Revenue Service. According to the letter, the couple owed twelve thousand dollars and change between taxes owed, interest, and penalties. She suspected there was no mistake about it.

"Can't you just call one of those numbers you hear advertised on the radio and make our tax problem go away?" the woman said.

Kim saw her own fee disappearing into thin air. "I won't know anything until I see all your tax records. If you don't have them, you'll need to request copies from your past and present employers. I can talk to an IRS representative on your behalf. The best that you can expect is that I'll be able to work out a payment schedule that you can manage on your present combined incomes."

The woman grew irate. "Well—that's just plain ridiculous," she managed to sputter before standing and turning to her husband. "Come on, Jeff. Let's go."

Kim wasn't sorry to see them leave.

The rest of the day didn't get any worse, but it didn't get better. She had a headache when she knocked on Laurie's door that evening. A light patter of rain had started falling on her walk to the house. It took a full minute before the door opened.

"I wasn't expecting anyone," Laurie said. "I've already eaten, if that's what you came to ask. Besides, it's raining."

The gentle patter had turned to a steady beat of droplets against the roof. "I didn't know it was going to rain," Kim said.

"It's all anyone talked about today."

Kim walked into the living room. She sat where she usually did, in the chair next to the bookcase. Laurie dropped onto the other chair and propped her feet on the coffee table. Neither spoke. Kim mentally kicked herself for failing to do the one thing she had promised herself she would do today—search the internet for a religious retreat currently in progress in Crestone, Colorado. Not that she expected the information to be terribly useful, even if the existence of the event was confirmed. She thought she knew why Natalie had appeared out of the blue on Sunday. She thought Natalie was working in tandem with Father Brian in a new plot to get Laurie's money. Natalie was merely the latest minion sent by the priest to regain the control he'd once had over Laurie and her assets.

"It was a long, lousy day," she said, startling herself with the complaint. She explained about her frustration with Mason Weld. She mentioned the young couple and their ignorance about tax law. Though she hadn't intended to, she complained of a wasted hour, one she almost certainly wouldn't be paid for.

"Is that why you do what you do? Just so you get paid?" Laurie said.

Multiple responses sprang to mind. Kim managed not to blurt out anything explosive in defense of her desire for an income. "People have to earn money, Laurie. It's the way the world works."

"That's the problem! I don't think it should be that way. I think people should be able to do what they love to do and be compensated for it. Like—" She didn't finish the thought.

"Like what?"

"Like me. I hate working with food. I'd rather work with people. With children." She met Kim's glance with a look of defiance. "And if by some miracle Cathy offers me my job back after I babysit the girls on Wednesday, I'm going to take it."

Kim steadied her emotions by rereading book titles in the bookcase. She reminded herself this wasn't the first time an ordinary conversation with Laurie had gone off the rails. She reached for a book. Rather than remove it, she fingered the spine. *The Varieties of Religious Experience*, written by William James. Laurie had said she'd read it for a college course.

Laurie started to say something.

"What?" Kim said.

"Nothing."

Kim didn't know how many times she would have to learn the lesson that she couldn't save Laurie. The weight of the knowledge settled heavily while the rain beat on the cottage's roof. Natalie—in the guise of repentant religious convert, Laurie's mirror image in many ways—might be the one temptation Laurie couldn't resist. Natalie would be back, and soon, Kim predicted. Whatever game she was playing, it had only begun.

Viewed in that light, it almost didn't matter what happened between Cathy Garrett and Laurie on Wednesday. If Kim was right, Laurie wouldn't be living in Creede much longer.

"I guess I'd better get going," she said.

"You're going to walk home in this weather?"

Kim didn't wait for an invitation to stay. She wouldn't have accepted one regardless. She tramped home through puddles that had formed on the uneven sidewalk. Deeper pools awaited her in the rutted dirt road leading into the canyon. The sudden deluge had sent everyone indoors. Miner's Haven still had a few cars parked in its lot, but she was too wet and cold to entertain thoughts of stopping in.

She was soaked by the time she reached the cabin. She took a long, hot shower and crawled under the down sleeping bag, still fighting off a chill.

CHAPTER 41

The rain stopped sometime overnight.

By morning Kim's shoes still weren't dry. She inspected one damp sneaker, then the other, as her hopes faded for going through the day with dry feet. She had only the one pair of shoes. Purchasing a second pair, specifically hiking boots, had been on her to-do list for weeks.

As soon as she arrived at the office, she removed her shoes and put on dry socks. She called Mason Weld and left a message that she wouldn't be at his shop until later. She read the morning paper and spent the next hour returning calls, several of which resulted in appointments scheduled for later in the week.

Dreading the work that lay ahead, Kim put on her still-damp shoes and left the office to spend the rest of the day at Mason Weld's shop. She and Weld spent the first fifteen minutes discussing her fee for processing the documents in the newly discovered box. Weld, per his custom, wanted to pay a flat rate; she wanted to be paid by the hour. They compromised. Kim shaved ten dollars off her standard hourly rate; she further agreed to do all the work on-site, enabling Weld to "watch her," as he insisted. She could have promised him she would be working as fast as possible to get out of there.

Her mild headache grew steadily worse through the afternoon. Her mood wasn't improved when it started to rain again. "It's supposed to rain off and on for the next week. Haven't you seen the forecast?" Weld said when she mentioned the dreary turn the day had taken. He added something about heavy rainfall moving west from Southern California and a high-pressure system holding the moisture in a band over the Rockies. The store was empty of customers. No one, it seemed, wanted to venture outdoors. When it became clear she wasn't going to finish today, Kim broke the news to the store owner that she would return in the morning.

The plan was to meet Mason at his shop at eight thirty the next day, Wednesday. Kim arrived on time. Weld was fifteen minutes late. He approached the front door smiling, proffering his personal mug as if it were to blame, and explained there had been a long line at the coffee shop.

Already annoyed, Kim followed him inside.

An hour later her headache was back. All work on the financial documents was finished. She'd left the pages with the assorted notes untouched. Kim handed them over and told Weld he could follow up on them if he felt they were still important. He balked.

"I've updated your system, Mason," she said, striving to keep the frustration out of her voice. "That was our agreement."

He started to argue.

She interrupted. "Look at this one," she said, having anticipated his response. "It says, 'Call Pete. Ask him about the dried flowers.' There's no date. I don't have a clue what this refers to."

After another five minutes of grumbling, he wrote a check. Kim went directly to the bank to deposit the money.

Lights were on in the office when she got there, but Dee wasn't in. She'd left a note on Kim's desk along with another message from a client. Kim checked her schedule and saw that she had two appointments that afternoon. The rest of her morning was blessedly clear. She propped her legs on the desk and leaned back in the swivel chair. After a minute, she sat upright and read her messages. One was from the young couple she'd met with two days ago. The ones who thought paying income tax was something only other people were supposed to do. They wanted another meeting. Kim didn't relish the prospect. Those kids might not know it yet, but they were in trouble.

Kids.

She laughed. They were likely only a few years younger than her, and she didn't feel much like a kid.

When she heard the click of the latch turning on the outer office door, she assumed it was Dee. She was about to call out a greeting. Before she had a chance, an unfamiliar woman's voice broke the quiet. "Hello! Is anyone here?"

Kim walked to the doorway. Standing in reception were the young couple from Monday and another woman. Someone's mother, she guessed, seeing a woman with neatly trimmed short hair, the dark strands beginning to go gray. Kim's first thought was to ask the woman where she got her hair cut.

Her second was a sneaking suspicion as to why the trio was there—the tax problem. On that point, she was correct.

"Kim Jackson?" the older woman said. "I'm Elaine Miller. Sasha's mom." She nodded at her daughter. "I left you a message. We need to get the IRS off the backs of these two. Do you have time now?"

Reluctantly, Kim signaled for the group to follow her into her office. On the way she pulled a third chair from its spot along the wall in reception and dragged it next to the chairs that faced her desk. She sat down and pulled out a fresh notepad.

Elaine Miller pushed a thick brown envelope across the desk. Jeff crossed one leg over the other and reclined with a clear look of annoyance. Sasha squirmed in the chair next to her mother. Kim opened the envelope and extracted the sheaf of documents. For lack of anything hopeful or sympathetic to say, she reread the top page, which she had read twice during the couple's previous visit. The letter from the IRS laid out in no uncertain terms the legal situation. When she finished, she set the page aside. "As I explained to Sasha and Jeff on Monday," she said. Some thought jabbed at her. She thought it had to do with Mason Weld. On reflection, she couldn't think what it might be.

"Unless they can come up with proof that they paid additional taxes during this period, beyond any deducted from their paychecks, the Internal Revenue Service will insist on collecting their due. I can make a phone call and discuss this on their behalf."

She stopped. She felt that jolt of a reminder again. "What day is it?" she said.

Elaine Miller looked askance at her. "It's Wednesday. What does that have to do with anything?"

Kim was moving before the woman finished speaking. She stood up and ordered the others to do the same. "You have to leave. I have another appointment. I'm sorry. You have to leave now!"

Ignoring the shocked looks on their faces, she brusquely shepherded them through the reception area and out the door. Gathering her jacket and keys, she checked the time, mentally kicking herself. Laurie was babysitting the Garrett girls. Right now. Kim had no idea how long she would be there. As it was already getting on toward noon, she doubted she had much time. Adding to her panic, she had left the tube she needed for collecting a saliva sample at home.

She sprinted home, sloshing through puddles. On her return trip, she drove.

Approaching the Garretts' front door, she rehearsed an excuse for being there, in case Cathy answered. She heard the chime ringing. She heard nothing else until a child's wail sounded from somewhere inside the house. She rapped on the door. "Coming!" Laurie shouted in a strained voice.

Kim stepped back. A moment later the door swung open. Laurie's look of expectation vanished, replaced by a frown. "Oh. You're not supposed to be here."

The child in Laurie's arms squirmed violently, nearly launching herself into the air. Kim took advantage of Laurie's distraction to squeeze past.

"Laurie!" the older girl yelled from another part of the house.

"As long as you're here, can you give Grace a glass of milk, please?" Laurie said. "I have to change Hannah's diaper. Then you have to leave, you really do. And don't touch anything. Don't look in any drawers or closets while you're here!"

"Got it."

Kim hurried to the kitchen, where she found the elder Garrett daughter kneeling on a chair, leaning precariously toward a bowl of berries. "I love strawberries," Grace said. "Do you love strawberries?"

"I do."

Suddenly aware of her surroundings, Kim glanced around, looking for a camera. She saw nothing in any of the corners. The top of the refrigerator was lined with bowls and a neat row of popcorn packages. A device might be embedded there or in the light fixture. If Cathy Garrett was monitoring the activities inside her house, she was probably on her way home now.

Kim leaned close to the little girl and spoke softly. "Do you know how to spit something out of your mouth?"

Grace nodded eagerly. "I'll show you." She reached for a strawberry.

"I have a better idea. Come with me." Kim led Grace to the hallway. She positioned the girl in a corner and leaned over her, shielding her from any videotaping that might be in progress. She took the tube from her pocket and removed the cap. "Okay, here's the game. Let's see if you can spit into this tube. Can you give it a try?"

"That's a weird game. I never played it before."

"Can you try?"

The girl tilted her head forward and dutifully spit. Some of the liquid went inside the tube. Some rolled down the sides, coating Kim's fingers in slime.

"I did it!" Grace said. "What's my prize?"

Kim would have preferred a larger sample. She had no chance to get one. Grace darted past her, running down the hall. "How about a strawberry?" Kim said to her back. She capped the tube and slipped it in her pocket.

"A strawberry's not a prize. It's fruit!" the girl said.

"What about fruit?" Laurie said as she emerged from a bedroom, holding a smiling, freshly diapered toddler. "What are you two up to?"

"We're playing a game. I won. I want my prize," Grace said.

"What about a cookie? Have you finished eating your lunch yet?" Laurie said to the child. To Kim, she said, "You have to leave."

"I know. Sorry. It looks like you have your hands full."

"They're both excited I'm here. What time is it anyway?" She glanced at the kitchen wall clock and said more emphatically, "You have to go now!"

Kim nodded and let herself out through the front door.

CHAPTER 42

Kim dropped off a prepaid package containing Grace Garrett's DNA sample at the post office on her way back to work. She sent her weekly letter to Lena. The thin envelope slid away into oblivion behind the narrow metal slot. On her way out, she veered toward the customer service window. Leaning nonchalantly against the counter, she waited for the postmistress to emerge from the building's nether reaches.

"Hello, Claudia. Anything in General Delivery for me?" she said affably, as if she'd never inquired before.

"Nothing today, Kim. I've told you a dozen times, the instant anything shows up, I'm popping a 'Closed' sign in the window and racing down Main Street, shouting your name. Until then, nice to see you, as always."

Kim smiled. The ritual gave her slim comfort in the absence of any reply from Lena. It warmed her to know that at least two people on the planet—herself and Claudia—continued to pay homage to the former Durango detective.

With the genetic material sample on its way to the testing lab, there was nothing left to do now except wait. Kim counted out the weeks. It would likely be early June before she could expect an email notice that the report was ready. With a gaze at the sky, she promised to ignore Cathy Garrett until she had something that counted as solid proof that Cathy wasn't who she said she was. *If* she got that far, she would take the information to Sheriff Preston. *If* any other evidence existed linking Cathy to Trip's murder, the sheriff would have to find it.

Satisfied, Kim returned to work.

She walked into her office to find Dee standing on a chair at the window, rag in hand and muttering, "What's the point in having windows if you can't see out of them? Oh hi, Kim. I saw you were in earlier. I didn't know if you were coming back. I'll be out of your way in a minute." She went back to scrubbing the window.

"Thanks. I can see the sparkle now," Kim said when Dee finished.

"Enjoy it while it lasts. More rain is on the way. Oh, I ran a dust rag over your desk and chased a few cobwebs out of the corners. I didn't disturb any of your papers."

"Thank you. I should have noticed and done the cleaning myself."

Dee waved off the suggestion. "Cleaning is my version of therapy."

Kim sat down and picked up the tablet where she'd left off taking notes in her hastily aborted meeting with Elaine Miller and the young tax rebels, Sasha and Jeff. She was relieved to see a phone number jotted next to Elaine's name. She called, and after apologizing for rudely curtailing the meeting that morning, though she wasn't sure why she needed to—the trio had burst in on her without an appointment—Elaine agreed to return tomorrow. Kim said she would look forward to seeing her and Sasha and Jeff then.

It was a lie. She wasn't looking forward to anything except holing up in her cabin until the skies cleared for good. On that note, she made a grocery list. She added window cleaner and several other cleaning products to it. She had her car in town. She might as well make good use of it and go grocery shopping.

—

The rain beat steadily on the cabin that night. The windows didn't get cleaned. Kim overbaked the chicken and under-cooked the rice. Of small consolation was that she barely tasted her food.

She spent the evening leafing through a sheaf of pages she had printed at work that afternoon. Her research had led her to over a dozen different retreat centers located in Crestone. The place, to her surprise, was a mecca for the wanderer in search of spiritual enrichment, Zen practice, community, or simply a fabulous view of the mountains. There were Buddhist temples, ashrams, meditation centers, monasteries, a host of sacred landmarks, and a smattering of Christian churches, including Catholic, Methodist, and Baptist. Kim had no idea which flavor of spirituality Natalie Beltran had chosen to devote herself to for the week. She didn't know whether Natalie had even gone there. But Natalie had known something about the place. Kim doubted there was a more perfect spot in Colorado to choose as a destination for an unspecified spiritual retreat.

Late in the evening, she tossed aside the pages and slouched deeper into the sofa. The rain drummed on the roof. She stared at the floor mop and thought about cleaning the floor. She would feel better. She knew that. But she stayed put.

She smiled, thinking about the package she had mailed that day. Backtracking further, she congratulated herself on making a clean getaway from the Garrett house with a child's spit ensconced in a plastic tube. She didn't know what she had expected to happen.

Well, she did. She had expected Cathy to come barreling through the door, fully aware of Kim's presence in the house.

She had expected to beat a hasty retreat, having incited Cathy's fury a second time. Or was it the third? She had lost count.

Her dealings with Cathy had come to feel much like a game. The glib thought caught her up short. She sat up straighter, no longer amused by the parade of her own thoughts. What was she thinking? This wasn't a game. A man was dead. Laurie could have been convicted of murder.

Cathy hadn't come to the house today, and that meant something too. Kim spent the remainder of the evening embroiled in a new worry that somehow, without intending to, she had played straight into Cathy Garrett's hand.

—

The next day dawned gray and damp.

Tired of getting her feet wet, Kim drove to work. At a few minutes past nine, Dee knocked on her door.

"Come in," Kim said.

Dee ushered in Elaine Miller, Sasha, and Jeff. For the third time in four days, Kim laid out the ground rules of income tax law to two people who really had no interest in hearing about it.

An hour later she deposited a check signed by Elaine Miller in the bank. It covered four hours of her time, a good chunk of which already had been spent in meetings. For her part, she agreed to contact the IRS and act as a liaison for Sasha and Jeff. Kim had an idea of what was coming. Sasha still did not. "You'll negotiate a smaller amount for us to pay, right? Because we're complying in good faith."

Kim resisted pointing out that the couple had done nothing of the sort. She promised to be in touch.

She stopped at Marla's café for lunch. After ordering, she asked if Laurie was working.

"God, I hope so, because we're slammed!" Marla nodded at the door to the kitchen and told Kim to go on back. "Put on an apron and start chopping something if you feel like it."

"Hey," Kim said, finding Laurie frowning at the nub end of a head of cabbage. Shredded leaves were mounded in a pile on a cutting board.

"I'm going to toss this," Laurie said. "Marla would probably say use all of it. I've almost cut myself twice." She tossed it in a garbage can. "I hate preparing food."

"I know. You've told me. I know you're busy. I wanted to ask you a question."

"Fire away," Laurie said as she transferred the cabbage from the cutting board to a large metal bowl.

"Did everything go okay while you were watching the Garrett girls?"

Laurie rolled her eyes. "It was going fine until you stopped by."

"Did Cathy know I was there? I hope I didn't get you in trouble."

"You didn't. She didn't know. Is that your question?"

"No. What I want to know is whether Cathy ever dropped in at the house when you were working there before—before Trip died. That one time when I was there doesn't count."

Laurie shot her an exasperated look. "I really don't get how your brain works. The answer is no. I was there. She didn't need to be home. That was the point."

Laurie had assembled the slaw ingredients and was getting ready to add them to the cabbage. Vinegar. Chopped carrots. Cilantro.

Kim had her answer. She didn't know how or where it fit.

"Okay. Well, I'll see you later," she said.

Laurie wiped her hands on a towel. "As long as you're here, I might as well tell you. Natalie called this morning. She wanted to know my work schedule. She's coming back through Creede today on her way to Santa Fe. I'm going to see her tonight."

Unsurprised, Kim nodded. "Enjoy your visit."

CHAPTER 43

Kim thought she should have been happy.

She had a new piece of the Cathy Garrett puzzle. She had little doubt now that Cathy had known she was in the house when Laurie was babysitting four or five weeks ago, and that Cathy had rushed home expressly to confront her. Likewise, she had little doubt that Cathy had known Kim was in her house yesterday. Inexplicably, Cathy hadn't raised a fuss. What was that about?

Something was in play. Each time she thought about it, Kim felt her stomach sink. Cathy had staged the morning by having Laurie babysit and Kim had waltzed right into a carefully choreographed trap. What Cathy had gained from it, Kim couldn't say. Her only consolation was that she had gained something too. Grace Garrett's DNA was winging its way to a commercial testing lab. Regardless of whatever else Cathy knew about what had gone on inside her house yesterday morning, Kim doubted that Cathy knew any of her daughter's genetic material had left the house in a tube. Now it was a waiting game. If the results revealed anything noteworthy, Kim intended to hand over the information to the sheriff and let him proceed as he saw fit.

The rain Dee had said was predicted to fall for a week stayed inside the thick band of clouds swaddling the town all day. Kim worked late. Her last meeting was with Wanda Jenkins, whose loan for renovation of the Berwick building into a craft brewery had been approved. Wanda was ecstatic. She invited Kim to come over to the restaurant for a meal to celebrate.

"Thanks. Maybe later. I want to reread the contractor's proposal and update your business plan. The sooner we get this contract signed and sealed, the better," Kim said.

"I agree." Wanda beamed. "Thank you, Kim. I know I wouldn't be this far along without your help."

After Wanda left, Kim updated the business plan and jotted down several key questions to answer. She could already see the old building glowing with new windows and lights, the buffed brick interior set off by gleaming wooden posts and moldings, and music playing above a crowd of people talking and laughing while they enjoyed the finely crafted beer.

When she finally called it a day, Kim didn't go to Wanda's restaurant. She drove home in the gray light, expecting raindrops at any moment. At the cabin door, a car approaching from behind startled her. She spun around and recognized Paula's Jeep. Paula slowed long enough to lower her window and wave. The artist wasn't alone. Kim didn't get a good look at her passenger. Nor did she get an invitation to dinner.

The sharp rap on her door came an hour later. Kim answered the knock and was taken aback to see Natalie Beltran standing on her stoop.

"Sorry to bother you. Is Laurie here?" Natalie said.

"No."

Thunder rumbled in the distance. Kim thought she ought to take it as a warning. Instead, she invited Natalie in.

"We were supposed to meet for dinner at six," Natalie said.

Kim glanced at the clock. It was approaching eight.

"She's not at her house," Natalie said.

"I haven't seen her since lunchtime. She mentioned you were coming through Creede today." When the silence grew long, Kim said, "She's probably with some of her other friends. Valerie and Joan, possibly."

"She's not. I went back to the café when Laurie didn't show up at the restaurant where we were supposed to meet. Marla made a few calls. When she couldn't find Laurie anywhere else, she suggested I come here."

Kim was having trouble getting a read on Natalie. In the cabin's dim lighting, all she could tell was that Natalie was subdued and reluctant to make eye contact. She seemed tired and markedly less polished than she had been the first time they'd met. That didn't change her belief that whatever Natalie Beltran was selling, she wasn't buying it. There was a priest lurking in the background who wanted Laurie's money.

"What retreat did you go to in Crestone?" Kim said abruptly.

Natalie looked up. Real interest showed on her face. "I went to the Zen center. It was fantastic. Have you been?"

"No." Kim squinted at her. "I thought you were Catholic."

"I was raised Catholic. Does a name matter so much?"

Kim's first impulse was to throw Natalie out. She had zero interest in playing any games, rhetorical or otherwise. Her second was to cut to the chase.

"Did Father Brian send you to Laurie?"

"What? What are you talking about?"

"It's a simple question."

Natalie's brow knitted. "He didn't send me. Not specifically. He did tell me where to find her. No one else would tell me. I've been wanting to see Laurie for a long time."

Kim had no clue how to proceed. She had lost the thread of what she wanted to sort out. "So he didn't send you? He didn't give you any instructions . . . about anything?"

"No! What in the world are you talking about? I don't even like that man, priest or not! Laurie always liked him. She felt so special being his chosen one." Natalie flashed air quotes around the word "special."

"I should go." She stood up. "I have a long drive home tonight. Obviously Laurie doesn't want to see me."

Kim walked her to the door. After Natalie left, Kim counted the ways she had blown it in her brief, very strange conversation with Laurie's sister.

Rain started falling again soon afterward.

The pattering was accompanied by occasional claps of thunder and white flashes of lightning striking somewhere far up the canyon. Kim watched the show through the north-facing window, which gave her the less welcome view of lights blazing in Paula's house. She didn't know which surprised her more: That Paula had a guest. Or that she felt a pang of jealousy about a stranger taking her place at Paula's table.

Presumably not a stranger to Paula, nor a table to which she had any legitimate claim.

Each new flare of distant white kicked off the quibbling anew.

She might have gone looking for Laurie, if only for something better to do than to sit at home, brooding. The monsoon storm that was stalled overhead dissuaded her from leaving her watertight abode.

Between the rain on the roof and the argument running in her head, there was too much noise for her to hear anything that might have served as a warning. White light flashed at the same moment as her cabin door exploded open. Kim was on her feet in an instant. Too late, she saw the woman framed in the doorway.

CHAPTER 44

Not one woman.

Two women stood in the opening. Cathy Garrett and Laurie were there. Cathy held Laurie tightly, with one arm wrapped around Laurie's neck and the other jamming a gun into Laurie's midsection.

"Sit. Down," Cathy ordered Kim.

She did as she was told. As her weight sank into the soft cushions of the sofa, she felt herself going under. Maybe for the last time.

Laurie appeared wobbly. From her glassy eyes and doll-like limpness, Kim suspected she'd been drugged. Her clothes and hair were soaked.

There was only one light in the room, an old lamp that gave off a weak glow. A hundred yards across the way, lights were still on in Paula's house. Even with binoculars, even if she happened to be looking this direction, Paula would not be able to see the drama unfolding inside the cabin.

There were no other houses in the vicinity, an element that once had lent the place charm.

Kim rapidly assembled pieces of a story she doubted she would ever learn in full. She understood enough to know that Cathy Garrett saw her as a liability.

"You don't have a problem killing, do you?" she said to the woman holding the gun.

"You don't get to ask the questions tonight. I'm the one asking."

"I'm really c-cold," Laurie said, teeth chattering. "Can I h-have a blanket?"

"No," Cathy said. To Kim she said, "I'm only going to ask you this once. What's your theory?"

Kim didn't even bother trying to figure a way out of the maze. There was none. Cathy was going to kill her and Laurie. The sociopath with the gun only wanted to know what Kim had discovered that might compromise her reputation as a devoted mother and grieving widow.

"You killed Trip."

"Brilliant, Sherlock. Now why on earth would I do that? Answer!"

"I think Trip found out something you didn't want him to know. He probably found out Cody's biological father is still alive. Genetic testing," Kim said, looking Cathy squarely in the eye. "Trip had Cody's DNA tested. I'm sure he couldn't understand why you wouldn't reach out to your ex when Cody needed a bone marrow transplant. If he's even an ex."

Cathy's eyes hardened. "How do you know what he did?"

Kim ignored the question. Buying time, she struck off on a different tangent. "Obviously Trip didn't tell you what he found out. Maybe he thought he could live with the knowledge that you had lied to him. It was probably tougher for him to accept the truth that you let your little boy die, perhaps unnecessarily. I think you sensed something different in him after he got the genetic results. I think Trip, unlike you, wasn't a very good liar. And you couldn't take any chances, though why, I don't know.

Plenty of people leave troubled pasts behind. By the way, he knew Cody's real name was Connor."

Cathy froze.

Kim knew she'd struck pay dirt. Little good that would do now.

The silence that trailed in the wake of her casual name-dropping shattered when Laurie spoke.

"Connor? Do you mean Connor James?"

Kim looked at her in astonishment.

Cathy screamed, "How the hell do you know—" She fired a shot into the wall.

Any doubts Kim had about how well Cathy could handle a gun vanished.

"Who told you that name?" Cathy shouted.

Laurie, released from Cathy's grip, teetered on the verge of collapse. Arms wrapped around herself, she barely managed to stay upright. "Trip did. The night he came to see me. He asked if I liked the name. I th-thought maybe you were pr-pregnant. With a boy."

Game over, Kim thought. Trip had left a clue, however feeble, on the last night of his life. Almost all the puzzle pieces were in full view. For all the good it would do her or Laurie.

"What was so terrible in your past that you had to leave it behind?" Kim said to Cathy, trying to take advantage of her distraction.

"None of your damn business."

"Tell you what. Let's trade stories. I'll tell you what's in my past, you tell me what's in yours. Then we can decide who got the worst deal."

Cathy stared at some indeterminate spot on the cabin wall.

"You won't get away with murder," Kim said. "Not again. Sheriff Preston knows I think you killed Trip. He knows I'm pursuing a couple of leads. He'll be all over you for shooting Laurie and me." It wasn't true, but Cathy wouldn't know that.

Cathy broke off from staring. She lowered the gun. "Who said anything about shooting you?" She switched the gun to her other hand. She gave Laurie a rough shove. "On your knees. Now!"

Cathy moved quickly. Laurie did not. Cathy grabbed Laurie by the shoulders and shoved her to her knees.

An execution, Kim thought.

In rapid, well-rehearsed movements, Cathy shoved the gun in the waistband of her jeans and took something from her jacket—a syringe, as Kim saw when Cathy flicked off the top to expose the needle.

"Laurie! Move!" Kim screamed.

Still holding the syringe, Cathy pushed up Laurie's damp sleeve to expose the flesh of her arm.

"What are you doing? Get away!" Laurie said. Her resistance amounted to little more than swatting at a fly.

Kim moved without thinking. She leapt to her feet and sprinted toward Cathy. Cathy released Laurie and had the syringe ready, pointed at Kim. It was poised on a perfect line to plunge into her. Too late, Kim saw the trap. She raised her hands. She juked sideways and fell. Cathy rolled on top of her. Fingers deftly holding the syringe, eyes gleaming maniacally, Cathy celebrated her victory with a triumphant smile.

There was an explosive sound of glass shattering. Next thing Kim knew, someone else was inside the cabin. *Paula,* she thought, catching sight of a blond streak of hair. The woman did a full body slam into Cathy. That quickly, the woman was on top, straddling Cathy. Using a rock, she smashed Cathy's head viciously.

Not Paula.

Natalie.

Kim rolled away and watched Natalie deliver one blow after another until, finally, Cathy stopped moving. Bloodied, Natalie dropped the rock and slipped off her.

"Call," Kim said hoarsely. "Call for help."

"You call," Natalie said. She went to Laurie.

Kim thought it was the wind whistling through the open door until she realized the sound she heard was her own breathing. She couldn't remember where she'd left her phone. She got to her knees. Blood pooled around Cathy's head. Cathy still wasn't moving. Kim wasn't sure she was breathing. The syringe lay on the floor near her. The gun was a bit farther away.

Get the gun, Kim told herself.

Natalie managed to get Laurie to her feet. With both arms around her, Natalie shepherded her sister to safety out of the cabin. Kim kept her eyes on Cathy, whose face was obscured by long, dark hair. The adrenaline rush abated. Kim sluggishly got to her feet and stepped around Cathy to get the gun.

Cathy's legs shot out scissorlike, catching and tripping her. Cathy was on top of her in a flash. Cathy had the rock. Kim screamed when the first blow came. Roaring in her ears obliterated every other sound, every sensation except the taste of blood on her tongue. She fought. But another blow followed. And another. However hard she struggled, Cathy's grip on her grew tighter.

The next thing Kim heard was a gunshot blast that came from somewhere much too close.

CHAPTER 45

It wasn't easy for Kim to admit she was wrong.

It wasn't easy for her to admit anything, not with her head bandaged and pain killers dulling mind and body. She could see out of only one eye. She couldn't speak, not with her jaw wrapped. She could nod yes and shake her head no, which she'd been doing while being interrogated by the Mineral County sheriff.

Paula came up with the idea of having Kim type her account of events the night Cathy Garrett broke into the cabin. The delay gave her time to think about what she wanted to say. During the interlude, she came to the conclusion that she had been wrong about Natalie Beltran.

Thank goodness.

"Start at the beginning. Tell me everything that happened that night," Sheriff Preston said.

By then Kim was sitting up in bed in Del Norte's medical center. The effort to get upright, even aided by the bed's motorized assist, had sapped most of her energy and all of her clarity about what she intended to say. She looked at the keypad on the tablet computer, puzzled by the layout of buttons. In addition to facial lacerations and a borderline jaw fracture, she had a concussion. She had a nasal feeding tube, an IV for fluids and pain meds, and a pulse oximeter attached to a fingertip and momentarily removed to allow her to type. She knew it was important to tell the sheriff something. As if she were a child, she began pecking at the keypad.

"Cathy bad. Natalie good."

The sheriff peered over her shoulder. "Right. Can you be more specific?"

Paula stood hovering at the doorway. Sheriff Preston had banished her there for the interview. Paula had her arms crossed and a tired, worried look on her face. She had worn the same clothes for two days. Kim wondered how she knew that. Then she wondered how she or anyone knew anything.

"Kim," Preston said softly.

Kim typed: "Cathy killed Trip. Wanted to kill Laurie and me. Needle!"

Preston read what she'd typed. "We found two syringes in your cabin. Are you telling me Cathy brought them?"

Kim nodded.

"Do you have any evidence that Cathy killed Trip?"

She shook her head. Somewhere in her scrambled neural pathways, she knew she should be telling Preston something crucial but couldn't recall what.

"Why do you think Cathy wanted to kill you and Laurie?"

Her fingers tapped furiously: "Don't think. Know!"

No one would tell her what had happened that night in the cabin. They were all waiting for her version of the events. She had seen Laurie once, briefly. Laurie, drugged by Cathy, was fine now but was hardly a credible witness. Cathy Garrett had been on a murderous rampage. Natalie Beltran was, at a minimum, a former psychotic who'd killed her own brother. Kim had a concussion.

She sympathized with the sheriff's dilemma in establishing the truth about events on a stormy night in Creede.

She tried to remember. In the darkness of her own mind, she saw lights. Paula's house was lit up like a Friday night football stadium. Lightning bolts flashed down the canyon, splitting the sky in ferocious bursts of streaky white.

Kim typed: "Search g house!"

Preston frowned. "Which house?"

"G! Grrtt!"

"The Garrett house? We did. We found several video cameras. I told you that."

He had. The moment Kim had learned about the cameras, she knew Cathy hadn't "needed" a babysitter that Wednesday morning she engaged Laurie. It was a setup. She'd likely been watching her home from a remote device, waiting to see if Kim appeared on camera, and of course she had. Kim hadn't been able to resist the temptation to snag DNA from a Garrett child. For Cathy, it was the last straw. Kim had proved she wasn't going to stop investigating Trip Garrett's widow. The next night, Cathy had put her plan into play to kill Kim and Laurie.

Kim's head throbbed with fresh pain. Her vision blurred in her one good eye. She felt dizzy and nauseated. The Garrett house—she needed to tell the sheriff something about the house. Paula spoke. Kim heard her voice but couldn't make out the words. Furiously she typed: "laundry boxes search!"

"Laundry boxes? What laundry boxes?" Preston said.

Kim collapsed against the pillow. She pushed the computer away. Paula rushed to her side. Paula sat down on the bed and read the last message.

"Presumably she means for you to search any laundry-detergent boxes you find inside the Garrett home," Paula explained to the sheriff.

Kim looked at her in gratitude. Then she closed her eyes in exhaustion.

One day later, she was discharged from the medical center. Paula took her home and installed her in a downstairs room, nominally a sitting room, newly outfitted with a hospital bed. Kim balked at the arrangement. Primarily she balked at being consigned to a hospital bed.

"It was the easiest, most economical solution," Paula said, completely unsympathetic. "Two guys in a van showed up and unloaded it. Two more guys will come and get it when you're well. I know the feng shui of the room has taken a blow, but presumably it will recover when you do."

Sofa, lamp, and table had been crammed into one corner to make room for the bed. Nearby were a chair and ottoman. The latter two pieces were appropriately situated either for a visitor or for Kim to sit in when she felt well enough to get out of bed. Both entryways, the one near the front door and the one on the opposite side of the room, were draped with dark cloth. The two window blinds were partially lowered. The room could be made entirely dark, a feature Paula suggested Kim would come to appreciate.

"You may have trouble believing this, but I've never aspired to being anyone's caretaker," Paula said. "I can't even promise to do my best. The truth is I'll probably forget you're here."

Kim tried to laugh but couldn't. Her jaw hurt. Her whole mouth hurt. Fortunately, she hadn't suffered lasting damage, according to her doctor. The physician couldn't predict when she would be able to chew and swallow pain-free. Or talk. The solution to the former, for now, was a diet of smoothies.

She undressed and got in bed. Paula lowered the window blinds. Kim immediately fell asleep.

Laurie was there when she awoke. She was sitting in the chair, legs propped on the ottoman. She might have been sleeping too.

"Paula says I can stay as long as I like while you're sleeping," Laurie said. "Can you pretend to be asleep? Why does she get to make all the rules?"

Kim smiled with her eyes. She reached for a paper tablet and pen and wrote "How are you?"

"Fine. I guess."

Laurie didn't look fine. She looked pale and haggard.

"How's Natalie?" Kim wrote.

Laurie shrugged. "Better. My grandparents came to see her. And to see me too. She's going to stay in treatment for a while. She needs the structure."

Natalie was in a private facility in the San Luis Valley. Paula had described the place to Kim as a gorgeous enclave for the rich and damaged. Most of the residents had addiction issues. Natalie was receiving treatment for PTSD after beating Cathy Garrett with a rock and, when that hadn't stopped her rampage, shooting her with the semiautomatic pistol Cathy had brought to the cabin. The act of violence against another human being had devastated Natalie and threatened to undo what years of intense therapy had accomplished. By now Kim knew Natalie had returned to the cabin after getting Laurie out of there. She knew Natalie Beltran had saved her life.

The bullet wound had been severe enough to disable Cathy until help could be summoned on that stormy night four or five days ago. Of all the things Kim was currently trying to keep track of, time was not one of them.

Her own thoughts and memories were proving disturbingly slippery.

Cathy Garrett, like Kim, had been rushed to the medical center in Del Norte. Unlike Kim, Cathy was under arrest. The sole charge currently against her was kidnapping. Sheriff Preston had assured Kim additional charges would be forthcoming. Authorities were still trying to figure out what to charge her with.

"Oh, I forgot to give you these," Laurie said. She handed over a stack of get-well cards.

Kim nodded her thanks. She picked up the pen and wrote, "What have you and Paula been talking about?"

Laurie rolled her eyes. "You won't believe it. Deconstruction. She makes me start with an idea. Or a belief. Or a whatever. Then she asks questions that make me take it apart—the idea or belief or whatever. The point is to see what it's made of. And to see if it actually depends on something else, a different idea. Or belief. Or whatever." Laurie frowned. She didn't look unhappy. "It's actually kind of fun. She says if I get good enough at deconstruction, we can move on to perspective."

Kim laughed. She reached for Laurie's hand. Yesterday she had confessed to Laurie that she knew her family history. Laurie, shocked, ultimately had been relieved. Given Kim's condition, they hadn't been able to talk at length about the tragedy, which was just as well for now.

Kim tired quickly. She was relieved when Paula came in to shoo Laurie out of the room.

CHAPTER 46

Three times in the next two days, Sheriff Preston came to the house to interview Kim. Between short verbal replies and longer, more detailed typed and handwritten responses, Kim gave her account of what happened the night Cathy Garrett broke into the cabin.

"She meant to murder Laurie and me," she said, slurring the words. She resorted to pen and notepad, writing: "I think she had the gun just to scare us. Her real plan was to have my death appear as an accidental drug overdose. Laurie was collateral damage."

"Hold on. Back up," the sheriff said. "Why did Cathy want to kill you?"

"I was asking too many questions. Cathy wanted to know how much I knew about her involvement with Trip's death. She wanted to know how much I knew about her!"

"Tell me again why Natalie was there? All this happened late. Not many folks moving around town at that hour, especially not in the pouring rain," Preston said.

Kim backed up in her story and described, for the third time in two days, Natalie's visit earlier that evening, when she was looking for Laurie. When Natalie left the cabin, Kim had assumed she'd driven to Santa Fe, as she'd indicated she would. Good thing she hadn't.

Preston wanted to know what Kim's interest in Cathy was and why she had continued to pursue her as a suspect after the murder charge against Laurie was dropped. "Seems like you could've been happy about that," he said.

She wrote her answer: "Trip found out something through an analysis of Cody's DNA! Something Cathy didn't want him to know. I wanted to know what he found."

"Probably got him killed. And nearly got you and Laurie killed too," Preston said.

Kim gave up the fight. She wrote, "What else do you want to know?"

"I think that'll do. Your story is consistent. That's what matters. In case you're called as a witness at trial. Which seems likely."

With the interview concluded, Preston didn't make any move to leave. Kim's head was pounding again. The pain regularly followed extended periods when she was forced to concentrate.

"How did you know?" Sheriff Preston said in a curiously conciliatory tone.

Her eyes flashed the question. *Know what?*

"About the laundry detergent."

The pain in her head intensified. She closed her eyes against sudden dizziness. It was hopeless to think she could order her thoughts and communicate them. "Different," she muttered.

"Excuse me?"

She wrote on the notepad: "Detergent. Three boxes. The packets. Made no sense."

She was afraid that she was the one not making sense, but for once the sheriff seemed to comprehend her cryptic remarks.

"You're telling me you took one look inside that laundry room and figured this out?"

Summoning determination, she typed, "Looked in whole house. Laundry different. Found?"

He nodded. "Yeah, we found."

He told her his officers had found packets of drugs, including Ativan—a brand name for lorazepam—and fentanyl in sealed plastic bags at the bottom of what appeared to be an ordinary box of laundry detergent. They'd also found cash, a gun, and a key.

"Key to what?"

"A storage locker. Found a whole lot more illegal shit there, but I'm not going to tell you what. I have to try and hold on to some control of this investigation." He stood up. "Nice work. I'll save the rest of what I have to tell you for another visit."

Kim slept the rest of the day. She was sleeping far more than usual. Paula insisted it was a good thing, nothing to worry about. Her brain needed time to heal.

Among the cards Kim received on a near daily basis, a letter came from Santa Fe. Fred Barnes's name and a PO box appeared in the envelope's return address corner. She assumed it was another "get-well" message and didn't open it.

A day or two later—time still wasn't high on her list of things to keep track of—she slit the envelope top and removed a handwritten page. Fred passed along sympathy for her injuries and his hope for a full and rapid recovery. Then it got interesting:

> Wanted to let you know that Robert and Janelle hired me to look into your and Laurie's kidnapping. They suspect Father Brian Jorgenson was involved. Robert and Janelle don't like that guy, and they really don't like his hold on Laurie. Took some digging, but I dredged up a name

from Jorgenson's seminary days. Guy's name is Brandon Tucker. Last name ring a bell? Tucker flamed out as a priest. He's bounced around working in nonprofits over the years, especially the kind raising funds for overseas missions. I have a lead on his current address in Arizona. I'm heading there in a few days to get some photos and to see if I can find a link to the woman who posed as Nell Channing. Whatever I get I'll turn over to your favorite sheriff.

There was another line or two, nothing noteworthy. Kim refolded the page, not sure what to think. Finally she decided she was seriously annoyed with Laurie's grandparents for hiring Barnes to track down the Channings but not raising a finger when Laurie was facing a murder trial. She wondered if there was something about having too much money that scrambled peoples' brains.

Still suffering the consequences of her own scrambled brain, she decided to be grateful there was a chance the Channings might be caught and charged with kidnapping and to let the rest go.

CHAPTER 47

Cathy Garrett's real name was Kathryn Symon James.

She hailed from central Florida, where she was married (currently) to Michael James. James was the father of a son named Connor James (aka Cody Garrett). Being a bigamist, or former bigamist, wasn't Cathy Garrett's worst problem. Nor was being wanted on an outstanding warrant for parental kidnapping of a minor child. Kathryn James had hightailed it out of Florida with her son and a treasure chest full of goodies that belonged to some nasty boys. The stash of goods included pharmaceutical and high-grade street drugs, guns, and cash. The attractive brunette, who gave every appearance of being a minivan-driving soccer mom, had at some point morphed into a minivan-driving drug mule.

Sheriff Andy Preston theorized to Kim that Kathryn James had worked her way up the food chain in whatever criminal network she called home. His counterparts in Florida agreed. Then, for reasons she wasn't divulging, she'd pulled the plug. She'd loaded up with as many "assets" as she could get her hands on and bolted. Law enforcement agents in Florida eventually hoped to trace her activities in the state through the seized evidence. At the moment the Mineral County sheriff wasn't giving up any part of the cache.

He had a murder to investigate.

Maybe two.

Kim had shared with Sheriff Preston her hunch that Cathy Garrett was responsible for Gerry Verkamp's death.

Preston had discovered Cathy's identity through the genetic test Trip Garrett had done on Cody. Preston got a warrant for the results and found a link to Cody's biological father. Dr. Michael James, a respected Florida internist, had had no idea his wife was involved in criminal activity, according to Preston. Again, according to the good sheriff, Dr. James had been devastated to learn of his son's death.

Kim was living in the cabin again. She had stayed longer in Paula's house than she had wanted to and had left before Paula thought she should. That didn't mean she didn't continue to see Paula daily.

As she was also seeing Laurie.

Presently, all three women were sitting outside the cabin. Kim's mouth had healed to the point where she could chew soft food and speak pain-free. In general, she preferred listening to talking. Reclining on a new chaise longue possessed of all its straps, she watched afternoon shadows creep up the rock wall opposite her cabin. Laurie and Paula were doing all the talking. To be perfectly accurate, Paula talked. Laurie was having trouble getting a word in edgewise.

"You're going to have to do a better job of explaining the Sermon on the Mount to me," Paula said. "I completely fail to understand why the meek should inherit the earth. Does a person merely have to be meek to get a share in the inheritance? Is that all there is to it?"

Laurie started to answer.

"Furthermore, does this mean the meek don't get to go to heaven? Logically speaking, it seems like it should be one or the other—heaven or earth. If true, that sounds like a potentially bad deal for the meek. Stuck on earth while everyone else is frolicking in heaven? Did they even have a say in this arrangement? Or were they too meek to speak up?"

"Stop," Laurie said. "Let me explain."

Paula didn't stop. "And another thing, were they—the meek—warned about climate change? Because I have to tell you, I think that's a serious game changer for the value of terrestrial real estate."

Kim smiled. The chatter went on. Paula had a long way to go to get through the beatitudes.

The subject of inheritance reminded her. Laurie—finally—had promised to deposit her stock certificates in a brokerage account. For the moment, the certificates remained in Kim's safe deposit box, where they'd been since Laurie had brought them from Santa Fe to Creede. As part of the arrangement, Kim had agreed to serve as Laurie's investment advisor. She hadn't promised how long she would stay in that role.

She was chuckling at Paula's latest string of non sequiturs when she heard someone calling her name.

"Kim! Kim!"

She was slow to become alarmed, but when she did, she sat upright, gripping the sides of the chaise longue.

A middle-aged woman was jogging up the canyon. She didn't much look like a woman who jogged anywhere. Her round cheeks were red. Her gray curls bounced. Kim recognized her long before Claudia, the postmistress, came to a stop near the trio of women. Huffing and puffing, Claudia had trouble getting the words out. "This . . . came . . ."

She handed Kim a small white envelope. It was addressed to her, care of "General Delivery, Creede, CO."

Kim stared at the neat print. She read her name over and over again. She read the return address in the upper left corner.

It was an unfamiliar address, different from the one she knew in Denver.

She slit the envelope open.

She unfolded the single page.

> Kim,
>
> Wanted to let you know I have a new address.
>
> I hope you're keeping yourself out of trouble.
>
> L.

She laughed. She became aware, slowly, of three women watching her. Laurie was first to speak. "Good news?" she said.

Kim laughed harder. "Yes. Good news."

CHAPTER 48

There was one last promise to keep.

Kim argued with herself for a week that a promise made to oneself didn't bear the same weight as a promise made to another person. She reasoned that a promise made to oneself might be made in the heat of passion. It could be construed as a cry for an anchor to hold on to at a very bad moment that when viewed at a calmer time might not be deemed necessary, or even a prudent pact to keep.

She wondered what a person of deep spiritual conviction would say about the argument. She wondered what Natalie Beltran would say.

Natalie, who had told Laurie that she was a practicing Buddhist, was in Santa Fe, where she had taken up residence in a Zen monastery. Natalie planned to return to Denver to continue her graduate studies in time for the fall term.

Kim digressed.

A day later, she was sitting in Paula's kitchen in the late afternoon, watching clouds weave into menacing patterns.

With the advent of summer in Creede came the advent of afternoon thunderstorms.

Paula had finished working for the day. She had finished cleaning her materials. Paint smells and turpentine filled the air, rapidly distributed by an overhead fan.

Kim studied the spot where she had once sat for Paula, sat for hours, all summed together. She thought she ought to be able to see the outline of her shape lingering in the space. But it was only an open expanse of gleaming wood near the windows.

She stared at her fingertips on the tabletop. They danced nervously. They had a right to. It seemed a very long time ago when she had stood at Trip Garrett's grave and promised herself that if she succeeded in uncovering Cathy Garrett's identity, she would reveal her own to someone. Lena, she had thought, but she had no plans to see Lena anytime soon. She could no longer remember why it had seemed so important to make that bargain. But she couldn't forget the deal.

She had succeeded in discovering Cathy's true identity. Sheriff Preston might have gotten there first, but Kim got there through the genetic test she had ordered for Grace Garrett. A match came back to a maternal aunt named Elizabeth Symon, Cathy's sister.

Kim bought herself a moment and stole a look at Paula, whose hands were resting on the dark wood. Then she bought another moment, one she hoped to hold in trust. Paula sat at the table, shoulders back, dark blond hair falling to her shoulders. Her blue eyes were piercing. And waiting.

"Once upon a time there was a woman who loved numbers," Kim said, beginning the story. "The woman believed that if all of the numbers in all of the columns added up to the right number at the bottom of the page, then all was well in the world."

She looked at her own hands, still for the moment. In her mind, she saw the thunderbolts of two worlds colliding. Oddly, the violence didn't yet seem great.

"Some of the numbers in her world were bad numbers. They didn't belong. When the little boy found them, Midas sent him to the dark place. Then Midas told her that everyone would blame her for hurting the little boy and banishing him to the dark place. He told her everyone would say it was her fault the bad numbers were there that didn't belong."

By now her hands were casually intertwined. She wondered that she felt even a shred of calmness. It was slipping. She hurried on.

"Afterward, a long shadow fell over her world. She crept into a smaller and smaller place inside herself, trying to escape the shadow, but it didn't help. Then one day she found a curtain between two worlds. No longer able to bear living in the world she had always known and thought she loved, she parted the fold of the curtain and stepped through it."

She drew a quiet breath.

"The new world wasn't a happy place, not in the beginning. No one she met there spoke the language of numbers. They all spoke the language of life. It wasn't a language she knew well, so it took a long time, but eventually she began to learn it. As she did, her heart started to grow. Strangely, she came to feel as if she had spent her whole life waiting for her heart to grow, and to learn how to live."

She took a chance and glanced at Paula. Paula's gaze was fixed upon her, steadfast and utterly serious.

Kim looked down. "Later, she never once regretted taking that step through the curtain, which was funny, because she had always had the audacity to think the other world—the one with tall buildings and people scurrying and numbers—was superior."

She faltered when she tried to speak. Then she knew there really wasn't anything left to say.

One moment of absolute quiet settled in the room.

"The woman in your story, was her name Kim?" Paula said quietly.

Kim flinched. "No."

She stood up. She walked over to the window. There was a lone pine tree halfway up the hillside amid the outcropping of rock. Above, the clouds continued to roll darkly into one another before separating with sudden bursts of sunlight.

She didn't know where she would find the strength to say it. She had no idea what the telling would mean for the next moment, or longer. If ever there had been a signpost telling her she had passed the point of no return, she hadn't seen it.

She turned around and looked at Paula.

"Her name was Emily. Her name was Emily Taggert."

AN EXCERPT FROM THE
NEXT BOOK IN THE
COLORADO SKIES SERIES

FALSE
CONVICTIONS

CHAPTER 1

"One of the first questions an investigator must ask at the scene of a suspicious accident or death is this: Has a crime actually been committed? Take the case of an incident that occurred five years ago at a nearby national park."

Dr. Abraham Craft cut an imposing figure as he paced back and forth across the front of the auditorium. Tall and distinguished, dressed impeccably in a dark suit, white shirt, and maroon tie, Craft had the air of a man accustomed to commanding an audience. His delivery combined a touch of showmanship with the ferocity of a courtroom lawyer, guaranteed to hold the attention of a room full of undergraduates.

"Most of you will have heard of the Black Canyon of the Gunnison National Park, located west of here. In early spring of the year in question, a man and woman touring the park literally fell victim to the terrain's hazards. While enjoying the view from the rim, they lost their footing and toppled over. The man fell hundreds of feet down the rocky cliff to his death. The woman slid seventy-five feet before she managed to clutch the trunk of a juniper tree with one hand and trap her feet on a narrow outcropping, thereby stopping her skid. From that precarious position, she was able to shout until her cries for help were heard.

"The woman suffered a broken left arm, a serious head gash, and severe bruising and abrasions. She also suffered the devastating news that her fiancé had died in the accident. But was it an accident?"

A late arrival to the lecture slipped into the vacant chair alongside Kim Jackson, causing her to jump. She glanced sideways, lighting up in a smile when she recognized Kent Dodge. Dodge, an assistant professor of criminology, taught one of the courses she was taking.

"Immediately on being rescued, which was no trivial affair in that environment," Dr. Craft said, "the woman gave a disturbing report. She insisted that she and her fiancé hadn't made a misstep and slipped over the rim. She claimed they were pushed. She hadn't seen their attacker. According to her report, she felt a violent heave on her lower back. She lost her footing and slipped over the edge at the exact instant that her fiancé also fell. Naturally, the report raised a host of questions.

"There were no witnesses to the couple's fall with the exception, if the woman could be believed, of their attacker. There was, however, an array of possible explanations for the tragedy. Consider the following: Perhaps it truly had been an accident and the woman's subconscious turned it into something else, as a coping mechanism. Perhaps it was a murder-suicide, and the deadly shove she felt came from her betrothed, who jumped at the same moment that she lost her balance. On a darker note, perhaps she was the perpetrator in the murder-suicide scheme, yet some survival instinct took over as she fell, and given the opportunity to save herself, she did. These various explanations were considered later, but the day she gave her report, an investigation was launched to determine, to the fullest extent possible, who was on the rim that morning and of those individuals, who might have had reason to attempt to murder these two people, succeeding once."

Dr. Craft walked behind the lectern, picked up a water glass, and took a sip. Kim's attention didn't wander from the man whom she first had heard speak seventeen months ago. On that night, with shirtsleeves rolled up and smiling more often than she had seen him smile since, Craft had seemed entirely at home in the Montrose, Colorado, community center, where he was pitching his latest book. Of African American descent and in his fifties, Dr. Craft had a voice that was deeply resonant, and his knowledge of his subject matter—crime scene investigation—was vast. Without ever once diminishing the profound solemnity of the cases he referenced, the professor had spun a seamless narrative that had kept Kim hanging on his every word. Since then, she had read his books. He was the reason she had come to Western Colorado University to pursue classes in criminology.

Finished with the water, Craft set aside the glass and continued speaking.

"Investigators interviewed dozens of people at the national park that morning. Most were unable to provide details of other visitors. After all, it was the spectacular scenery that drew them there, not interest in their compatriots. Names were gathered along with contact information. Statements were taken. Of special note, every person interviewed had observed something in common. Each interviewee said he or she had noticed a group of young men dressed alike—black leggings and black hoodies—running in the park that morning. The men weren't always together. Some had been seen running alone, some in pairs or small groups. No one knew precisely how many men were there. Estimates ranged from a handful to a dozen. Likewise, age estimates ranged from late teens to early twenties. In this instance, investigators caught a break. One of the park employees was able to identify the group as Gunnison

High School cross-country runners who periodically came to the park to train."

Kent Dodge nudged Kim on the shoulder. He leaned over and whispered, "This is where the story gets good."

"The names of five young men ranging in age from fifteen to eighteen eventually emerged. When interviewed, they proved to be a tight-lipped bunch. Each one was unfailingly polite, answering 'Yes, sir,' or 'Yes, ma'am,' 'No, sir,' or 'No, ma'am' to questions. Each one insisted he hadn't seen anything, and by God, he certainly hadn't done anything so heinous as what was suggested. Investigators were struck by one odd thing. It was as if the young men were reading from the same script. Their answers and their demeanor raised a host of red flags.

"The lead detectives finally got a break while interviewing the youngest member of the group. 'Seth,' as I'll call him, eventually admitted that his running buddies once had joked about doing *something* like this, namely, pushing someone off the rim. Seth swore he'd been horrified by the mere suggestion, though he said he might have laughed at the time. He swore he didn't believe any of his buddies capable of committing this crime, but if one had, he had no idea who it could have been.

"Seth maintained a swagger in his step and attitude throughout successive interviews, but it was clear to seasoned investigators that, as time passed, the young man was in a world of hurt. I had the opportunity to interview him during this period. I'm not a trained psychologist, though even I could see the terror in his eyes. By giving voice to what he considered an outrageous proposition, a joke, really, Seth didn't realize he was allowing his subconscious to entertain the possibility that this crime could have happened, committed, in fact, by one of his friends. From there it was a short walk mentally to *this did happen*. Not long afterward, the young man's behavior grew increasingly worrisome. He was given to tantrums that often resulted in him shouting at his parents, 'I didn't tell those cops anything! The guys won't believe me! They'll think I said something!' The fear for Seth, not the reality, became unbearable."

Dr. Craft's words sent a jolt through Kim. Recognizing their truth, she hurriedly scribbled them down: "The fear, not the reality, became unbearable."

"Seth's life continued to unravel. Within a few weeks his parents felt they had no choice but to send him out of state. Word was he went to live with relatives in the East. He didn't. He went elsewhere, enrolled in a new school, received extensive counseling, and as far as I know has never returned to Gunnison.

"Think about it for a moment," Dr. Craft said, raising his hands in front of him as if to frame his point. "Consider the fear that consumed Seth at this time. I suspect he became persuaded that someone he formerly trusted had committed a brutal, random act of murder with the only purpose of fulfilling some dark, private fantasy. If a person could do such a thing for no reason, what worse thing might that same person do if he believed he had a *good* reason to kill someone?

"Well, so much for Seth. As for the other guys who went running at Black Canyon that day, investigators never could shake their stories. In a blow to the case, the manner of death of the man who fell and died was ruled undetermined. There simply wasn't enough evidence to support a finding of homicide, accident, or suicide. The woman recovered from her injuries and went on with her life, for a time." Here, Dr. Craft paused for one poignant moment before adding, "In a cruel twist of fate, she was murdered three years later."

A collective gasp rose from the audience.

Dr. Craft hadn't finished. "Fate, do you say? Or was her death the result of a more malicious design?"

For the next thirty minutes Kim listened, spellbound, as Dr. Craft recounted details of the investigation that had led Gunnison police to a twenty-year-old man who had been among the original five suspects in the canyon attack. In a meticulously planned crime, the man gained access to the woman's second-floor apartment in the middle of the night, garroted her, and pushed her through a window. She was dead before she hit the ground. The act of pushing her out the window was ludicrous, except possibly to someone for whom it held symbolic value. Ultimately, evidence was found at the scene linking the man to the crime. He was tried and convicted for the woman's murder. No charges were ever brought against him for the canyon attack.

"It's Craft's most famous case," Kent Dodge said to Kim when the lecture ended. They were outside, walking across campus on a September day awash with autumn sunshine. "He wrote a book about it. Publication is on hold. The kid's appealing his conviction. The book's considered inflammatory. Apparently it's a real page-turner. Where are you headed?"

Kim glanced at her watch. "The library. I have more reading to catch up on. Speaking of books, congratulations on yours. I heard a couple of classmates talking about it the other day. I hope the rumors are true."

Kent Dodge stopped and put his hands on his hips. "Thank you. Yes, there is a book in the works. It's a multibook deal, actually. It's been so long in coming, I doubted I would ever see this day. Quite gratifying to have my manuscript accepted by a publisher. Still, there's a long way to go before it makes its way into print. Listen, there is something I'd like to talk to you about. Can you stop by my office tomorrow, say sometime around two?"

Kim didn't have plans. Ordinarily she didn't stay that late on campus on Fridays, but it wasn't a major inconvenience. "Sure."

"Great. I'll see you in class in a bit, and tomorrow at two," Dodge said.

"See you then," she repeated.

ABOUT THE AUTHOR

Amy O. Lewis lives in New Mexico. Her debut novel, *A Mountain of Evidence*, is the first book in the Colorado Skies mystery series and was released in 2021.

"A multilayered thriller with a sympathetic protagonist. [. . .] It unfolds at a brisk, action-packed clip, with enough suspense to satisfy thriller fans."

—*Kirkus Reviews*

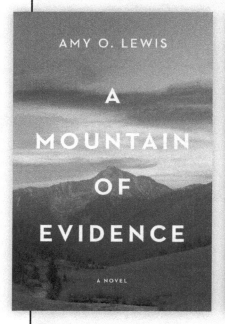

Follow Kim Jackson's story from the beginning with the first books in the Colorado Skies mystery series.

Now available on Amazon.com, Barnesandnoble.com, and Indiebound.

CPSIA information can be obtained
at www.ICGtesting.com
Printed in the USA
LVHW100756090123
736731LV00003B/263